MASTER OF THE MOORS

Kealan Patrick Burke

Copyright 2008 by Kealan Patrick Burke
Cover Design by Elderlemon Design

ISBN-13: 978-1479135899 (CreateSpace-Assigned)
ISBN-10: 1479135895

This is a work of fiction. Names, characters, businesses, places, events and incidents are either the products of the author's imagination or used in a fictitious manner. Any resemblance to actual persons, living or dead, or actual events is purely coincidental.

MASTER
OF THE
MOORS

KEALAN PATRICK BURKE

For the readers, without whom I'd be lost in the fog.

1

Brent Prior,
Dartmoor, England
1888

SHE IS WEEPING.

The cold eye of the moon peers at her over a pillow of fog. Arms crossed over her breasts, eyes swollen from crying, the woman stumbles blindly across the moors, her clothes torn, hair in disarray, streaks of shadow like dark fingers on her cheek. The air thickens as if it has gained the weight of her misery. Around her, half-glimpsed ghosts rise with imploring arms from the fog, shifting and stretching, then are just as quickly consumed. She stumbles on across the uneven landscape, once her haven, now the canvas upon which her fear is painted in pale strokes. Sphagnum moss breathes its cloying scent at her; unseen creatures flee at her uncertain approach, and the ground shifts from cushioning loam to unyielding stone.

She is lost.

Then a sound, a footfall, and she whirls, the fog rushing away from her in cyclonic waves. Eyes wide, she struggles to discern the slightest sign of life from this maddening colorless void between earth and moon. "Hello?" Her whisper dies before it crosses her lips. There is someone there. She sees nothing and has yet never been so sure of anything in her life. Amid the roiling clouds of fog, someone is approaching.

She is frightened.

Without direction, every step is treacherous, for mires and bogs punctuate these fields, but in the absence of visibility she allows her other senses to guide her, trusting in them as she has trusted them all her life, relying on instinct to spirit her away from harm. Head down, and despite the best efforts of her skirts to send her sprawling, she quickens her pace. Ahead, there is nothing but a wall of shimmering, shifting white.

A bird cries out and it is akin to a scream.

She stops. Face upraised to the veiled moon she closes her eyes and draws in a breath. Sudden pain carves fiery lines across her stomach. *There is so much left to do*, she thinks, *it cannot end now. They will need to know what they are.* A moment passes, marked by a sound that might have been her pulse thudding against her skull, or the protest of the child in her womb. She puts her hands to her belly, and whispers. "They'll need you. They'll need their savior."

She is cold. The moon peers like a frightened child around the edge of a cloud.

Serpentine shadows sprawl at her feet.

When at last she opens her eyes, there is a man standing before her, smiling, a shard of stolen moonlight gleaming in his hand.

***

Grady awoke from dreams of thunder to a pounding on the door. For a moment he lay still in his bed, the sheets clutched tight to his chest against the early morning chill, and waited for the impatient knocking to reveal itself as nothing but the lingering echoes of the dream. But when the window above his bed shuddered in its frame as fist met wood again, he sat up, blinking away sleep, and slowly got out of bed. As he dressed, he heard the floorboards creak in the room above his own. The din had roused Mrs. Fletcher and it would make a devil of her for the rest of the day. With a sigh, he shrugged on his dressing gown and made his way out into the hall. The brusque persistence of the man at the door filled the hallway with muffled gunshots, inspiring Grady to quicken his pace, despite the protestations of joints unaccustomed to such urgency.

"All right, I'm on me way," he complained, flapping a hand in the direction of the door, as if the displaced air might expedite word of his irritation to the visitor.

Mrs. Fletcher's voice startled him. "Heaven save us, Grady, the bloody sun isn't even up. Whoever's there, I hope you intend to give them what-for for wakin' the house."

Grady looked over his shoulder at the large scowling woman standing at the head of the stairs. The reddish cast of her face emphasized the few locks of white hair that had escaped the confines of her crumpled nightcap.

"That I will," he murmured and opened the front door.

A slender figure all but fell in on top of the old man, who backed away as if someone had thrown something unpleasant over him. Startled, Grady aided the gentleman in righting himself, realizing as he did so that the man was none other than Edgar Callow, yeoman and master of the hunt club.

"Lord save us, Sir, whatever's the matter?" Grady asked, alarmed.

The huntmaster's face was only a shade darker than the morning fog. He composed himself, brushing some imaginary dirt from his greatcoat. "Is your master here?"

"What's happened?" Mrs. Fletcher inquired from the stairs.

Callow opened his mouth and closed it again, then braced himself against the doorframe. "It's my wife," he said softly. "Sylvia...she didn't come home last night."

Though he had little love for Callow, who on any other day would have treated him in a manner usually reserved for vermin, Grady felt a pang of pity for the man. He had only recently married, and whether fate or betrayal had spirited his wife away, it was obvious he already feared the worst. Grady was no stranger to loss, though he had never been able to blame it on anything but his own foolish decisions. With a sharp nod of assent, he moved out of the doorway. "You'll come in out of the cold?"

"There's no *time*," Callow protested. "I have men waiting at the Fox & Mare, horses at the ready. We'll need them all in this horrid weather, but your employer knows the moors better than any of us and I'd consider him an *invaluable* asset. Please...rouse him, won't you?"

Grady turned and met Mrs. Fletcher's expectant gaze. There was no need for words. She sighed heavily and went to wake Mr. Mansfield.

***

The fog was a living thing, creeping across the moors like an animal and making twins of earth and sky. From within the low clouds came the sound of clopping as hooves met stony ground, then stopped. Then all was quiet, but for the occasional shrill cry of a lapwing.

There were six of them in the party, including Callow, who surveyed the terrain as if he could see through the fog. Behind him rode Peter Laws, owner of The Fox & Mare, and whipper-in for the Sunday foxhunts, and Greg Fowler, the local shopkeeper. Alistair Royle, coal merchant and inveterate gambler, followed at a pace that reflected his sluggish mood, with Mansfield and Grady bringing up the rear.

"He's mad if he thinks we'll find her in this," Royle muttered, his face still red from the strain of leading his intemperate mare up the slope to the rocky tor—a misshapen spire of weathered granite bearded by fog. The heavyset old man had been hungover and still half-asleep when Callow had roused him, a condition reflected by his shabby state of dress. His breeches were stained, coat buttoned only at the top, allowing his swollen gut to hang over his belt. "Would've been far more practical to stay at home and send for a constable."

Eyeing the red ribbon cinched around the tail of Royle's horse—a warning to those in the rear that the mare was known to kick—Mansfield rode up beside him and leaned in close so they would not be overheard.

"If he hears you, you're likely to get a thrashing."

Royle scoffed, spittle flying from his piscine lips. "Oh, come now." He smiled slyly. "Are any of us here surprised his little foreign lass has run away?"

Royle's inability to keep his thoughts to himself frequently got him in trouble, but on this occasion at least, Mansfield had to concede that no, he was not surprised it had come to this. Though all outward signs suggested a gentleman, Callow was known throughout the village as a cruel man, quick with his fists no matter the sex of his chosen targets. He had, on one drunken night at The Fox & Mare, even confessed a certain respect for the so-called Whitechapel Murderer, who he believed represented 'a force of purification in those Stygian ghettos.' How he had managed to woo a striking and intelligent woman like Sylvia Callow, who must surely have seen through his charismatic facade as soon as she'd set eyes on him, was a mystery to the villagers. But not to Mansfield, who had heard from her own lips how Edgar had been little more than an escape for her from the poverty of Calinesti, her village in Romania, where Callow had spent a year fulfilling the stipulations of his philanthropist father's will.

"Do you realize how much medicinal whiskey I drank last night?"

Mansfield shook himself out of his reverie and looked at Royle. "No, and I don't care to know. Just listen to Callow and do what he says."

"Bah! I'll wager she's on a train to Paddington right now. If she has any sense, that is."

Mansfield sighed and moved his horse along the line until he was level with Callow.

On a clear day, the rolling, rugged moors were awe-inspiring, but today there was nothing but a dense floating field of gray ahead of them. Here and there more tors could be seen poking their craggy heads through rents in the clouds, but it wouldn't be long before even those were obliterated completely. Mansfield could feel the cold fog pressing against his skin searching for a way into his bones.

"What do you wish us to do?" he asked Callow.

The huntmaster, eyes glassy, didn't respond, and for a moment Mansfield wondered if he'd heard the question at all. Then, without looking at him, Callow said, "I loved her, you know."

Although it unsettled Mansfield to hear the man refer to his wife in the past tense, he nodded his understanding. "Of course. And I assure you, if she's here, we'll find her."

"Why wouldn't she be here?"

"Well you have to consider the possibility that she..." He trailed off, unsure how best to suggest that Sylvia might simply have left him.

"That she what?"

"That she might *not* be here."

For the first time since he'd gathered the search party, Callow smiled. It was faint and not at all pleasant. "She knows better than that."

Mansfield stared at him for a moment, then at length said, "I'll go scout up ahead."

"By all means."

Mansfield rode away, finding himself in agreement with the boorish Royle now more than ever. A search on a day like this was a preposterous idea, and yet here they were trouping blind across an unpredictable landscape. He was also bothered that Callow had recruited him for his 'navigational skills'. Mansfield had, like Laws and Fowler, grown up by the moors, but such intimacy with the terrain did not guarantee safe navigation, especially in the fog. Callow would have known this. There were boulders, bogs, excavation pits and mires scattered throughout, all of which could be lethal to man or mare alike. Only total dark could be more forbidding, and dangerous. Today, superior navigational skills were worthless, which begged the question of why Callow had asked him, or any of them for that matter, to accompany him at all.

Just as Mansfield reached a black, stunted oak he recognized, Grady, his groundskeeper, rode up beside him, peaked cap raised high on his head, allowing a few spidery strands of silver hair to poke out. Despite the considerable differences in their ages, the men were steadfast friends. Ned Grady had been tending the grounds at Mansfield House for twenty years. As a result, it was impossible to picture the place without his slightly stoop-shouldered form ambling to and fro in the foreground.

"There's more hope of findin' Jesus out here today than that woman, I'd say," he said in his distinctive Irish brogue. His horse snuffled and rattled his bridle, drawing a gentle admonishment from Grady.

"You'll get no argument from me there. Any other man would have put out a telegraph to Merrivale. They'd have sent constables and bloodhounds. That he'd settle for us instead..."

"Doesn't feel right, sure it doesn't?"

"Not a bit."

"When he came to the house this mornin' he looked like a man who'd been to hell and back an' stopped for a few pints along the way. Now he's calm as anythin'."

Mansfield observed the striations of age that bisected the groundskeeper's cheeks, the red-veined, hawk-like nose, and the calm blue eyes that peered out from beneath the brim of the cap. He was not yet sixty, but he looked a decade more.

"What do you think he's up to? A facade, maybe, to cover the fact that she's left him?"

Grady squinted into the fog. "I don't know, sir. Honestly. The man has me flummoxed. But I'll say this much: You can usually tell what a fella's thinkin' by the look in his eyes. I looked into *his* eyes today an' they were just holes. Like lookin' into two pools of oil."

"We'd all look the same in his situation."

"That may be, but it might be best to stay on yer guard with him anyway, sir." He raised his whip and pointed it back the way he'd come. "Just to be safe."

Mansfield nodded.

"Oh, by the way," Grady added. "Did you happen to notice that Fowler brought his pistol?"

"No, and I'd rather you hadn't told me."

"I wouldn't worry," said the caretaker with a smile. "The way he shoots I'd say his foot's the only thing in danger."

A muffled groan told them the group was close, and when at last they resolved like a funeral march from the fog, Callow like a specter in front, Mansfield saw that Royle was slouching in his saddle and perspiring heavily.

"He's lookin' fairly crawsick," Grady noted.

The man who had summoned them here, the huntmaster, drew to a halt in front of them and Mansfield felt his insides writhe. Grady had not been exaggerating. Callow's face was like a theater mask, the eyes elliptical slits of darkness.

"Anything?" he asked.

"Not yet," Mansfield told him, "but I can tell you where we are. The Tavy River should be about half a mile straight ahead."

"Good." He turned and looked over his shoulder. "Help him off his horse." His gaze was directed at Royle, who looked moments away from sliding out of his saddle.

Royle smiled and raised a hand. "I'm sorry, awfully sorry, but perhaps it *would* be better if I turned old Lightning here around and headed home. I'm really feeling rather ill. Too much of the old vintage last night, I imagine."

Laws dismounted and helped Royle from his horse.

Callow's mouth twitched, as if the ghost of a smile had momentarily possessed it but found no reason to linger. "Good riddance."

Royle gaped at him. "I beg your pardon?"

"It is, I believe, rather typical of you to back out of any situation in which you do not stand to benefit directly. You've made a career out of being a parasite, so much so that to do something as a favor or—God forbid—out of the goodness of your heart, seems a preposterous notion."

"Now wait just one bloody second—" The color had returned to Royle's face.

"Laws," Callow continued, "since you provided him with the spirits that are now making him ill, you can accompany him back to the village. Besides, you know the terrain better than he does and I would hate to have to feel responsible if he fell and cracked his worthless skull."

"I'm not altogether sure what *you* imbibed last night, Mr. Callow," said the furious Royle, "but it must have been a devil of a drink to leave you with the impression that you can address your fellows in such a manner." He wiped a hand across his mouth and shrugged off Laws' attempt to pacify him. "Why...I wouldn't talk to a dog that way!"

"I sincerely doubt you could find a dog inclined to listen."

As if attuned to the mood of her master, Royle's horse snorted and backstepped. He made a half-hearted attempt to soothe it before turning his glare back toward Callow. "If that's how you speak to that woman of yours, then it's no wonder she ran off and left you."

All trace of a smile vanished from Callow's face.

Mansfield raised a hand. "Royle, leave it alone for God's sake."

But he was not to be silenced. "The nerve! Say what you like about these others if you feel compelled to, but you won't talk down to me no matter how bloody high your horse might be!"

Grady stepped forward. "Hold yer tongue, Royle, an' have a bit of compassion fer the man. He's out here lookin' for his wife, not a quarrel."

Royle turned on him. "Ah, the Catholic peasant speaks. How *humbled* we are to hear from you. Too bad you're not worth a—"

"That's enough," Mansfield interrupted. "One more word and I swear I'll blacken your eye myself."

"Easy, gentlemen," said Fowler, with a nervous laugh. Now that Grady had brought it to his attention, Mansfield noticed the holster strapped to the man's belt. A polished walnut handle protruded from the sheath like the top of a question mark.

The tension curdling the air was eventually broken by Callow. "We're wasting time."

"Agreed," Mansfield said. "Laws, take Royle home. We'll carry on from here." Laws nodded and moved behind Royle's horse to where his own mount awaited him.

It then became horrifyingly clear that the tension had not only affected the men. Royle slapped a hand against his horse's flank in frustration and the mare started, it's eyes wide and frightened as it rose on its hind legs and whinnied.

"Royle, calm that blasted nag!" Grady yelled.

Royle, cursing, grabbed the horse's reins and tugged. "Steady there! *Steady*, Lightning."

"Laws, get out of the bloody way!" Grady called.

But despite the sudden ruckus, Laws attention was elsewhere. He had turned almost fully away from the group and was squinting into the fog, one finger raised and pointing back the way they'd come. "I just saw—"

"Laws!"

Lightning threw a kick so fierce and sudden it proved with tragic finality the aptness of her name. There came a sound like someone hitting a sack full of meat with a hammer and Laws was knocked off his feet, arms aloft as if he were trying to fly. He landed heavily on his side and flopped over on his back, a single shuddering breath sweeping about his head like an attentive ghost. Royle, still struggling to calm the mare, looked around, confused by the sudden flurry of motion as the group hurried to Laws' aid. Only Fowler and Callow remained on their steeds.

Mansfield got to him first. The innkeeper lay with his legs apart, mouth moving soundlessly, expelling nothing but blood. His eyes were like swollen red rubies. Mansfield, unsure whether or not the man could still see, resisted the urge to grimace, and put his hand on the man's shoulder.

"Laws," he said. "Peter. Can you hear me?"

Grady squatted down on the other side and put his index and middle finger to Laws' wrist. "He's gone," he said a moment later.

"But he's still moving!"

"Nothing but sparks, sir. His head's been pulverized."

Royle, who had finally managed to placate his mare, moaned loudly. "It was his fault. I did nothing to him. He knew better than to—"

"Shut *up,* for feck's sake," Grady said, and all there knew that on any other occasion, such a command would have earned him a world of trouble. But, perhaps unwilling to draw the ire of anyone else, Royle did as he was told.

Mansfield looked down at Laws, at his caved-in head, and swallowed dryly. A single slim shard of bone protruded from his shattered cheek as his head slowly drifted to the side. Mansfield feared he'd see that detail over and over again in his nightmares for years to come. He looked up at Callow, who seemed impossibly unaffected by what had just occurred.

"We have to keep going," the huntmaster said.

***

"Sir, we can't just leave the poor sod out here," Grady said.

Callow gave a curt nod. "You're correct, of course. Royle can stay with him until we return."

Royle looked as if he'd been slapped. "Me?"

"Yes. He was willing to accompany *you* home, wasn't he? And as it was your mare that killed him, I'd expect you'd be only too glad to oblige. If nothing else, it will give you some time to compose your thoughts before you have to inform his widow of the tragedy."

Royle's mouth dropped open.

"And keep the gadflies off him," Callow added, turning his horse.

Mansfield's unease deepened. Callow didn't look all that put out by the innkeeper's death. Worse, he saw that Grady was again correct, in that even the panic the yeoman had exhibited earlier was no longer evident. It was as if he really had been wearing a theater mask, and now it had slipped off, revealing the cold and impassive face beneath.

"Sir, if I may..." Grady said. "This isn't right. Laws was a friend. Someone should bring him back to the village, not to have him lyin' out here in the cold and damp."

"I take it then, that you're volunteering for the task?"

"I am."

"Good. Then do it, but I'll suffer no more delays. We're not on a hunt, gentlemen. The lives of my wife and unborn child are at stake." He looked at Royle. "Help Grady with the body. Then take your mare with you back into town and present it to the widow Laws. I'm sure she'll appreciate being granted a look at her husband's killer."

For a brief moment, it looked as if Royle might object, but instead he muttered something to himself and went to help Grady.

"Would it not make more sense for us all to go back?" Mansfield said. "What just happened doesn't bode well for the rest of this day. Perhaps if you summoned the constables in Mer—"

"It's too late for that," Callow interrupted. "But if any of you want to head back, then do so. I'll find them myself if I must."

Mansfield considered doing just that, but knew if he did, he'd be at the mercy of his conscience forevermore. He looked at Fowler, whose face was positively gray with fear. Nevertheless, the shopkeeper cleared his throat and nodded. "I'll stay and help. We've come this far..."

They mounted their horses.

"Be careful," Mansfield called back to Grady, who waved before leaning down to grab Laws by the shoulders. Royle grimaced and did his best to avoid touching the body until the groundskeeper glared at him.

Callow led Mansfield and Fowler onward at a steady pace.

"Mansfield," Fowler called at one point, "what do you think he saw?"

"Who?"

"Laws. Before the horse kicked him he was pointing into the fog. Didn't he say he saw something?"

"Maybe it was the Beast of Brent Prior?" Callow said over his shoulder.

Fowler didn't look as if he found the reference at all funny. "I can't believe he's dead. Poor Sarah will be destroyed."

"She will," Mansfield replied, "but there's consolation to be found in the fact that it was quick. I don't think he suffered." But as the land fell into a gentle slope, the horses' hooves crunching across the patch of stony ground that carpeted the hollow before the terrain softened again, he wondered if he truly believed that. An awful yawning emptiness had opened inside him and he realized that for a long time after this day he would walk into The Fox & Mare expecting to see Laws there, making jokes and polishing glasses as normal. But the gray faces gathered in the shadows of the tavern and the lines of mourning on Sarah Laws' face would forever bring home to him the reality of what had happened here today.

They rode faster into the fog, damp earth flying in their wake.

"Callow!"

The huntmaster looked back at Mansfield, who asked, "How far did she normally go on her walks?"

Callow didn't answer. The fact that he was leading them now only served to reinforce Mansfield's belief that they were being drawn into something, that this whole search was nothing but a show, perhaps to aid Callow's case if Sylvia turned up dead, and that angered him. Even if it resolved that she had indeed taken that train to London, it wasn't going to undo the tragedy that had befallen Laws. He had to struggle not to remember how the innkeeper had looked, had to wrestle with images of Sylvia lying out here in the cold and fog.

Generally, people who lost their way on the moors were never seen again, and while superstitious villagers were always quick to blame ghosts and devil hounds, Mansfield knew the mires were filled with the preserved remains of fools who had simply wandered too far or succumbed to the myriad natural dangers. But Sylvia Callow was no fool and he desperately wanted to believe she hadn't set foot on the moors at all.

They halted at Callow's order, the horses circling until the verve left them.

Fowler looked around, uneasy. "Why are we stopping?"

"I saw something," Callow mumbled. "Over there."

Mansfield followed his gaze but saw nothing but fog. "What do you think it was?"

A crow cawed somewhere overhead. The horses snuffled.

Callow frowned. "Fowler, be a good man and take a look will you?"

"Why me?"

"Because if it's not anything we wish to know about then you're well-equipped to handle it."

Fowler looked down at his holster and sighed resignedly. "Yes. I suppose so. Where did you say you saw it?"

Callow pointed off to their right. "There. A shadow of some sort. Like someone hiding from us."

Fowler looked positively terrified, which in turn affected Mansfield's already tenuous nerve. The dread seemed woven into the fog itself.

"Fowler," Mansfield said. "If it's Sylvia, try not to shoot her."

"Perhaps you should come with me, just to be sure I don't."

"Perhaps I should." He started to dismount, but Callow put a hand on his forearm.

"No. Let him go. I'd like to speak with you for a moment."

Visibly disappointed, Fowler trudged through the sodden grass. A moment later the fog erased him from sight.

Mansfield sighed. "We'll find her. You have to believe we will."

"Oh, I'm fairly certain we will."

"You are?"

"Of course. In fact, I imagine in the next few moments you'll hear Fowler's proclamation to that effect."

"How do you know?"

The huntmaster smiled. "Because this is where I left her."

2

"WE SHOULD STOP FER A FEW MINUTES, Mr. Royle, see if this fog lifts."
Royle said nothing. Instead he watched his feet squelching in the sodden grass and occasionally grimaced, as if in pain.

"D'you hear me?" Grady persisted, anxious to stop before the ground gave way completely, or they walked right into an icy river and froze to death. He hoped the saddle blanket they'd used to shroud Laws would help contain the scent of blood long enough for them to get home. If the horses caught wind of it, they'd go berserk and they'd certainly had enough of that for one day. For now, at least, they plodded dutifully along, no hint in their demeanor of the tragedy Lightning had caused. In that, Grady envied them, for he was finding it increasingly difficult to erase the ingrained image of Laws flying backward through the air, the blood soaring upward from his face like an elongated tongue.

"We should have stayed with them," Royle said, rubbing his brow with the back of one pudgy hand. "We'll get lost out here. End up like Laws. Mercy..." His face creased into a grin and a laugh bubbled up out of his considerable gut. "Wait until my tyrant of a mother-in-law hears about this!"

Grady stopped, halted his horse, and looked squarely at Royle. "Listen to me," he said, "what happened was an accident. Laws has been around horses long enough to know that the red ribbon on Lightnin's tail wasn't there fer decoration. He was distracted, that's all. A case of bein' in the wrong place at the wrong time."

"But his head...did you see what Lightning did to his head?"

"I did."

"What will I tell her? What will I tell his wife?"

"The truth. That he wasn't payin' attention an' the horse kicked him."

"Nothing else?"

"What else is there?"

"Plenty."

"Try to keep yer mind off it."

"Do you think the others will be all right?"

"Yes. I wouldn't have left 'em if I didn't."

Stones crunched beneath their feet, which to Grady signified that they'd reached the Hay Tor, although there would be no hope of seeing the gravel marker in the fog. Still, it would be a good place to rest and it told him they were headed in the right direction. Of course, there was also a chance that they'd been going around in circles and had come back to the same tor they'd passed with the hunt, but he doubted his tracking skills had atrophied that badly since he'd last been called upon to use them.

"We'll stop fer breath here," he said, looping the mare's tether around a small boulder, which he also used as a seat.

Royle, fist white around Lightning's reins, sat down opposite him on a rotted stump Grady feared would collapse beneath the man's weight.

The fog passed between them like a parade of ghosts. Once or twice, the rotund man's gaze shifted to the shrouded body dangling over the side of Grady's horse, but never lingered for too long.

"The shadow of death," Grady said, once he'd settled himself.

"What?"

"Laws said he saw somethin' in the fog. A couple of seconds later he was dead. Few of death's recruits get to share what they see before he takes 'em. I think, given another minute, our friend would've been able to describe him fer us. In that regard, I think we're better off."

Royle scoffed, but there was uncertainty in his eyes. "You really believe in that nonsense?"

Grady shrugged, but said nothing.

"Then I suppose you're also convinced there really is a spectral fiend haunting this very moor?"

"Not at all. The Beast of Brent Prior is a myth."

"How can you be sure?"

Grady shook his head. "A large dog ravagin' a farmer's livestock, half-glimpsed in the dark, heard howlin' in the dead of night, eyes blazin' when lit by lantern-light, and seldom glimpsed in the day—isn't that mysterious enough to warrant speculation, an' turn rational man's thoughts to the unnatural? The superstition has always been there, Mr. Royle, fueled by old wives' tales. Give our hardy farmers a shadowy figure an' a brace of mutilated sheep an' they'll quickly lean toward legend before logic."

"And what of those who've claimed to have seen more than just fleeting glimpses of the thing?" Royle asked. "Jim Potter saw it loping toward the village one night as he was closing his living room curtains. Passed straight through the light from his window. 'A long dark shape, of a reptilian nature,' he said. And other people have seen it too. You remember old Dan McGowan? He claimed the abominable thing was circling his house, like a vulture, until the night he took his Winchester to it and blew a few sizable holes in its rump."

"Stories," Grady said, glancing over at his horse and the crooked shape atop its rear. "Nothin' but fanciful tales told to make heroes outta cowards. All it takes is fer the story to be told once an' you can be sure everyone who heard it will have some kind of a terrifyin' encounter of their own soon after." He produced his briar pipe and a small pouch and began to fill the bowl. Then he touched a match to it, drew deeply and exhaled blue smoke into the fog. "Let me ask you this, Mr. Royle. Have *you* ever seen the Beast of Brent Prior?"

Royle stared, but in his eyes Grady could see a man weighing the benefit of tainting a cordial exchange with an untruth. Eventually he slumped and shook his head, as if ashamed of being unable to endorse his beliefs with a testimony of his own, or of having to concede a debate to a mere groundskeeper. Grady had no illusions that this brief spell of amiability would ever extend beyond the ragged circle of the tor's pedestal. For Royle, it wouldn't be proper to have associations with the lower class that were not strictly practical.

"Well," Grady said, upturning his pipe and emptying the bowl onto the hard ground, "let's just say this: I hope I'm right, but if I'm not, then let us both pray we never discover the truth of it."

Royle nodded. "Fair enough."

"Good." Grady rose on painful legs, his knees like rusted hinges. "Then we'll head off before the dark decides to creep up an' let us know her secrets, shall we?"

"Can we not wait another while? I haven't yet caught my breath."

Grady smirked. "Hard to do that when you're talkin'. Anyway, we best head off now. The fog's not showin' any signs of dispersin'."

Both men stood and it seemed the air was colder than before.

"It's awfully dense, isn't it?" Royle said, alarmed. "Will we be able to find the way?"

"Have faith, Mr. Royle," Grady told him, though in truth his own had faded a little. He resisted the instinctive urge to bat at the fog as if it were nothing more than smoke from his pipe that could be cleared with the swipe of a hand.

"Callow is out of his mind," Royle muttered, and tugged on Lightning's reins. "Even our imaginary Beast would have better sense than to come out in weather like this." When he turned, he saw that Grady was still standing next to the boulder he'd been sitting on. He wasn't moving. "What's wrong?"

For a moment the groundskeeper said nothing, then he spoke in a quiet voice, as if afraid of being overheard. "She's gone."

Royle frowned, confused. "Who?"

"Alice. Me mare. She's gone. I have her tether but there's nothin' on the other end of it."

"She got loose?"

"Must've." Grady gave a short sharp whistle but the fog seemed to swallow it, as if he'd whistled into a wall. They waited for a sound: a snuffle, jingle, trot or neigh, anything to signify the mare's presence amid the rolling clouds.

Nothing. The time stretched out until it seemed as if hours had passed before Grady turned to look at Royle.

"She's out there all right," he said, clearly unimpressed by the horse's mutiny. "Somewhere. But I haven't a hope of findin' her in this. Maybe the other lads'll come across her on their way back. If not, then she can spend the night on the moors."

"Couldn't you follow the tracks?"

"In this? Even if I could, God knows where they'd lead me."

"So, you're just going to leave her?"

"Christ almighty!" Grady said, clapping both hands to his mouth, startling Royle in the process.

"What? What is it?"

The color had drained from the groundskeeper's face. "The *body*. Jesus, Mary and Joseph, the bloody mare has gone off with the body!"

He turned as if to storm off into the fog, but Royle grabbed his arm. "Wait! Where are you going? You just said you'd never find her out there."

"Yes, but now I have to."

"But you'll get lost!"

The groundskeeper paused, head cocked, listening.

Royle froze. "What is it?"

"Listen."

Moments passed without a sound. Then, just as Royle was about to ask again what it was they were supposed to be hearing, there came the unmistakable clop of a hoof striking stone.

Grady, with a relieved smile said, "There she is. That's her."

"Thank God."

Grady walked slowly in the direction of the sound. "C'mon Alice," he called. "C'mon girl."

A rattle. Then: *clop-clop-clop*. She sounded close. Grady cursed the thick shifting clouds and took another few steps, pausing to check that he hadn't lost sight of Royle. The fat man stood by his horse, looking worried.

"Alice, come on love." The groundskeeper moved forward, hand outstretched. The mare whinnied, danced on the spot, nervous.

He could see her now. "Come on..." She was less than five feet away.

The horse screamed. It was a horrifying, unnatural sound, like rusted steel being grated together, or mangled. Grady, startled, staggered back and collided with Royle. Lightning reared up, eyes whiter than the fog, head thrashing. Royle turned to placate her. Grady was already moving back toward the dreadful sound of his horse in agony.

A loud hissing sound stopped him.

"What on earth is *that?*" Royle said, fear rattling his voice. "Easy, Lightning." But the horse was not to be calmed, no more than Grady's horse was to be saved from whatever was tormenting it. The groundskeeper dared another few steps. There was a sudden tearing sound and Grady was struck full in the face by a warm wet spray. He gasped in horror and looked down at himself, at the dark red liquid that had saturated him.

Blood.

Royle cried out.

The fog parted and a lumbering shape staggered forth. For one soul-freezing moment, Grady thought he was just about to have his first dreadful glimpse of the fabled Beast of Brent Prior, but as he backed away, he realized it was nothing so complicated as that, though the mythical creature might well have been the instigator of this horror before him. He leapt aside, just in time to avoid the collapsing ruin of meat that had once been his horse. Lightning shrieked and struggled to be free of Royle's restraint, the blood inciting the mare's instinct to flee.

"God save us!" Grady yelled and swept his arms around him in the fog, as if they were swords that would excise the killer, cutting through the curtains of gray like Hamlet skewering his lurking traitor.

The stuttered hiss came again, as if the moors had suddenly become infested with snakes.

"Royle, we have to get out of here."

"I know, I know. Dear God, what *is* that?"

"Just get on your mare. We'll be sharing the ride home."

"You're covered in blood!"

"Get on the feckin' horse!"

Royle obeyed, though it took a considerable amount of effort to get Lightning to stay still long enough to mount her. Once astride, he lowered his arm to assist Grady. Grady took it and seated himself behind the saddle, so he was riding bareback. He looped his arms around Royle's voluminous belly. "Turn around. Whatever's out there, we don't need to chance ridin' past it."

Royle tugged on the reins. The horse, still shaking its head and whinnying, turned away from the gruesome remains of Grady's mare.

They took off as fast as the fog would allow, which wasn't very fast at all—a realization that made Grady nervous. Whatever had killed Alice was bound to be moving quicker than they were. Assuming it was following—*hunting*—them, they'd need to increase the pace. And yet to do so was to risk flying blind into territory made unfamiliar by the fog. They chanced crippling the horse among boulders or riding straight into a mire if they took it too fast.

"Is it following?" Royle called over his shoulder.

Grady looked back. He thought he might have seen a shadow running—no, not running, *bounding*—in the swirling wake of their flight, but then it was gone. "I don't know, but let's not stop to find out."

"What about Laws?"

Grady shook his head. "Forget about him fer now."

"Do you have any idea which direction we're heading?"

"I think so. Just keep *goin'*."

They rode on, jolted by every rise and slope that slipped from the fog.

Royle lashed his crop against the lathered horse's hide. Lightning responded, the speed increased, and then a blanket of darkness flashed before Grady's eyes, so sudden and brief he feared he was about to be knocked off the horse. It was as if someone had whipped a dark coat across his face. His hands slipped free of their grip around Royle's belly and he quickly grabbed the sides of the saddle to keep from falling. He heard a deafening hiss, felt a slight pressure against his chest and then the hazy light returned. Shocked, he looked to his right just in time to catch a glimpse of black dissolving into gray.

"Jesus," he whispered. Then louder: "Royle, did you see...?"

Grady looked down at his hands, at their furious trembling, and noticed the long thin scratch marks in the rear of the saddle where the thing had clawed its way over the horse. Its nails had missed his nethers by less than an inch.

"Royle?"

He looked up and, to his horror, realized two things at once. First, Royle was dead. The fat man's hat was gone, as was most of his head and what remained brought to Grady's mind the image of a boiled egg cracked open and ready for salting. Only the momentum and the man's weight were keeping him in the saddle. Secondly, the horse would soon react to the blood again, and when that happened, Grady was as good as dead. Even if he survived the fall, whatever was out there wouldn't be long finishing him off. He reached around Royle and grabbed the reins, then, with both fists pressed against the man's left arm, heaved him off the horse. The body hit the earth with a sickening thump but Grady did not look, nor did he glance over his shoulder to see if Royle had suddenly grown a ravenous shadow.

***

"What have you done?" Mansfield said as he dismounted. "What have you done to her?"

Callow's smile faded. "What any man would have done in my place."

"You're insane!"

"Oh please, I did you a favor. I did everyone in this godforsaken village a favor. You, my poor misguided friend, have no idea what it is you've been meddling with."

Dumbstruck, Mansfield turned and ran into the fog.

"You'll do her no good!" Callow roared after him, but he wasn't listening. All that mattered now was finding Sylvia. Finding her *alive*. Anything less and he would tear Callow apart with his bare hands and to hell with the consequences. The man was a raving Bedlamite. He cursed himself for not realizing it sooner, for not taking Sylvia's words at face value. And now he'd harmed her.

I'll kill him.

He tore at the fog as if it had gained substance, cursing under his breath as his feet almost slid from under him. Somewhere up ahead, he heard a voice, Fowler's perhaps, offering low words of comfort, and that gave him hope. He thrashed at the gloom, tears leaking from his eyes, desperate to see her, to know she was—

A moment later, he found them.

"Oh God," he sobbed, as Fowler looked up at him from where he knelt beside her, holding her arms at the wrist as he might have held her hands, had they not been missing.

Sylvia was lying on her back, breathing short hitching breaths, eyes wide open and staring. Beneath her, the grass was dark. Too dark. He couldn't tell if the blood on her bodice had come from her wrists or from other wounds on her chest.

"She's dying," Fowler said helplessly. "I don't know what to do."

Mansfield went to Sylvia's side and brushed his fingers against her cheek. Her eyes found him, the pupils almost completely dominating them. "You didn't come," she whispered in her clipped accent.

He shook his head. "I didn't *know*."

"Save the child."

She looked away, her breathing so irregular he feared each breath would be her last. Then he kissed the corner of her mouth. Her lips were like strips of cold leather. He rose, one trembling hand held out over her body. "Fowler. I need your gun."

"What? Why?"

"Just give me the bloody thing!"

Fowler obeyed, flinching when Mansfield snatched it from his hand. "Stay with her," Mansfield commanded. He stalked off, back the way he'd come, teeth clenched so hard his jaw muscles hurt, tears streaming down his cheeks. He expected to find that Callow had fled with all the horses to make pursuit impossible, but to his surprise, the huntmaster was still there. He'd come down off his horse and was standing with his back to Mansfield, peering into the fog, muttering to himself.

Mansfield, trembling with rage, stopped a few feet away from him. "Turn around."

Callow didn't move.

"I said turn around and face me, coward."

"There's no time for such melodrama I'm afraid," said Callow and nodded at the wall of white in front of him. At first Mansfield saw nothing, and was about to say as much, or pull the trigger, whichever suggested itself to him first, but then he noticed twin orbs of white fire rising from the fog like will o' the wisps. He took an involuntary step back as a dark mass materialized from the gloom. *It's the devil himself*, he thought.

"Goodbye, Mansfield," said the huntmaster as the shadow drew back and, with an awful hissing sound, lunged forth from the fog, eyes blazing.

3

Brent Prior,
1904

GRADY SAT BY THE KITCHEN HEARTH, the occasional puff of smoke from his pipe threading through his view of the moors and the low-lying mist that had risen as he'd watched. The heat from the flames was reassuring; it soothed the feeling of age and uselessness that sometimes threatened to overwhelm him whenever he sat for too long.

On this particular morning, he felt nervous, so much so that, rather than eschewing breakfast completely—a steadfast ritual—he'd opted for a glass of hot whiskey, ostensibly to chase away the chill of dawn. His true motive had been to settle the almost suffocating ache in the pit of his belly that told him things were coming to an end, that soon Brent Prior and Mansfield House would be little more than a scattering of memories culled from his countless years of service here. It was a depressing thought and one he had to struggle to subdue.

The back door opened and Mrs. Fletcher bundled into the room, her cheeks scorched by the cold wind, silver hair knotted into a severe bun that lent her eyes a shrewish cast. She stomped the mud from her shoes and hurried to the fire. "My word," she said, rubbing her hands together, then offering her palms to the flames. "It's bitter out there this mornin', Mr. Grady. The sheets I left on the line are stiff as a board."

"It's a harsh one, all right. Perfect mornin' for one of yer fine cups of tea, I'd say."

"Is that so? And you couldn't have made one yourself?"

"I'm afraid I don't have the necessary skills with which you've been blessed."

"I see."

He smiled and countered her scowl with a roguish wink. He would miss their banter if Mansfield House died. He had always liked Mrs. Fletcher. Despite losing her husband and youngest son to consumption years before, her spirit remained indomitable, the agony that must have been worrying away at her soul kept hidden from her employer and charges. Grady could not recollect ever having seen her upset, and, on more than one occasion, she alone had kept the household together when outside forces had tried to tear it apart. Nevertheless, he knew there was a vulnerability to her. It lurked in the corners of her eyes and in the deep lines around her smile.

"You seem a bit under the weather today, Mr. Grady. Is anythin' the matter?"

Inwardly cursing himself for letting the melancholy penetrate his mask of good humor, he smiled and waved away her concern. "Just the thought of fixin' those fences. 'Tis too cold a day to be gettin' bit by wire on one side and the chill on the other."

"If I were you I'd leave it," she said quietly, her eyes glassy and full of reflected fire. "It's not like anyone's goin' to inspect it. Besides, what do we have to keep penned in anymore? All the animals are sold off."

"You're right." He leaned forward with a groan and tossed a log onto the flames from the stack by his feet. Sparks blossomed and danced their way up the chimney; heat flared, prompting Mrs. Fletcher to move back a step. "But I'd much rather get it done," he continued. "Just because the master isn't well is no excuse to be lax in our duties." The truth of the matter was that he *needed* to keep working. If he didn't, he was afraid he would only be contributing to the ruin of Mansfield House, to his *own* ruin.

The charwoman scowled. "Oh, now, I didn't mean that we should! Only that there's little use in mendin' things that haven't got no use anymore. You'd only be wearin' yourself out for nothin'. Then what have I got? You stuck in bed recoverin' from a broken back and none of the work that *needs* doin' gettin' done!"

Grady grinned. "You make a fair argument, Mrs. Fletcher."

"I make an even better cottage pie," she replied, shrugging off her coat. "The perfect thing to smite the chill on a day like this, I think." As she spoke, she looked up and over Grady's shoulder. The hall door creaked open. "And speakin' of things to chase away the chill, I dare say you'll find nothin' warmer in this house than our little missus," said the charwoman, with obvious affection. Grady turned in his seat, wincing as his roasted pant leg scorched the skin beneath.

"Well, good mornin', young Katherine," he said, and beamed at the auburn-haired girl who plodded into the kitchen, her eyes at half-mast, a hand raised to stifle a yawn. She gave them a lazy salute, then slumped into a chair. Mrs. Fletcher raised an eyebrow and grinned at Grady, who said: "Long night, was it Kate?"

"Mice in the walls," she murmured. "I thought they'd eat their way through and nest in my hair. Where's Neil?" She rubbed sleep from her eyes.

"At work since six," Grady remarked.

Another yawn and Kate sat up, blinking. "Wonderful. I couldn't stand to listen to his griping at this hour of the morning. Could I have a cup of your famous tea, Mrs. Fletcher? If not, you may have to scrape me off the table."

The charwoman spoke as she filled the kettle. "You'd be better off gettin' a few more hours of sleep. You need every bit of rest if you intend to go to the dance tonight."

Grady caught her wink and shrugged to indicate that this was news to him. "What dance would this be?"

Kate swiveled in her chair and let her chin rest atop the backrest. "The *October Dance*. I told you about it last week. You said you'd help me hollow out some pumpkins, remember? Everyone attending has to bring something to celebrate Halloween. Neil's bringing a turnip."

"A turnip?"

Kate nodded. "Because he's lazy. He says if they ask him about it he'll tell them it's not like he could *see* it wasn't a pumpkin."

Mrs. Fletcher rolled her eyes. "That boy would use his handicap to get out of anythin'. I imagine he'll cross the oceans of the world and visit all four corners on the strength of pity, and yet you dare offer him assistance and he'd nearly strike you!"

"I don't recall anything about a dance, or pumpkins, or turnips," said Grady. "I wish I had, or I'd never have offered to take Mrs. Fletcher out for the night."

Mrs. Fletcher gasped and tossed a tea towel at him, which he caught before it reached his face. An involuntary grimace surfaced at the arthritic pain that flared through his knuckles. He quickly recovered and gave Kate an apologetic look.

"I'm afraid your benevolent charwoman swore me to secrecy. She wouldn't have the whole village gossipin' about our illicit affair."

"Oh, you rascal! You'll hold your tongue or it'll be the kettle that comes your way next!"

Kate laughed loudly, drawn from her sleep-daze by their humor. To Grady, the sound was like a breeze through spring blossoms.

The mirth faded as a blushing Mrs. Fletcher tended to her tea and muttered about old men and their improper propositions. As Grady was massaging the pain from his fingers, Kate asked, "Has anyone been up to check on Father?"

Grady nodded.

"And, how was he?"

The old man straightened in his seat and stared into the fire. "Little change."

"I thought I heard him weeping last night. I went in to his room but his eyes were dry. Must have been a dream."

"If he wept it might be a good thing," Grady said, then added, "a sign that he's ready to come back."

"Well," Kate said defiantly, "I don't care what Doctor Campbell says. That crotchety old lout—"

"Don't talk like that about the poor man," Mrs. Fletcher interjected.

"—doesn't know what he's babbling on about half the time. I think one of these fine days Father will be back to himself and running this place like the tight ship it once was."

"And what does *that* mean?" the charwoman said, hands-on-hips. "Are you implyin' that we've let the place fall to bits while the master's ill?"

Kate, with a sly smile, nodded once. "Precisely."

"I'll take the broom to you, young lady."

Grady chuckled. "She means it. She's already swept me off my feet."

This time he was not swift enough to halt the arc of the tea towel. It struck him full in the face and he moaned. Kate fled on a wave of laughter. Mrs. Fletcher grabbed the broom and began to swipe at the girl's heels, the occasional scream of delight startling Grady as he watched with a small sad smile on his face.

This morning, happiness held court in the kitchen, while upstairs the master lay dying. It felt wrong somehow, but all present knew that a break from the sorrow was a necessary thing if they hoped to keep their wits.

He dreaded the day when laughter was merely a ghost in a house of memory.

***

"Hello," the voice said and Neil almost dropped the box he'd been lugging into the shop from the small storeroom. The voice registered immediately, but the scent that followed confirmed the presence of Tabitha Newman. His heart fluttered, butterflies with sharp wings scything their way around his stomach. Carefully setting the box down on the counter, he looked in the direction of her voice, letting no trace of his excitement reach his face.

"Who is it?"

"Tabitha, silly."

He shrugged. "Well how was I supposed to know? You could have been that old hag Mrs. Crowther for all I knew."

"I think you knew it was me." She sounded terribly close.

"Think what you like."

"Here, smell this. It's pretty."

It took him a moment to realize what she was doing, and when her wrist brushed against his nose, he jerked away and almost slammed into the shelves on the wall behind him.

"Oh...I'm sorry," Tabitha said, embarrassment in her tone.

"What are you doing?" Neil said, faking outrage. "I could have broken my neck!"

But even as the venomous words spewed from his lips, the sensation of her skin was being committed to memory, to be studied later at his convenience. She smelled of soap, and some kind of fancy new perfume, an alluring scent that made the hair prickle on the back of his neck. It made him wish with all his might that he could see her, just for a heartbeat, just long enough to commit her face to mind so that he would no longer have to rely on his feverish imaginings for her portrait. He would never tell her so, however; she would only take it as an invitation to act as his guardian, and there were already far too many people assuming he needed one. Besides, even if he dared confess his feelings, there was her older brother Donald to consider. He, for one, cared little about Neil's welfare. Thus, he buried his affection where no one could reach it, and feigned indifference.

"It's a new perfume; supposedly quite expensive," she told him, "though my father isn't known for his generosity, so who knows how much truth there is in that? He probably picked it up at a common market."

"Probably."

He heard her feet scuff the floor. Then, "Why are you like this?" she asked.

"Like what?"

"So... I don't know...mean."

He shrugged. "How would you like me to be?"

"A little nicer. After all, I'm not mean to *you*."

"And that's supposed to make a difference to the way I am, is it? Just because you're all smiles and roses all day every day?"

"If you took the time to show a little interest you'd know that isn't the case at all. I have my share of bad days."

He scoffed. "Really."

"Yes, as a matter of fact, and it's more than a little arrogant for you to assume otherwise. Need I remind you that I have a brash, foul-mouthed ogre for an older brother? You try living with him for a week, never mind fifteen years, and see what it does for your disposition."

He sighed deeply and drummed his fingers on the countertop. "Was there something you wanted besides someone to bore?"

"You're impossible. Anyone would think in a dull village like this you'd be glad to have a friend."

"Is that what you are? Well, I'm frightfully sorry to disappoint you, but I have no need of friends. I do quite well on my own. Now, I repeat, was there something you wanted? This is after all, a shop."

"As a matter of fact, there are two things, although your usual absence of cheer has made me doubt the sense in proposing the second of them."

Inside his stoical shell, Neil's excitement grew.

"Firstly, I need flour," Tabitha said. "My mother's baking a cake for the October Dance."

"That's nice." His heart was in his throat.

"Which brings me to my second order of business: Are you going?"

"What's it to you?"

"Just once can't you answer a question with some degree of civility?"

He made a dramatic sigh. "Kate wants me to take her. I'd rather be eaten by wild dogs."

"I'm sure that could be arranged," Tabitha said. "But in the meantime, you should know that if you *are* there, I expect you to ask me to dance, assuming you know how."

Instinctively a crude insult arose in him but he bit his tongue. Instead he said, "Why on earth would I want to dance with *you*?"

When she spoke, her words were shaped by a smile. "I happen to think you'd like that very much."

"Then you're mad."

"We'll see."

He went to fetch the flour, his heart racing, forcing him to double his efforts in order to conceal his delight.

He'd envisioned the scenario that had just taken place a hundred times over, with only the feeblest of hopes that it would ever transpire beyond the realm of his imagination. Now that it had, he wasn't sure what to do. A bolder man would attempt to initiate courtship in a more forward manner, and while Neil was plenty bold on the surface, his insides felt like jelly now. But then doubt swept over him. What if she was toying with him? What if it was merely a ploy, a means of repaying him for his bitter treatment of her over the past few years? It certainly made more sense, for at no time had he given her an opening from which she might draw the slightest hint of interest on his part. This was a crushing thought, but sadly, easier to swallow than her sudden invitation.

He returned with her order and carefully set it out on the counter. "Do you need anything else?"

"No," she said as he put the small sack of flour into a cardboard box. "But I would appreciate it if you'd carry this to the door for me."

"I'm sure you would." He made no move to do as she'd requested and had to restrain a smile at her exasperated sigh.

"Very well. Until tonight then, and I do hope you're more of a gentleman at the dance."

She left the store, the fragrance of her lingering in the air, as intoxicating as any drug and twice as potent, insinuating its way into his brain, shaping his thoughts, bending them, until he knew he was deceiving himself by pretending he wouldn't be at the dance to take her up on her offer.

The Hounds of Hell themselves couldn't keep him away.

4

A GHOST LAY STILL AND SILENT ON THE BED. From the doorway, a slender shadow watched.

"Father?" Kate was almost afraid to speak too loud, for fear the words would slice through his palsied body and shatter him like glass.

There was little sense in expecting a response—Doctor Campbell had told her not to—and yet she continued to speak to him, knowing without a doubt that someday he would answer. She persisted, because people didn't just vanish out of themselves without saying goodbye.

The stark white face was turned to the window, shadows nestling in the hollow cheeks, silvery stubble catching the muted morning sunlight. His eyes were open and unblinking. Kate might have thought him dead but for the low rasp of his breathing and the gentle rise and fall of the sheets around his painfully thin chest.

Through the window, the sun skewered the lazily drifting mist, making swords of smoke that angled toward the house, the dew glistening on the moors like scattered diamonds. Kate liked to think her father was contemplating the beauty of the scene, but when she'd mentioned this aloud, Doctor Campbell had, as was his custom, dismissed it as preposterous. *His condition suggests cancer or some other form of degenerative disease. But in other ways it doesn't. His muscles are atrophying at a rapid rate, his breathing is shallow and there is no response to stimuli. He's losing weight, and hair, and teeth. But I'm confounded as to the source of it all. Despite the symptoms, there doesn't seem to be a point of origin. It's almost as if he's already died and the body is just slow in following. So, young girl, what you're looking at is an empty vessel. It sees nothing, feels even less. Don't upset yourself with idle fantasies.*

Looking at her father now, Kate was convinced more than ever that the doctor was an incompetent fool. That Campbell drank to excess was no secret, and there had been rumors that his relocation to Brent Prior from London hadn't been of his own volition. It wasn't hard to believe, for despite its beauty, there were few places more isolated and desolate than the moors. To an appreciative eye, it could be a place of splendor. To a man accustomed to the hubbub of London's thoroughfares, gin-palaces and markets, it would be the ultimate punishment. A prison.

"Father?" she whispered again and sat down on the bed. He didn't acknowledge her—no sudden catch in his breathing, no blink to indicate he was aware of anything beyond whatever nightmare capered behind his eyes. "I'm going to the dance tonight." She reached out a hand and stroked his cheek. Stubble rasped beneath her fingers, the skin cool beneath. "I wish you could be there to see us. It's been such a long time since you've danced with me. I know you'd love it."

She let her hand slide lower and rubbed a thumb over his cool lips. Outside, a raven cawed, its shadow sweeping across the sheets before it moved on.

"That mountebank Doctor Campbell thinks you'll never get out of this spell of yours, but he's a fool. You know that too, don't you? I remember you used to say so." She smiled. "You used to say he was probably just some tramp masquerading as a medico to get the respect he was sure he deserved. Well, I think you were right. He was in here on Saturday reeking of whiskey and tobacco. What self-respecting doctor would dare show up to the house of an ill man in his cups? Even Neil says the man can't wear cologne because it would crawl from his own cheeks at the stench of him." She laughed, but the sound was so hollow in the room, it almost summoned tears.

"Why won't you wake up?" She drew her hand down to his chest, to where the faint thump of his heart assured her of life, and leaned in so that her hair trailed over her fingers. "He says you're going to die," she said in a broken whisper. "And Grady and Miss Fletcher, they don't say it, but I know they already think you're lost to us. Sometimes I think even Neil has given up on you."

Her brother seldom visited this room, but when he did he never spoke to their father, but sat, as if waiting, only to leave moments later. Once, when Kate questioned him about the brevity of his vigils, he'd retorted, "Unlike you, I can't see him, so all I can do is listen. I can't stand to hear that terrible tortured breathing. He breathes like a dying man. But it should be much worse if the room fell suddenly quiet, so I do not linger long."

In truth, there was no question in her heart that Neil loved him, and yet she could never quite convince herself that his love for their father was quite as strong, or as pure as hers. A pronounced streak of callousness ran through her brother's heart. She had, on occasion, caught him with the most unsettling look on his face, as if he were envisioning scenarios too awful for benevolent minds to comprehend. She tried to tell herself that she gave those looks far too much import, when perhaps he was only daydreaming. If so, however, she did not want to know the nature of the things that kept him enthralled.

As she watched her father, a slight shape beneath the sheet, she felt a sorrow so deep it caused her stomach to clench. She grimaced, and the gasp that escaped her ended in tears. "What happened to you?" She lowered her head to his chest. "I know you can hear me."

She closed her eyes and cried quietly, her hand smoothening out the wrinkles in her father's shirt. She imagined his arms moving suddenly, the thrill that would overwhelm her as his fingers clawed his hands up around her back. He would embrace her, his mouth opening to whisper words of comfort—*I'm here my love, everything's going to be fine*—and she would cry until she felt as if her own life were draining from her. She would hug him until he protested, and scream for all to hear that the damnable Doctor Campbell had been denounced as a fraud by his own patient, who had defied him by coming back to life. There would be a celebration, festivities that would last until Christmas, and the house would be alive again.

"Come back," she said again, her chest filled with mourning. "Come back to us."

She raised her head.

Upon the moors, a bird cried. The sunlight shifted ever so slightly as the mist twisted in on itself. There was no breeze. No sound.

But for a single, gurgled breath.

Kate gasped, a chill scurrying down her spine.

Her father's head was still turned toward the window, but his gaze had shifted, the eyelids wide. He was watching her, in apparent fear, out of the corner of his eye. She saw the angry red veins stretched across the whites, like tiny ropes attempting to drag his attention back where it belonged, and as she stared, petrified despite the implications of this startling new development, his lower lip twitched.

She was on her feet in an instant. "Oh God...*Father?*"

Everything in her wanted to cry out, just as she had envisioned, but for the moment, she was not yet certain enough to summon anything but the slightest of whimpers. *He heard me*, she thought, her nerves humming with excitement. *He's waking!*

He stared at her from the corner of his bloodshot eye. There was a click as he swallowed, a slight *pip!* as his dry lips parted.

Kate moved back to him. "It's me," she said, her voice choked with tears, "I'm here. It-it's all right now." She had never given much credence to the power of prayer, but what was happening now—though she scarcely dared believe it—was nothing short of a miracle.

The eye widened until it seemed there was only red-veined white. A shudder passed through her father, his breath emerging in stuttered hisses, his chest rising and falling rapidly.

"Daddy..."

Then the mist reached up and choked the sun, darkening the room and sending confused shadows sprawling across the bed.

Kate felt a cold uncertainty at the stark, unbridled terror in her father's eyes. Did he not know her? Was he seeing a phantom in her place? The petrified look seemed to be screaming a silent plea to her: *Stay away stay away stay away...*

"Don't be afraid," she sobbed. "It's me, Father. Please don't..."

He convulsed, once. There came the sound of what might have been a splintered cough, quickly followed by a tortured gurgle, as atrophied organs struggled to reacquaint themselves with life.

Then she did scream, as, from her father's slightly opened mouth, something began to run.

***

"Tobacco."

"Who's that?" Neil asked. The customer brought with him the smell of wet clay and burning leaves, an autumnal odor that might have been pleasant if not for the underlying stench of death that accompanied it.

"I do apologize if I startled you."

"You didn't." Neil heard no apology at all in the unfamiliar voice. While the accent suggested someone local, the deep, rumbling timbre was completely alien to his ears.

He turned his back on the man and began to feel the notches in the wood for the appropriate shelf. Greg Fowler, the storeowner, had carved symbols in them to indicate what each one held. Neil only had to run his fingertips over them to find what he was looking for. Of course, initially he'd protested what he'd perceived as 'special treatment' but Fowler had marked the shelves anyway and secretly, Neil was glad of them.

"It's up there, one shelf to your right."

Neil clenched his teeth in irritation. "I *know* where it is." He grabbed the small pouch, turned and tossed it onto the counter.

"You must be Neil Mansfield," the stranger said. "Jack Mansfield's boy."

"Who are you?"

"A past acquaintance."

"Well then, I'll be sure to tell my father that a *past acquaintance* says 'hello.'"

The man laid his coins out on the counter. "How is your father, anyway? I'm surprised I haven't seen him ambling about."

Neil collected the money, ran his thumb over the coins to ensure he'd been given the correct amount, then deposited them into a small tin box behind the counter. "He's sick. Has been for a long time."

"Sick? Really? Well, that is indeed a shame."

Again, Neil was struck by the lack of sincerity in the stranger's voice. "Can I get you anything else?"

The man said nothing.

Neil frowned. "Well?"

"If you were offered your sight, would you take it?"

Neil clenched his fists. Few things angered him more than when people assumed they had to right to discuss his disability just because he didn't hide it. "I beg your pardon?"

"I think it's a rather simple question. Your eyes are quite remarkable as they are. Don't misunderstand me. I'm merely hypothesizing. Say if you could see again, if someone could return your sight to you, would you accept the gift?"

"No."

"Why not?"

"It's an absurd question."

"You think so?"

"It's not something that can be cured, so if you're done being ridiculous..."

"Oh, don't be so sure of that, young Mansfield. Small villages breed small minds incapable of seeing the breadth of the sky above their own chimneys or the world beyond their gates. But not everything is so simple, or clearly defined. There are ways of fixing even the most impossible problems. There are *other* ways of seeing."

"Yes...well right now nothing would satisfy me more than to have *you* see yourself to the door."

"Aren't you at all curious why I asked?"

"Are you a doctor?"

"Insofar as I offer people what they need, I suppose I am."

"I don't have much time for doctors. Our current one leaves a lot to be desired. To describe him as shabby genteel would be complimenting the drunken lout."

"So I've heard." Boots scuffed the floor as the stranger drew closer. "But right now, I'm more interested in you, Neil."

The boy felt a pang of unease and slowly moved away until his back was pressed against the notched shelves. "Why?"

"Because I believe I can change your life."

"What makes you think I *want* my life changed?"

"Come now, every boy your age has a wish, something that they'd give everything to have. And, as preposterous as it might sound, I do believe I'm in a position to give you exactly what it is you need."

"I need you to leave. Can you grant that wish?"

"My, my, aren't you the spirited one."

It was not a question, so Neil made no attempt to answer it, but the silence wrought by his lack of response made him uncomfortable. To his relief, it didn't last long.

"I've upset you," the stranger said, "and for that I apologize, but I do believe we'll speak again, young Mansfield. In fact, I dare say we're bound to become steadfast friends, once you realize I mean you no harm. Quite the opposite, in fact."

"Believe what you like. You've wasted enough of my time." Neil turned back to the shelves and began to trace the notches, even though there was nothing he wanted but to preoccupy himself with something other than the stranger.

"You're correct. We'll have ample time to discuss our secrets," the man said. "Perhaps when our paths next cross you can tell me more about that pretty young girl who came to see you earlier."

Neil froze. The idea that this foul-smelling, deranged stranger might know about Tabitha disturbed him more than it had any right to. "Mind your own business," he grunted, but the sound of boots crunching gravel told him the man had already left. He turned to face the breeze soughing in through the open doorway. The man's voice, seductive and cordial and yet colder than anything he had ever heard before, echoed in his mind.

I believe I can change your life.

5

"I WOULDN'T CELEBRATE JUST YET," Doctor Campbell said, as he stepped into the hallway and pulled the bedroom door closed behind him. The sleeve of his oversized coat snagged in the jamb and he muttered first an apology, then a slew of obscenities as he struggled to worry it free.

Typical, Kate thought.

At last he tugged and the door slammed shut with a bang, the echo like thunder in the quiet house. The doctor grimaced, ran a hand over his coarse hair and licked his lips. As usual, he reeked of whiskey. While Grady waited patiently, Kate tapped her foot on the floor in a staccato rhythm.

Pale light washed the walls and cast the winding staircase in shadow. Wind swept the chimney dust from the roof, scattered it across the moors and into the thickening fog.

Campbell set his battered Gladstone bag at his feet and straightened with a grunt. "He's awake. I can tell you that much."

"That's very illuminating." Kate crossed her arms to avoid kicking the information out of the doctor. "But is he all right?"

Campbell leaned against the banister of the stairs. Grady winced at the creak it gave and stepped closer to the old man. Kate guessed it was in case he might be required to save the doctor from a sudden fall if the railing chose to give way. *I'd let him fall*, she thought, *it might teach him some manners*.

Campbell was sweating profusely and, when not gesturing emptily at the air—a habit Kate assumed was his attempt to coax forth long forgotten medical terminology—daubed his brow with a soiled linen handkerchief.

"He's conscious, but not speaking and, I dare say, not entirely lucid. What you might see as a step forward may indeed be a whole leap in reverse."

"But he woke up," Grady said. "Surely that means somethin' after all this time?"

Campbell shrugged. "Haven't you ever heard the expression 'waking up just in time to catch your death'?"

Kate, fists and teeth clenched, stepped forward. Grady reached out a hand to stay her. She kept her glare fixed on the wheezing doctor, who seemed oblivious to the proximity of the chestnut-haired dervish.

"Don't you ever have any good news, you incompetent sop, or do you have so little to live for yourself that you delight in being the bearer of misery?"

Campbell looked at her. "Young miss..." He paused to hack a cough into his soiled handkerchief. "Believe me, I wish more than anything that I could tell you your beloved father will be up and around in a matter of days. But I have seen nothing to contradict my belief that he is slowly collapsing under the weight of some great and mysterious malady. That he has managed to cling to life this long is in itself a wonder!" He wiped his mouth before continuing; spittle still glistened on his lips. "I've gone to great lengths to try and understand what it is that's plaguing him. I've spoken with some colleagues of mine in London and though they have put forth some theories—Doctor Joyce even suggested some kind of tropical virus!—not a one of them could shed any light on the cause of this illness, or indeed what it might be. Therefore, you can see how difficult it is to treat a disease alien to me, and how equally difficult it is to offer you the hope you so desperately seek. To do so would be merely raising the height from which you'd eventually have to plummet when you learned the truth. I'm truly sorry, but it is not in me to deceive a dying man's children."

"If you can't identify his illness, then how can you say he's dyin'?" Grady asked.

Campbell scoffed. "*Look at him* for Heaven's sake!"

Kate moved before she was fully aware she was going to, but just as quickly she could move no more. Grady's hand had attached itself to her shoulder and one squeeze extended her patience, but not by much. Campbell raised a hand to his throat, as if fearing she might yet try to take a bite out of it.

"He's *not* dying," she told him. "And I believe it's quite probable that you insist on drawing such a conclusion only because your drunken mind has long since shredded your expertise, allowing you no alternative but to fall upon the simplest of diagnoses to save you the labor of having to strive for a cure."

Campbell was appalled. He turned to Grady. "Are you going to permit this...this...*child*...to talk to me in such a manner? I'd cuff her ears if I were you."

"Fortunate for the lady then that yer *not* me," Grady replied.

"And don't you dare call me a child," Kate added, bolstered by Grady's support.

Indignation stiffened Campbell's posture. "*Lady?* Well, then it's clear who holds court in this house."

Kate glowered. "You're a charlatan and a drunk and I'd rather you not befoul the precious air in my father's room again."

The color drained from the doctor's face. Again he appealed to Grady. "Will you not even raise a hand to this obduracy? Does her tone not embarrass you as her guardian?"

"She's her own guardian," Grady said. "And she's not herself. None of us are, with the master bein' ill. I would think, as a physician, you'd have seen grief and fear in all its incarnations and would understand how ugly it can make a mourner."

Kate felt her guts tighten at the caretaker's words. She looked beseechingly at him. "We're not mourning. There's no *reason* to mourn, for God's sake."

"I have seen all kinds of grief," Campbell replied, ignoring her, "but never such insolence. Not from a child. It's a disgrace. Furthermore, I believe it's your responsibility to remind her in this instance of her place, and her manners."

"Of course you do. But perhaps yer outrage needs reinin' in, Doctor. Try to understand what this lady's been goin' through. She's very close to her father and the thought of losin' him..." He shook his head, glanced at Kate. Her eyes were filled with dark fire.

Campbell, flustered, moved to a safe distance at the head of the stairs and continued to mop his brow. "I admit I've been wrong before," he said. "Not often mind you, but only a fool would claim to know the secrets of the human body inside and out. I'd just feel better not offering false hope, that's all. I didn't mean to cause upset." His hands were trembling and suddenly, he looked a decade older.

"Then perhaps you'd better work on yer beside manner, Doctor," Grady suggested.

Campbell's mouth grew tight. "Mr. Grady, you should not mistake my willingness to compromise as an admission of ineptitude. I'm merely explaining my reasons for not giving you the diagnosis you're looking for, nothing more."

"What about the physicians in London? *Qualified* doctors. Surely they'd know more than this...this—?" Kate floundered for an adequate insult, and Grady interjected before she could find them.

"We've already tried that, Kate, and the master is here at home on the strength of their recommendations."

"Nor, may I add," said Campbell, "would it be wise to move him at this late stage."

"We're talkin' about a man who hasn't moved an inch in almost two years 'cept to be cleaned and fed, a man who stares out the window as if tryin' to figure out where and what he is. Today he moves, he actually moves *on his own*, and yer tellin' us 'tis a sign he's on the way out?"

"All signs suggest—"

"If 'tis all the same to you," Grady continued, "I think we'll keep hopin'. At least until Master Mansfield tells us himself 'tis a futile pursuit."

The doctor shrugged, and donned his bowler. "Of course. But I must caution against investing too much hope in his recovery. It will only make it harder for you afterward."

"Understood."

"I've given him a dose of morphine. It will tide him over until I return."

Grady nodded.

"Why bother?" Kate grumbled, not loud enough for the doctor to hear.

Campbell trotted down the stairs, one hand braced on the banister for support. Halfway down he paused, stared straight ahead a moment, and then set his bag down on the step. Kate and Grady watched as he produced a slim glass test tube from inside the bag, which he raised before turning to look up at them, a sad smile on his face.

"Do you know what this is?" he asked, giving the vial a violent shake. The silver liquid within moved sluggishly.

"Mercury?" offered Grady.

Campbell shook his head. "I show you this in an effort to convince you that it would be best to mourn your father now," he said, looking at Kate. "And get the worst of it over with."

Kate huffed. "I'll do no such thing, you—"

"Emetics do nothing," Campbell said, interrupting the imminent insult, "and salts are worthless. This," he said, and gave the tube another shake, "is what my lancet drew forth from your father."

Grady expelled a stunned breath and when Kate looked at him, she saw him struggle to regain his composure for her benefit. Heartsick, she looked back at the doctor. "What is it?"

"His blood," Campbell said, as he returned the tube to his bag, snapped the clasps shut and descended the stairs.

***

She was like a cyclone. Grady wished he'd just gone ahead and started mending the fences, but it was too late now. Kate slammed the parlor door behind her hard enough to set the ornaments on the mantel rattling, her eyes wild as she looked around the room. Grady, who feared she might break something in her turbulent state, went to her, arms held out for an embrace. To his surprise, she pushed him away, took a few steps and then turned, her face contorted with rage and frustration.

"You're a man of the world, aren't you?" she demanded, but continued before he could answer, "Or so you keep telling me anyway. So tell me this: What makes a man bleed silver?"

"Kate, I—"

"Don't *lie* to me, Grady, just don't bloody lie to me or I swear I'll send you out of this house for good."

He had weathered a thousand of her tempers, but never in all his years had she threatened to expel him from the house. It hurt, but he reminded himself that she was incensed by the doctor's disturbing announcement and most likely didn't mean it.

"I've never lied to you," he told her.

She stepped close, eyes blazing. "Then tell me now what you've been afraid to tell me before. What happened to him? What happened to Father to make him this way? There was a search for a missing woman of which he was a part, that much I know. But what *aren't* you telling me about that day? Something was done to him, some kind of a seed was planted in him on that hunt that eventually felled him, made him what he is now. What made him sick?"

"Darlin'...there are things people should—"

"Grady, I'm not a fool, so don't treat me like one."

"I'm not," he protested, but she wasn't listening.

"The villagers, those who haven't fled far from here still talk of that search on the moors." she said. "I've seen you struggle to get those fences up even though we have no animals left to keep in. Are you're trying to keep something *out?* On those few occasions when you go into the village, you cross yourself whenever you pass by the gate to the moors and I've seen the way you look at it from your window. I *demand*, right this bloody second, that you tell me why you're so afraid and what has made a breathing corpse of my father."

Grady felt a cold finger trace a path down his spine at the thought of having to tell her anything about that day. But the steely set of her jaw and the fury in her eyes told him she would persist until he did so. And he had to admit that she deserved to know why her father was dying after all these years of watching over him. Only his desire to protect her had kept him from telling her the truth.

He rubbed a hand over his face and sat down with a sigh. "I don't know enough to satisfy you. I only know what I saw with my own two eyes, and over time I've grown to doubt even that. But if you insist on hearin' my account of it..."

"I do." She was calmer now, but only a little. He knew it wouldn't take much for her to fly into a rage again. She was scared, and he wondered if on some level she already knew, or at least suspected, some of what he was about to share.

She sat on the rocking chair opposite him, her arms crossed, waiting.

Grady looked out the window at the gloom. "It started with an early morning visitor," he began.

***

Mansfield shuddered, came awake. Immediately he felt the cold fire overwhelm the sluggish tide of morphine. His hands began to tremble, his head snapping to the left and the right, teeth clenched behind lips tightly shut to silence the scream. He grunted softly, opened his eyes and saw the room had turned white—bone white, fog white...moon white. Mist rose from the foot of the bed, curled up like surf around the sheets and collapsed back down into the seething white mass. He convulsed as if shocked, his heart ramming against his ribcage as if desperate to be free of the torture. A single drop of silver blood trickled from his nose.

He closed his eyes, and concentrated on the sound of his own ragged breathing. Prayers—and there had been a century of them whispered to the dust in this room—had no effect. The pain remained, crawling like snakes beneath his skin, pausing often to chew and bite his organs, to tear like maddened dogs at his nerves, to push against his skin as if seeking an exit. Sometimes he saw them; their diamond-shaped heads heaving against the skin of his chest, forcing it upward like hands beneath rubber, until he could watch no more, could only dream of screaming before he passed out. At first, he had assumed they were hallucinations, vile imaginary representations of an even viler pain. But then he touched them, felt them shift beneath his flesh, felt them press against his trembling fingers, and knew they were real. This most hideous invasion instilled in him a rage, a grim determination to linger, suffer on, and deny the parasites their meal.

He thought of Neil, sitting quietly on the window sill, almost close enough to touch and yet a million miles away; Kate, sobbing against his chest while his arms ached to hold her and his tongue yearned to speak, if only to let her know he heard and felt everything, that he was still here. But he couldn't, the parasite stemmed the flow of words before they ever reached his mouth. He could only lie beneath blankets that felt like steel wool, while snakes writhed inside his skin, maddening him, torturing him.

Changing him.

6

HIS TALE TOLD, GRADY ROSE FROM THE SOFA and went to the sideboard by the window. As he poured himself a glass of brandy, he caught a glimpse of Kate's pale face reflected in the sideboard mirror. Her eyes were wide, her fingers interlaced to keep them from shaking.

"I'm sorry. I know how it sounds, and before you remind me: yes, I am a mad old fool." He replaced the crystal cap on the decanter and returned to his seat with the brandy. "I'm not even sure *I* believe it anymore."

"But it's preposterous," Kate declared. "Beasts on the moor? Father used to tell us such things to scare us!"

"He was right in tryin' to scare you. Perhaps he thought if he could make you fear the moors, you'd keep away from 'em."

"I mean, such a fanciful tale belongs in the pages of *The Strand*, not in real life!"

"I'm only tellin' you what I saw. Maybe the fog was to blame fer blurrin' things, but whatever it was, it killed Royle with one swipe of its claws and cut my poor horse to ribbons."

"A wolf then, or a wild dog?"

"Maybe," he said, making no attempt to hide the doubt in his voice.

"Didn't anyone try to run it down after what happened? Didn't they try to find out what it was?"

"No. Why would they?" He took a sip of his brandy. "No matter how brave a man might be, he won't go tryin' to chase down the devil fer fear he'd return without his soul, and nothin' scares a man more than that."

Kate glanced at the mullioned window and the fog pressing against the pane. "Then it's still out there."

"It hasn't been seen since," Grady reassured her, even though that was not altogether true, but he felt, given the fear that had possessed her, that this small white lie was justified; anything to spare her the kind of permanent dread that had made its home in his heart ever since the day of the search.

When she looked at him again, sadness had replaced the fear. "What did it do to Father?"

Grady slowly shook his head. "I don't know. It hurt him, infected him somehow."

Her lower lip trembled, and tears filled her eyes. "With what?"

He offered her a feeble smile. "I don't know that either, but whatever it is, I know he's strong enough to beat it. And when he does, he can answer fer you all the questions I can't."

"I won't care by then," she said, her voice wavering. "If...*when* he comes back to me, I won't care what made him ill. It won't matter anymore."

A heavy silence descended and hung between them and after a while, Grady composed his best smile and said, "Do you still want to go to the October Dance tonight?"

She nodded. "I have to, or go mad thinking about these things."

"Then we best get prepared. I'd rather not have the wrath of Mrs. Fletcher on me for keepin' you talkin'.

Grady stood, took her hands and gently brought her to her feet.

"I'm sorry," she sobbed, and slipped her arms around his neck. "I would never cast you out. You and Mrs. Fletcher are all I have."

He stroked her hair and hushed her tears. "And you'll always have us."

She nodded, obviously not convinced, and pulled away from him. He understood her reluctance to accept his promise. After all, she'd lost her mother, and now her father would in all likelihood succumb to whatever disease had him in its grasp. Promises meant nothing to her anymore. Not when she'd long been aware of the transience of life.

"I'd better get cleaned up," she said, averting her eyes so he wouldn't see the fresh tears. As she walked toward the door, Grady wondered when she'd gotten to be such a young woman. He'd been here all along, watching her grow, and yet somehow it felt as if he'd missed it, as if she'd hidden herself away in some secret chrysalis and emerged a beautiful young lady. He smiled at her when she looked over her shoulder at him. But the swell of affection he felt soon faded beneath a black cloud of worry. Perhaps it was the master's waking, All Hallows and its inherent superstitions, or the awareness that soon Kate would leave to face the world beyond their little haven, but an ominous feeling had nestled in his chest, as if a storm was coming, a storm so fierce it might tear them all asunder.

***

The nerve of that little wretch, thought Campbell, as he wiped his nose on his sleeve and studied the glistening trail that remained on the fabric. The morning chill breathed against his bones, even though his coat was wrapped so tight around him a sneeze would rend it apart. Nevertheless, he was possessed of a trembling that set his teeth clicking; he could feel the fingernails of winter splitting his lower lip, a discomfort he would not fully appreciate until he reached The Fox & Mare and the heat aroused it. He did not relish the thought of removing his ungloved hands from the warmth of his pockets, but since one of them held a flask of whiskey, it was a sacrifice that would have to be made. Tensing his shoulders and pausing by the cold stone wall that separated the road from the rolling moors, he fished out the flask, quickly unscrewed the cap and drank deeply, until he felt the fire filling his belly. A belch of appreciation and he was on his way, hands and flask returned to pockets.

Insolent cur.

He'd delivered that little whelp from her mother's womb and clothed the fluids from her tiny body. He'd even slapped the first breath out of her. Now, as he remembered the insults she'd cast his way earlier, he wished that damn fool groundskeeper had permitted him an opportunity to do so again. The way her eyes had bulged with fury at him, the way the veins in her throat had stood out like cords beneath a cape, her mouth twisted into a hateful sneer, and all because he'd opted to tell the truth rather than deceive her into believing anything but grief lay ahead. Her impertinence clung to him like a shroud. Why, had he dared to show his tongue at that age it would have been pulled from his mouth, and rightly so. Had he been alone with her, he might have attempted that very thing. With Grady there however, he'd have been asking for trouble. The groundskeeper was like her loyal hound.

He sighed. At least he could delight in remembering the confusion on her face when he'd showed her the blood. That had shut her up in a hurry, as he had known it would, though he was just as puzzled by the oddly colored serum as she had been. It wasn't at all natural for something so metallic in hue to come from a living creature in place of blood, but he couldn't for the life of him figure out what had caused it.

It was something he imagined the boys in London—his former colleagues—would have a field day with, if he chose to share it, and he had not yet decided if he was willing to take that step. There was every chance that the serum might prove to be a significant find, an anomalous precedent that might make him a fortune, and return him to the level of prestige and respect his nocturnal imaginings told him he'd once commanded. The prospect filled him with excitement. But reality, as had been proved today, was often quick to bring him down to earth.

The world was going to hell. Was it any wonder then that he frequently sought the solace of oblivion, the panacea whiskey offered against the seething contributions of the impudent, the pious and the treacherous? Not at all. His own microcosmic existence had imploded at the realization not so long ago, that his days were a blur, his nights a time for febrile dreams and haunted recollections. His wife had cast him off like an old suit and quickly found another, better tailored than he. He'd become a pale empty shell with spidery cracks for veins and a mouth used only to dictate diagnoses and consume the fuel necessary to ensure he remembered to breathe, or more accurately, to fool him into believing he *wanted* to breathe when another morning came around to cast its spiteful light across his eyes.

And Lord, how angry it made him. Angry that he had wasted so much time trying to fit the mold of the caring husband when all the while he'd known he didn't care at all. Marriage, to him, had been an institution in the literal sense. There had existed no middle ground, no fairness, only the gradual emergence of dominant and submissive roles between two people locked in a cage of fake smiles and dutiful intimacy. Worse still, the dominance had not been his, and soon his role had been relegated to that of a silent observer, forever watching but scarcely understanding just what it was he had wed. Overnight it seemed as if Agnes's natural reticence had vanished, replaced by an inexplicable temerity he was not capable of sharing. She became a chattering whirlwind concerned only with her appearance and social standing, and frequently taken by a maddening need to be free of Brent Prior and what she termed 'its grubby underlings.' A woman of airs and graces, of lofty aspirations; a woman with striking beauty and no depth at all. Over the years, as he listened without word to her tirades and feverish monologues—all spoken as if she addressed a theater crowd and not her husband—the hard shell of irritation in him had cracked, producing shoots that spun upward into dislike, which in turn branched out into loathing.

Then the jewelry began to appear.

At first it was a brooch, an inexpensive—by Campbell's estimation, at least—cameo he assumed she had picked up on one of her increasingly frequent trips to Devon. But as the months went by, more lavish accoutrements began to gather in her nightstand. At first, perhaps at the behest of deliberate ignorance, he'd told himself she was buying these things for herself, but this excuse, flimsy to begin with, shattered completely the night she came home drunk, reeking of gin and a musky, manly stench, and wearing a pearl necklace she made no attempt to conceal from him.

"Who is it?" he'd demanded, sure he wouldn't know the name she gave him, but unable to stop himself from asking. The lack of anger he felt shamed him. He didn't even rise from his seat as she danced, *flaunted* her betrayal in front of him as if he were her brother, or friend, a confidant, anything but a husband. He simply sat, hands hanging between his knees. Her response should have enraged him. It didn't, but merely ran stiffened fingers over heartstrings gone taut with age.

"His name is Simon, and he's a gentleman."

What bothered him the most was not the treachery itself, but the complete lack of guilt she displayed. She seemed almost proud, and acted as if he should have known of her affair all along, or at least expected it.

Four days later she was gone, no note, no farewell, just the lingering scent of her in a cold dusty house.

It took weeks for the anger to come. To quench the flames, he returned to drink after fifteen years of abstinence at Agnes's request. In some small way, it felt like a betrayal of her, and he relished it, latched onto it, until it became his sole reason for being. Until he could no longer clearly remember why it was he hated his errant wife, only that he did and would continue to do so.

"Who's that?" someone asked, jarring Campbell from his reverie. He leaned against the wall and squinted through the fog of his breath at the boy slowly making his way toward him.

The Mansfield boy. Another young pup, uncouth and undisciplined, using his blindness as an excuse to insult whomever he wished without fear of reprimand.

Bloody children. Bastards, all of them. They should all be left to choke on their first breaths.

The boy, white eyes rimmed with silver, frowned as he tapped a long thin stick against the gravel surface of the road, one hand outstretched, grubby fingers reaching. "Announce yourself."

He has his father's eyes now, Campbell thought, and smirked even as he recoiled. Cold stone knuckled his spine as the blind boy's fingers swept through the air inches from his face. He remained silent, hoping the child would move on.

Neil sniffed the air, a slight grimace passing over his face. "Oh, it's *you*," he said and continued along the path toward the monolithic sandstone manse that overlooked the village from its perch on Barrow Hill.

Campbell watched him for a moment, then spat and reached into his pocket for the flask. The Mansfield boy had always repulsed him, and it was something more than the child's disposition that inspired that disgust. It was not the blindness, for Campbell had been too long a doctor for such things to bother him. It was something else, something he couldn't quite identify. With a shrug and a long slug of his drink, he capped the flask, stowed it and hurried to The Fox & Mare, where, he hoped, less unnerving company awaited him.

7

THE STICK THWACKED AGAINST THE FOOT OF THE OAK TREE. Neil ran his fingers over the warped bole and turned left, the antenna-like probing of the cane leading him off the gravel and on to the carpet of leaves and dirt that would bring him home.

A low breeze hissed through the trees, carrying with it the scent of wood smoke, and making bare branches tap together like old bones. Dead leaves scratched across the path. The chill increased.

Neil imagined the house up ahead—an oblong of cold stone, as Grady had once described it to him, and wondered if today was the day when he'd come home to find his father awake. He doubted it, and realized that, for now at least, he didn't mind that their father was bed-bound. He relished the freedom that came with having him confined to his room. There were no orders, few chores, and a distinct lack of discipline due to Mrs. Fletcher and Grady's unwillingness or inability to dictate household policy. Their father had never ruled Mansfield House with an iron fist, but there were still things he had forbidden Neil to do, and as a result, the boy had yearned to do them all the more, his curiosity inflamed.

Stay off the moors, his father had said. *There are plenty of other things you can find to do to occupy your time, but I won't hear of you mucking about out there. It's full of dangers, and it's no place for a boy who can't see.*

A boy who can't see...

The memory of his father's words filled Neil with resentment. It had been just one of an endless parade of inferences designed to make him feel useless, helpless, an imposition on those forced to look after him. Before his father fell ill, every rule had been doubled for Neil, every simple command punctuated with sympathy for the poor little blind boy until he'd felt compelled to prove his independence. But his body hadn't been possessed by the same need, and each attempt to assert himself only succeeded in justifying his father's treatment of him. It frustrated the boy until he was forced to choose an alternative route: if he could not venture out on his own, he would not venture out at all.

The house became his prison; everything he touched quickly grew ugly in its familiarity. The sawing of mouse claws in the walls threatened to drive him mad; the wind gurgling through the gutters, the rain tip-tapping on the window, the always distant rumbling of thunder that became malicious laughter, the subtle shifting of the slates on the roof, Mrs. Fletcher's humming, Grady's tuneless whistling, the swishing sound of Kate turning the pages of one of her blasted books, the floorboards groaning, the flutter of candle-flames, his father's voice, insisting Neil let someone take him outside, the grumbling, the clucking of tongues, Kate's relentless teasing...all of it became a whirlwind of noise, a cacophony that might deafen him with the banality and intrusiveness of it, until he couldn't endure it any more.

Everything changed on Kate's birthday. Their father fell ill; the house grew quiet and even as time passed and the seasons changed, the gleeful racket never returned. Neil went outside, alone. On the first occasion, he decided to see if he could make it as far as the village but stumbled, fell, and ended up clawing his way back to the house in silent terror. As expected, Grady and Mrs. Fletcher were outraged.

Neil didn't care.

There were countless attempts after that, few of them allowing him to make it any further than the tree at the end of the lane. Then, one morning, after much arguing, he allowed Kate to accompany him, not to guide him, just to stay with him as he tried to reach the village. He fell and smacked into a low branch, opening a gash on his forehead large enough to make Mrs. Fletcher blanch later at the sight of all the blood, but he persisted, stopping only when Kate caught his arm. He pulled away, about to launch a volley of insults her way, but her voice gave him pause. "We're here," she'd said. "You made it."

"Of course I bloody well made it," he'd snapped, but was secretly ecstatic.

From then on, he ventured out on his own and used the sounds of nature to guide him. Grady fashioned for him a sturdy cane from an oak branch, and though Neil had resisted at first—reminded once again of the pity with which people tended to view him—he soon saw the sense in it, and after a time, that thin piece of oak became his faithful guide, its tapping preferable to the coaxing and muttering of any human or the whining of any hound.

Now that cane caught against a large flat stone, jarring Neil from his thoughts. He had veered off course, and quickly righted himself, using the stick to find the narrow space between the stone markers Grady had set along the path to prevent him from wandering off onto the moors.

The moors.

He could hear it out there, encroaching on the house, and clearly remembered Kate laughing at him when he'd told her what it sounded like. "A muted voice," he'd said, "like it has a secret to tell, but can't find the words. And when there's fog, it sounds like it's breathing." Kate had found this so utterly hilarious, he'd had to pull her hair to quiet her, and had refrained from mentioning it again, or sharing with her the other sounds he'd heard, those whispers that drifted in through his bedroom window at night, calling to him, daring him to seek out their origin. There was something on the moors, he knew, something that scared the villagers enough to make them leave their homes and everything else behind to be rid of it. Something ugly and hungry had scared them away, something that moved beneath the veil of dark and fog. The Beast of Brent Prior, perhaps. Neil smiled at the thought. Mere fancy, of course. He didn't believe in such things, but liked to imagine great big ancient hounds darting across the moors at night, snatching silly old sheep away before they knew what had hit them.

The smile faded when something invaded his imaginings, and his senses.

As he'd traversed the path, the autumnal smell had intensified. Up until now, he'd ignored it. After all, it was autumn, and the path was lined with trees that had laid down a thick carpet of foliage to die at their feet.

But this was different. The smell was too strong, too cloying to be natural.

It summoned a memory of the summer before, when Neil had awoken to a faint, unpleasant smell that had grown stronger as he descended the stairs for breakfast. His nose had led him to the closet beneath the stairs, but when Grady investigated, he found nothing and couldn't detect the odor Neil had described. A week later, with the temperature outside slowly rising, the smell was horrendous. This time, when Grady opened the closet door, he noticed the stench and after a short search discovered a badly decomposed rat inside one of his old forgotten work boots.

Now Neil detected the same stench again, woven into the natural scents of wood smoke and dead leaves. Had something crawled beneath the leaves to die? Reason suggested so, but doubt nagged at him.

He's here.

It was a foolish, childish notion, but it persisted.

He's here, watching you.

No, he's not. You're being ridiculous. Why would he follow you?

Because he's mad.

He quickened his pace as much as he could without tripping himself up.

The house was close. He knew by the slight angle the path had taken.

Behind him, blood-chillingly close, leaves crackled beneath a footfall not his own.

A gasp caught in his throat as the cane betrayed him. He stumbled, almost fell but managed at the last second to steady himself. The wind strengthened, making the bones of the trees clack with more urgency. He whirled, cane raised defensively.

"Who's there? Kate, is that you?"

It would be just like her to try and scare him, but unless she'd been rolling around in dead things, someone else was standing there watching him.

"Who are you?" he said, forming a picture in his mind of what his unseen pursuer might look like, but the pieces refused to come together.

Stop it. If he knows you're scared, it'll only encourage him. He didn't know where this wisdom had come from. He was certainly too frightened to have conjured it up by himself, but he heeded it nonetheless.

"C'mon then," he said, gritting his teeth and swishing the cane in a threatening arc. "What are you waiting for?"

Only the wind replied. He waited for another few moments, the cane still raised and trembling in his hand, and now new doubts began to enter his mind. Maybe it really had been just the leaves that he'd smelled, and maybe something *had* crawled beneath them to die. It certainly wouldn't be anything unusual, and far more credible an idea than a total stranger following him home where anyone who happened to be looking out the window might see him.

"Imbecile." He lowered the cane and turned back in the direction of the house. It wasn't far now. He would be there in a few hurried steps.

More leaves crackled, then again, and again, so close Neil knew if he turned and waited a heartbeat the follower would be upon him. He whirled and, with a cry equal parts fear and rage, lashed the stick at the air before him. There was a sudden smack and the cane halted halfway through its arc so unexpectedly that Neil lost his grip on it and staggered forward.

He raised his head, arms out in front of him, terror playing havoc with his thoughts. *He caught it*, he thought, struggling to keep the dam of panic from breaking. *And now he's going to use it on me.*

He flinched and let out a startled yelp when someone grabbed his hand. He struggled, kicked, flailed and screamed, knowing beyond a doubt that he was going to die, so impossibly close to the house. Nails dug into his sleeve, fingers clutched at him, forcing open his hand. Terror overwhelmed him. The man had followed him and would kill him, for reasons unknown. He had read Neil's thoughts somehow and he would leave the boy's battered and bloodied body buried beneath the leaves so that *he* would be the dead thing the others would smell when the heat returned.

In his personal darkness, he imagined a darker shadow looming over him.

Leaves crackled. Closer.

Neil's scream became a sob. "Why are you doing this to me?"

Then the wind faded, sighed through the leaves and fell still for a moment. It was long enough for Neil to realize he was alone again, and that his cane had been shoved back into his hand. In the distance, he heard the faintest sound of leaves crackling underfoot.

"Who are you?" Neil whispered, the tears warm against frozen cheeks.

The memory of the stranger's voice was the only reply.

We'll have ample time to discuss our secrets.

***

"So, you went shopping," Donald said.

Tabitha glared at her brother as he sauntered over to meet her. His thick rubbery lips were stretched into a mocking grin, revealing large yellow teeth, his peaked cap pulled down over large ears made red by the cold. Snot leaked from the bulb of his nose. "Well?" he asked again when she didn't answer. He fell into step with her as she made her way toward the house, a large two-story building with a gabled roof. The white shuttered windows looked like tired eyes peering through the veil of ivy that smothered the walls and reached into the gutters with delicate fingers.

"I would have thought that was rather obvious," she said, hoisting the box to give him a better look. "Now leave me alone."

"Well, well," Donald said, stuffing his hands into his pockets. "Aren't we contrary? I was just trying to show a little interest in my sister's life, that's all."

Tabitha clenched her teeth to keep from responding. She knew if she voiced the insults that frolicked across her tongue, he'd pull her hair, or punch her in the arm, not hard enough to draw blood or leave bruises, of course, just enough to hurt and make her entertain the notion of crying. Worse, even if her parents were in plain view of his persecution of her, they would shake their heads and go back to whatever they were doing. Donald had always been their favorite and apparently that gave him permission to abuse her whenever he saw fit without fear of punishment.

He kept abreast of her when she walked faster and she felt the combination of fear, loathing, and self-disgust roil within her. At last she reached the door, but as she raised her hand to the latch, he grabbed it and spun her firmly around to face him.

"You're not being very friendly today, Tabby."

"Don't call me that." She avoided his gaze.

"Why not? Is it because it reminds you of a cat? I wouldn't imagine you'd mind all that much. After all, you do have a lot in common. Both sly, and cunning, and always eager to catch a mouse." He giggled maniacally and she tried to pull free of his grip. He tightened it and moved closer, until she could smell the tobacco on his clothes.

"You've been smoking," she said and watched him shrug.

"So what? You've been doing a lot worse, haven't you?"

She closed her eyes and thought, *one of these days I'll hit him back. I truly will. One of these days I'll bloody his nose for him.*

At last he released her, but she knew he wasn't finished. Not until she told him what he was waiting to hear. She shivered, hoping he might suggest they continue the conversation—if that was what it was destined to be—indoors, in the warmth of the house. But he just stood, still grinning that ugly grin, and waited.

"He's going," she said at last. "He'll be at the dance."

Donald nodded. "Good girl. I'll wager you promised him the time of his life."

He winked and started to move into the house but she grabbed his coat. He turned and looked at her hand as if it had grown an extra finger. She quickly released him.

"What?" he asked, all trace of humor, however forced, now gone.

She hesitated, cleared her throat. "Is our agreement complete, then?"

He shrugged. "We'll see how you do tonight, won't we?" With a chuckle, he went inside, slamming the door behind him as if she was indeed a cat who'd been shunned from the house.

I'm sorry, she thought, as tears spilled welled in her eyes, *I'm so sorry, Neil. So sorry for what I've done. So sorry for what they're going to do to you.*

8

CAMPBELL WATCHED HER, WAITING FOR ACKNOWLEDGMENT. When it didn't come, he sighed silently and made his way toward the bar.

Sarah Laws had, at one time, been known as the 'smiling wench' of The Fox & Mare. It was not a derogatory term. Sarah had jokingly, and in retrospect unwisely, coined it herself in a crowd of benevolent drunks, who'd latched onto it immediately and thereafter favored it over her given name. But the nickname had died with her husband. After all, it was hardly appropriate to call a grieving widow a wench of any kind, and all who gathered beneath the smoky veil in the tavern knew it.

On the day a horse killed her beloved, she became Sarah again.

On the day a horse killed her beloved, her jovial nature vanished, replaced by a severity and bitterness that aged her, painted silver strands in her red hair and turned the corners of her mouth down, pointing the way for the beginning of new wrinkles.

On that day, Doctor Frank Campbell commiserated with her, offering his condolences, even while unbridled excitement and hope frolicked behind his eyes. He was one of the few not discouraged by the change in her demeanor or the obvious atrophy of her spirit. To him, it was the sign of an opening, a door left barely ajar but ajar all the same, through which a man, armed with love and honorable intentions, might squeeze through.

Brent Prior was filled with women who'd married young and withered in the marital snare, the light of hope and ambition long since diminished in their eyes. They went about their days with barely restrained sorrow in their eyes, perhaps wishing for a miracle they knew in their hearts would never come. And for those lucky enough to discover companionship, love and the happiness it brought, fate frequently intervened to reduce them to their basest level. Typhoid fever, consumption, cholera, cancer, influenza, enteric fever, pneumonia, scarlet fever, smallpox, and of course, violent death at the hands of fellow man or beast, or simple treachery, all waited in the wings to tear the worlds of lovers apart, erasing the fantasy of eternal bliss.

But while sorrow and grief often robbed a woman of her beauty as well as her spirit, Campbell thought it had had the reverse effect on Sarah Laws. Gone now were the coy smiles and flirtatious winks to every man but him. Gone were the whorish crimson lips and painted cheeks, allowing the world a glimpse of the natural beauty she'd kept hidden behind a plastic mask. It was a faded beauty, the vitality drained from it by parasitic grief, but it was there. The doctor could see it, like a low light burning in a dirty lamp, and it drew him like a moth. Throughout his days of drunken self-pity, disgust and rage, Sarah Laws remained the prize that could keep him alive. She was a slender thing, her hazel eyes like dimming embers awaiting the heat of companionship to rekindle their flame.

Campbell seated himself at the bar, ostensibly to distance himself from the guffaws and raucous celebrations provided by the cluster of dirty farmers seated at the round table in the corner, his real motive to be as close to Sarah as he could manage. She looked even more bleached of color today, so much so that his affection toward her was diluted by concern for her health. She was all angles, her shoulders and elbows forming points beneath her blouse. Her face was ashen, her eyelids at half-mast, as if her presence here was simply a dream from which she yearned to awaken.

"Good morning, Sarah," Campbell said, drumming his fingers on the wood. He watched, with some disappointment, as she cast him a noncommittal smile, flung the rag she'd been using to polish the glasses on the counter, and set about fixing him a drink. This was far from the first time she'd paid him no mind, so he was not discouraged by her dismissal. As she turned away from him, he let his gaze drift from her carelessly tied hair to the pale smooth skin of her neck, speckled with the tiniest cluster of moles, and down her back to the swell beneath her skirts. She was divine, and he prayed to all that was holy that he'd be given the chance to see beneath those clothes. He could weather her standoffishness and indifference for decades more if he knew that eventually she'd be waiting for him, arms and legs spread invitingly.

She all but threw the drink down before him.

He smiled. "Thank you."

She didn't meet his gaze. Instead, her eyes moved to his purse, and the clumsy fingers he used to procure the cost of the drink. He gingerly placed the coins in the open palm of her hand and nodded. "There's sum enough for you to have a drink of your own," he said.

Another perfunctory smile and she was gone, back to the other end of the bar where she tended to her glasses with more fervor than such a menial task demanded. Campbell sighed, and stared into his drink.

The bar was a small, gloomy, smoke-filled square, with pine wainscoting and three Y-shaped poles spread across the length of the room, keeping the rafters safe above their heads. The Fox & Mare always gave the impression that it was crowded, even when only a few souls occupied the place. This effect was due in part to the stuffed foxes that guarded the corners and the pheasants and grouse frozen in mid-strut atop the rafters. Above the bar itself, an enormous stag's head protruded from the stone wall, the look of death in its eyes carefully erased by a taxidermist's hand. The magnificent antlers twisted outward like gnarled roots seeking ground from which the beast might grow again. On the wall opposite the door, a row of pictures hung, each frame containing a face grinning in victory—the huntmaster's gallery. Near the end of the row, a picture had been removed, leaving a noticeable white space on the smoke-tainted wall. Beneath these grinning heroes, seven circular tables pressed close to the wall sat empty, while the farmers continued to laugh uproariously in the corner opposite.

"Another?"

Campbell looked up to see Sarah standing before him, hands on hips.

"Pardon?" It was then that he realized he'd finished his drink without even being aware of it. "Oh, yes of course."

Sarah nodded and took his glass. Again, he watched her, until she returned with the drink and, as before, set it roughly down on the counter. She waited with tangible impatience for him to produce the money. This time he deliberately delayed the transaction.

"It must get frightfully tedious attending to us louts," he said.

She shrugged, held out her hand.

"Perhaps you should consider getting out some night. Have a few drinks and maybe a dance or two. It might be just the tonic."

When she smiled, his own smile dropped a notch. Scarcely had he seen such a humorless, bitter expression on a pretty girl's face.

"I suppose that's your medical opinion, is it Doctor?" She pronounced the last word as if it were a kind of disease.

"Not at all. I just think it's an awful waste for you to stay cooped up in here all the time, condemned to play sympathizer to drunkards and ruffians. It would do you the world of good to get out of here some night."

He hoped the proposition was obvious and yet feared he'd been too bold. The last thing he wanted was to scare her off, or anger her, now that she was, at last, focused solely on him.

"Tell me, Doctor," she said, leaning closer, "of what interest is it of yours what I do with my hours?"

Campbell pursed his lips. "I just think they could be better spent, that's all. You're still a young woman, and an attractive one, but no one ever lived a full life breathing in the fumes from those content to waste theirs."

She stared then, and in his mind he saw her reach out and touch him, her fingers brushing against the stubble on his chin, her tongue parting her lips to moisten them, preparing them to meet his. Or perhaps she would step back and frown, fold her arms and consider him in earnest, only for the severity to leave her face for one fleeting moment. Long enough for her to nod curtly and tell him a time and a place for him to meet her, to take her out and show her the life she'd been missing, the love she'd had and lost, the passion she hungered to regain.

But instead she looked over his shoulder, grunted and said, "Leave your money on the counter. I have other customers to attend to."

Annoyed, and more than a little frustrated, Campbell turned to see who had quashed his chances. He froze, his foot slipping off the rung on the barstool. "Dear God," he whispered, and then quickly realized everyone must have heard him. The room had fallen deathly quiet, the farmers' mirth forgotten as they stared over their drinks at the man approaching the bar.

Despite the thickness of the smoke from the farmers' pipes and cigarettes, the room was suddenly filled with the smell of damp earth, and death.

***

A faint rustling roused Mansfield from a dream of Hell.

With fear caught in his throat, he opened his eyes, dreading whatever apparition might be sharing his room tonight. No longer did the waking world offer him respite from the torture of sleep's menagerie of horrors. No longer could he trust the sounds that dragged him from slumber, for more than once he had traced them to an unspeakable thing towering over the foot of his bed, its jaws wide, bloodstained teeth gleaming, pale tongue lolling, as if in quiet laughter at his helplessness. It wouldn't linger long, but its dissolution left Mansfield with a clear view of another monstrosity—an image of himself, beaded with sweat and wide-eyed, peering over the coverlet from the mirror across the room.

Sometimes it was Callow he saw standing in his room, grinning at him, whispering, "All prey is equal when hunted," and chuckling with the sound of coal tumbling down a pipe.

Full consciousness brought with it the familiar pain and Mansfield groaned low in his throat at the sensation of a thousand knives skewering his legs. If felt almost as if the bones were attempting to rearrange themselves, to knit themselves into impractical shapes, an illusion reinforced by the occasional crackling and popping sounds he heard at night, each sound signaling the onset of a fresh wave of ferocious agony. Whatever it was that was killing him, was spreading upward, caressing his spine, his ribs, his arms, with tongues of fire, twisting them until he felt sure he would die from the shock of having to endure such torment.

He was not dead, though he wished to be, as selfish as he knew it was to entertain such yearnings. The children awaited his recovery, but he knew if he could find his voice he would tell them to leave this house, to leave Brent Prior and everything it represented to them without delay. But they would resist, their faith in his convalescence leading them to defy him. Here they would stay until he died and set them free.

It might not be death at all, he thought then, alarmed at the intrusion of a long-stilled voice inside himself. *It might be an awakening.*

Perhaps, but an awakening to *what?*

He narrowed his eyes at the glare as the mist shifted and sunlight once more filtered through the windows. He blinked, once, twice and exhaled a ragged breath as invisible claws scrabbled at his ribcage.

The pain washed over him.

Hissing air through his teeth, he jerked with the shock of the onslaught, the tendons in his neck straining beneath the skin. His body went rigid, his head thrusting back deep into the pillow as molten lava replaced his blood.

"NNnngghh," he grunted, hands contorting, twisting the sheets. He shut his eyes tight, saw crimson fireworks explode, and opened them again.

Think of Kate think of Neil think of anything something anything...

Dust motes danced in the fall of light. He focused on them until his vision wavered with tears.

Please...

He blinked them away and looked up, to a gathering of shadows he had detected in the periphery of his vision.

At last, the pain began to ebb.

Thank God.

The shadows began to uncoil from where they'd been nestling above him.

Mansfield stiffened.

There was a dead woman on the ceiling.

9

JESUS, MARY, AND *all the blessed saints.* Campbell had to restrain the urge to cross himself. The bar was quiet but for the sound of the stranger's boots thudding across the floor. The doctor was aware he was staring, aware that his gawking was hardly the appropriate way to greet a man, and yet he couldn't look away.

Leprosy, he thought with a shiver of revulsion. *Some kind of skin cancer.* The stranger carried himself with an air of confidence, which Campbell assumed false, a gait contrived to foil the sympathy and pity he inevitably attracted. He seated himself three chairs down on Campbell's right and, "Ale," he said as he tossed his coins on the bar.

The farmers recommenced their celebration, but it was more subdued now. The lamps flickered, sending shadows jerking across the floor.

At last Campbell managed to tear his stare away from the stranger. He spent the next few moments watching a curiously unperturbed Sarah fill the man's glass, then looked down at his own drink, and frowned. The smell of earth and rot had grown stronger, tinged with an acrid scent like burnt leaves. It invaded the nostrils as surely as having one's face thrust into the filthy ground. Struggling to preoccupy himself so he would not feel compelled to look in the sick man's direction again, Campbell drummed his fingernails on the countertop and thought of Kate Mansfield, the audacious little whelp. That only served to touch a flame to the kindling of his ire, however, so he sighed and decided to make this drink his last one. Here, at least. He would finish off a bottle at home, away from the leper and the stench he carried with him, and away from the potential heartbreak of having Sarah continue to act as if his existence were a burden in a list of the many she had to bear. But as he was raising his glass, he felt the stranger's gaze on him, and turned to meet it.

"Do I know you?" Now that he was facing him, Campbell used the opportunity to examine the man further. His face was wreathed in soiled, ragged bandages that revealed only his eyes—two small dark holes—and a pair of light pink scaly lips curved, it seemed by scarring, into a permanent grin. Tufts of dark hair poked out from loose gaps in the bandages and what skin could be glimpsed here and there glistened and wept, as if only his bindings kept it from sloughing off. He wore a long filthy overcoat, missing its buttons, the hands that emerged from the tattered sleeves unusually large, with far too many knuckles, as if he'd broken his fingers so many times the bones were now packed like pebbles beneath the skin. The fingers themselves were long and thin, ending in splintered, mud-encrusted nails.

"I'm not sure you do," the stranger replied. The strong, sanguine voice was unexpected, given the scabrous mess of his mouth.

"Well, I'm Doctor Campbell."

"Are you."

"And your name?"

"Stephen."

Sarah appeared with his drink and scooped the money from the counter without sparing either of them a glance. Campbell couldn't resist taking a surreptitious whiff of the air she left in her wake as she passed him by. He then became aware that Stephen's eyes hadn't left him. He smiled, embarrassed, and sipped his drink.

"Stephen, eh? You're not from around here."

"I used to be."

"Is that so? How might I know you?"

"I doubt you would."

Campbell raised his eyebrows. "I've been this village's physician for close to twenty years now. I'm sure I'd know your family. What did you say your surname was?"

"I didn't." Stephen hefted his glass and took a tentative sip of his pint. The skin of his lips separated into dry red grooves as he did so, prompting Campbell to avert his gaze.

"So, what brings you back?"

Stephen lowered his pint and carefully wiped his lips, a motion that brought an involuntary wince from Campbell. When the man looked up, there was the slightest gleam to his eyes, like a hint of diamonds in a pile of coal. "A reunion," he said.

"Oh yes? May I ask with whom?"

"You may," said Stephen, humor stretching his burnt grin. "But you'll be waiting a considerable amount of time for an answer."

Campbell searched for a response, but found none. He waited a few moments, long enough for him to realize that his vision had started to blur slightly from the alcohol, before he spoke again. He knew if he was sober, he wouldn't have bothered trying to engage the man in conversation, but in his current condition, he needed the company. Listening to the farmers cackling about their wives, the wind whistling through the cracks in the door, and with Sarah shunning him, he was alone with his thoughts, and even they had turned bitter. He firmly believed conversation to be the saving grace of unhappy folk, which rendered him unparticular about his choice of drinking partners, even if, as evidence on this occasion, they sometimes took the form of half-rotted men.

After a long sip of his whiskey, he raised the glass to indicate to Sarah that he was ready for another, then turned back to the bandaged man.

"I didn't mean to pry," he apologized. "Strangers tend to arouse the curiosity in villages as dreary and banal as Brent Prior, that's all."

Stephen said nothing. After a moment, Campbell sighed and turned in his chair to look at the muted light pressing against the glass. As he watched, a dead leaf smacked against the glass. The sun had all but drowned beneath the thickening mist. "Dreadful weather," he remarked.

"I quite like it."

"Really? Well then you must like this area of the country. One month of sun, eleven of gloom, and that's if we're lucky!" He chuckled and shook his head in wonder at his own wit. "So, are you staying close by?"

"You ask a lot of questions." The humor had left Stephen's voice.

Campbell spread his hands in a placating gesture. "I'm just trying to make conversation. It wasn't my intention to bother you."

"A fire."

The doctor frowned, wondering if he'd missed some bridge in their conversation. "I beg your pardon?"

"It's the question you really want to ask isn't it?" He gestured with one gnarled finger at the bandages. "What happened? I sincerely doubt you'd be so curious about me if not for the bandages and the tantalizing hint of ravished skin beneath."

Campbell shook his head in protest. "Sir, I assure you—"

"I look for no assurances from you, Doctor Campbell, and I am not offended. If you were a layman, scrutinizing me like some rare biological prize, then I'd have you rent apart before you saw me rise from my chair. You, however, are a physician, and I choose to take your interest as strictly professional, borne of concern and not morbidity."

Campbell was a little shaken by the threat. He was less afraid of an altercation (which at his age, and in his condition, he would surely lose) than he was of being *touched* by the man. He repressed a shudder of repulsion and swallowed. "I meant no disrespect, Stephen. My staring—and I apologize for being so obvious about it—is as you say, strictly a professional thing, not a result of any ghoulishness in my nature." When Stephen offered no response, Campbell persisted. "A fire, you say?"

"Yes, quite a blaze." He spoke of it with undisguised awe, his eyes glassy and distant.

"Well..." said the doctor when the silence began to stretch. "I'm truly sorry to hear that."

The focus returned to Stephen's eyes. "Don't be," he said. "We can't shutter ourselves away in the dark and moan about the unfairness of fate, the cruel caprices of destiny. Everything happens for a reason, as they say, and I believe that to be true. I may no longer have the looks that carried me so easily through my younger years, but I find I have no need of them now, nor have I any use for costumes, capering, or social graces. Not here, oh no. These are the wilds, Doctor Campbell, and here everything has its place. There are hunters, and there are the hunted, the prey. Sooner or later we all discover in which category we are best suited. Of course, like destiny, the balance is not always fair."

To Campbell, the man's words seemed to echo, and linger. He was getting very drunk and couldn't for the life of him think of a coherent response, so he nodded thoughtfully instead.

"I wonder..." Stephen continued after another sip from his glass, "...which one are you?"

Campbell chuckled, hoisted his drink in a silent cheer and drained it. "My father used to take me hunting," he said, stifling a burp, "but I wasn't very good. Made him very frustrated with me. I was quite a good shot, if I remember correctly. But as soon as a pheasant stepped into my sight, I froze and started quivering. No matter what I tried, no matter how many threats my father threw my way, I couldn't pull the blasted trigger. Eventually he gave up on me. In more ways than one." He raised his glass and hailed Sarah, who gave him an irritated look before snatching the glass from his hand. When he looked back to the burned man, he saw the ruined mouth had once more tugged itself into a crooked smile.

"What?"

"You may be more of a hunter than you think."

"How so?" Campbell said, with a frown. The room was beginning to move faster than his eyes could follow, so he blinked a few times and squinted.

"You seem intent on that prize there," said Stephen, nodding in Sarah's direction. "I saw you sniffing the air earlier. Her scent excites you, and now that you've caught it, you intend to pursue her until you've run her down. Ambitious prey for a man like you."

Campbell found it difficult to ascertain if he'd just been insulted. His head was beginning to swim, a development that annoyed him considerably and he pressed a hand to his temple. "A man like me," he mumbled.

"Yes." Stephen leaned close, so close that Campbell's mouth and nose filled with the stench of burning flesh. He almost gagged. "A frail, alcoholic, wasted man who spends his days trying to remember who he is, and more importantly *why* he is. You probably dream of murdering your patients, because despite their sicknesses, no matter how chronic, they will *always* be better off than you. If they die, they get the kind of peace you only dream about. If they live, they get another few years to spend their money, to be happy. In the meantime, you stumble about in search of oblivion, fantasizing about a woman who would rather see you in a casket than in her bed, trying to ignore the total lack of respect you command in your own community." He shook his head in mock admiration. "My, my. What a symbol of healing you are."

This time, Campbell straightened, teeth clenched. Gone was the fear of having to touch this ruined man. The bastard was goading him now, demanding he strike back with word or fist, and with alcohol bolstering him, he was suddenly willing to oblige. Twice today his integrity had been insulted, and while he could do nothing about the first offender, he could certainly put this sneering leper back in his place. He rose and the chair spun away from him. Gripping the edge of the counter, he leered at the bandaged man, whose ugly grin only maddened him further.

"Who asked you for my life story, you putrescent blackguard?" he said, rolling up his sleeves. "What I do or who I am is none of *your* bloody business."

"Doctor Campbell," Sarah said chidingly. He ignored her.

"You swan in here with your bloody face in tatters and have the gall to degrade one of Brent Prior's finest citizens. I should add some more scars to that shredded countenance of yours."

If Stephen was offended, his eyes didn't show it.

"Who the hell do you think you are?" All the hatred and bitterness poured from Campbell in a torrent. "Stand up," he said through clenched teeth.

"Doctor Campbell," Sarah said, as if addressing a particularly troublesome child. "You'll not do anything in here."

"I said *stand up*," Campbell repeated and swatted his hand in the air. It missed Stephen's face by mere inches, but connected with the man's drink, which toppled off the bar and smashed on Sarah's side of the counter. The bandaged man didn't even spare it a glance. He remained intent on the doctor's outrage. But still, he made no move to comply with Campbell's demand.

"Campbell, that's *it*, get out and go sleep it off," Sarah raged, fetching the dustpan and brush from beneath the counter. In some distant part of his mind, Campbell found it sadly ironic that this was the first time she'd ever spoken to him so passionately.

"Not until this bastard apologizes," he said, though the anger had already begun to fade, perhaps at the sobering realization that he was attempting to pick a fight he couldn't possibly win, and angering Sarah at the same time. He leaned in close, once more forgetting the revulsion, his nose almost touching Stephen's. "You'd better hope you don't fall ill anytime soon," he said and whirled, almost losing his balance in the process. Through bleary eyes, he noted the bulky shadows rising in the corner—the farmers, eager to get their knuckles bloody, but not from assisting Campbell. He scoffed at them as he made his way toward the door. "Blasted bumpkins. Good for nothing but shoveling manure." They glared but made no move toward him.

The only sound was the tinkling of glass as Sarah emptied the dustpan. When Campbell looked over his shoulder before exiting the bar, he saw her smile as she put a fresh pint of ale before the bandaged man.

He spat on the floor as he marched out into what had been a low morning mist before the breeze fled. Now a cold fog hung in damp veils around him as he shook with temper.

That bastard. That no good bastard, I should have rammed his rotten teeth down his throat. It was an empty threat, he knew, but it satisfied him to entertain the thought and the image of the big man pinwheeling backward off his chair, mouth bloody, eyes wide in surprise that an aged country doctor had put him on his back. Perhaps the bandages would have come off, revealing to Sarah and the chuckling farmers the hideous visage that had been so content to smirk from behind them.

He smiled and buttoned up his coat. The weight of the flask in his pocket was reassuring and, with shoulders hunched, he headed home.

***

When Grady and Kate entered the kitchen, there were two grinning heads on the table. Wielding a wickedly sharp knife, Mrs. Fletcher was busy sawing the scalp off a third, her tongue protruding from the corner of her mouth as she strained to cut through the skin.

"Well, well," Grady said. "You've been busy."

Kate, still unsettled by Grady's story, composed a smile and made her way over to the charwoman. She ran a hand over a pumpkin's firm orange hide. "I can't believe you have two of them done already."

Mrs. Fletcher paused to wipe her brow. "Well if I was waitin' on you lot there'd be nothin' done."

"They look fantastic."

The pumpkins were fat and shiny, freshly plucked from the field behind the house. While much of the land used for planting had turned fallow over the years, the acre directly behind the house was still used to grow potatoes, cabbage, carrots, parsnips, turnips, onions, lettuce, and occasionally pumpkins, albeit in much smaller proportions than it had when the master of the house had been well enough to aid in tending it.

Before thoughts of her father could anchor themselves in the forefront of her mind, Kate rounded the table and, using her hands as a shovel, began to scoop up the mountain of pumpkin guts that had amassed behind the orange heads. "Where should I put these?" she asked Mrs. Fletcher with a grimace. The innards felt cold and slimy against her skin.

"Just pile them in the sink for now, love."

Kate did, rinsing her hands immediately after, even knowing she was about to sully them again. She gazed out the small window above the sink. "I'm so tired of this fog. It started out to be such a lovely day."

Mrs. Fletcher shrugged. "It always does, doesn't it?"

"I suppose." She dried her hands on a cloth dangling from the cupboard beneath the sink. "Have you seen Neil yet?"

The charwoman sighed. "He came home lookin' a little rattled, whatever was goin' on in that head of his. But he said he was fine, just tired."

"Where is he now?"

"In the field, fetching a turnip."

Grady laughed. "So, he's goin' ahead with his plan, then?"

"It would seem so." Resting a forearm on the crown of a pumpkin, she added, "Honestly, sometimes I think that boy must have been adopted. He didn't get that laziness from his father, that's for sure. Or from his mother for that matter." She recommenced her sawing, nodding in satisfaction when the top of the pumpkin dropped to the table.

Kate selected a knife from the assortment Mrs. Fletcher had spread out on the countertop next to the sink, and joined her at the table. She set to work on the fourth and last pumpkin. "Grady, I thought you were going to help me with these?"

"That's right, he did," Mrs. Fletcher said with a wry smile. "But I think by the looks of it he was hopin' to let us women handle all the work."

Grady lowered himself into his usual seat by the fire and waved away their remarks. "Don't think fer one minute I don't know who'll be saddled with the task of carryin' them blasted things to the dance tonight. If I pulled a muscle laborin' over them now, ye'd be in fierce trouble."

Kate rolled her eyes as Mrs. Fletcher muttered, "I think we're supposed to be grateful."

"They're almost all done anyway," Grady said, hiding a grin. "'Twould be unfair of me to steal yer thunder."

The back door opened and Neil stumbled in, face reddened by the cold, a large dirt-caked turnip held to his chest. The chill crept in around his thin frame; the flames fluttered in the hearth.

Grady cringed. "Cripes. Close the bloody door lad, will ya, before we all get pneumonia."

Neil said nothing, but aimed an expression of distaste at the old man before shoving the door closed with his foot. Kate broke off from her pumpkin to guide him, but he shrugged her off with a mild look of irritation and, balancing the turnip in the crook of one arm, slowly made his way over to the table. Kate hid her own exasperation, though she had to admit her brother knew the layout of the house well enough to manage on his own, and had told her as much a thousand times. Nevertheless, she found it difficult to restrain herself; she always felt compelled to assist him, perhaps out of some worry that he might hurt himself, leaving her with no family at all.

Neil let the turnip thump to the table. Dirt scattered across its surface. The pumpkins shuddered.

"That's a fine turnip," Grady quipped, and winked at the others.

Neil shrugged, and that was typical of him. To an observer, he would appear a creature of apathy, his disposition marred by disability, making him sullen and indifferent. But Kate knew differently. She had seen him cry, had experienced his warmth and kindness. Everything else was but a mask to protect him against the vagaries of an unkind world. He'd found strength in defiance, and, as hard as it might be to bear it, she recognized it for what it was.

"It'll have to do, I suppose," Neil said, in response to Grady's comment. He reached out a hand and ran it over the nearest pumpkin's triangular eyes. "If nothing else, it will be a lot easier than these fellows to hoist down the road."

"Those wenches don't care," Grady complained. "They won't be the ones carryin' 'em."

"Ah, so they've hired you instead of a mule, have they?"

"An ass, more like," Grady replied. Kate and Mrs. Fletcher chuckled but Neil's smile was visibly forced. Kate watched him carefully, trying as always to read the thoughts in her brother's face. When he began to feel the surface of the table for a knife, she slowly and silently placed her own within reach of his fingers. She had barely withdrawn her hand when he latched onto the knife and grinned victoriously. She mirrored his grin, but knew how outraged he would be if he knew she'd assisted him. But sometimes she found it too hard to resist.

"Mrs. Fletcher told me Father woke today," Neil said, his tone unreadable as he dug into the turnip.

Kate nodded. "Yes, but only for a short time. Did you go see him?"

"Not yet. Maybe later. I expect he needs all the rest he can get."

More excuses, Kate thought with a bitterness that shocked her. If fear was the primary cause of his avoiding their father, then why now, when a glimpse of hope had been offered, was he still so reluctant to enter that room?

"All he's been *doing* is resting," she said. "It wouldn't kill you to look in on him."

"I said I would. Later."

Grady rose, clucking his tongue. "I suppose I'd better lend a hand if all you two are goin' to do is quarrel." He shook his head. "I'm tellin' ya. 'Tis gettin' so a man can't even relax by the fire around here."

"Just wait till our young miss has you dancin', then you'll feel the need to relax. You may have to be carried home," Mrs. Fletcher said with a grin. Grady's scowl coaxed a laugh from Kate and soon the brief moment of tension was forgotten, all of them hacking, sawing or carving their fruits and vegetables.

"Are you expectin' to do a bit of dancin' tonight, Neil?" Mrs. Fletcher said.

"Hardly."

"Oh come now," she teased. "I bet they'll have to drag you off the floor kickin' and screamin'."

Neil scoffed.

"They will if Tabitha Newman is going," Kate murmured. Neil glowered at her, thick black brows drawn down over narrowed white eyes.

"Tabitha Newman?" Grady said, obviously impressed.

"Dan Newman's daughter," Mrs. Fletcher said. "He's quite the gentleman. I'd say you could do a lot worse than the daughter of a cotton broker, young Neil."

Neil's face was puce, his fingers so jittery on the turnip, Kate feared he'd cut himself. And yet she couldn't resist saying, "I'll bet she's quite a dancer too."

"Shut up," Neil snapped.

"Neil, please," Mrs. Fletcher said, "She's only makin' fun."

"Well she shouldn't," he replied. "It's none of her business."

Grady grinned. "Come now lad, it's—"

"Or yours," Neil said and slammed the knife down on the table.

Awkward silence filled the kitchen, until Kate said, "What on earth is wrong with you? We were only joking." It alarmed her to see that he was trembling with rage.

"You're always 'only joking'. I'm sick of it."

Grady put a hand on the boy's shoulder. Neil flinched and moved away. "Don't."

"All right," Mrs. Fletcher said calmly. "No need for us all to get upset with each other. Obviously, we've intruded upon Neil's business and shouldn't have. Let's keep our noses where they belong from now on, shall we?" She reached across the table, her large bosom almost sending a pumpkin toppling but Kate lurched forward in time to stop it. "Are we forgiven, Neil?" the charwoman said, lightly stroking Neil's cheek. For a moment he looked as if he would turn away from her touch, but gradually his expression softened, if only slightly. "Yes."

"Good," Mrs. Fletcher said, but Kate saw the upset in her face.

Grady returned his hand to Neil's shoulder and this time the boy left it there. "This young man works hard. He needs to let off some steam like the rest of us, isn't that right?"

Neil nodded, then slowly picked up the knife and returned to his hollowing. Peace was restored, but the cheerful spirit had been sacrificed to allow for it. They continued to work in silence, Kate slicing her thumb twice as she tried to finish her pumpkin and watch her brother at the same time.

She was more worried than ever now. The expression on his face might have relaxed, but she sensed the temper still there, beneath his skin, simmering inside him. Why was he so angry? It had to be more than embarrassment at having his courtship, or his hope for one, revealed. *Maybe I'm jealous*, she thought, and had to admit there might be some truth to that. What if Neil and Tabitha fell madly in love, married and moved away as soon as it was deemed acceptable to do so? It would be akin to him dying. She'd have lost him, just like she'd lost her mother, just as she was losing her father. She would have nothing but Grady and Mrs. Fletcher and although she loved them, she longed for someone her own age to keep her company. Someone who'd love her and never leave her.

Yes, it was jealousy, she decided. Her fear of being alone was forcing her to attribute more significance to her brother's behavior than was due. Yet, when she looked at him again, at the tautness of the muscles in his neck, the barely noticeable vein pulsating in his throat, she couldn't help but wonder.

10

CAMPBELL AWOKE IN A DITCH and into what he thought must be a dream. Wherever he looked he saw nothing but white—a dream of Heaven, perhaps, but then the cold hit him so severely it felt as if someone had replaced his blood with ice water. And he was wet. His immediate assumption, that his bladder had let go while he'd slept, was dismissed when he tried to roll over on his side and the ground squelched beneath him. He blinked, one last attempt at dragging himself out of this preposterous dream, and realized to his dismay that he was fully awake. Disorientated, he sat up and a wave of nausea swept over him.

What happened? Where in God's name am I?

He groaned and put both hands over his face. A deep throbbing ache pounded against the inside of his skull. With great effort, he planted his hands on the wet grass and levered himself up. Eyes narrowed against the pain, he struggled to make out anything in the fog, but there was nothing to see.

I'm in a field.

He tried to remember how he might have ended up here but his thoughts were as sluggish as his movements.

All right, think. I was in The Fox & Mare...

He stepped forward, hands pressed against his temples as to keep the brain within from seeking solace without, and his foot sank up to the ankle in a soggy hole. To keep from falling, he reached his arms out and staggered back, tugging his foot free, but leaving his shoe behind to fill with brackish water.

"Bloody *hell!*" he roared and bent down to retrieve the sodden shoe. Blood rushed to his head, making him dizzy and aggravating the relentless ache. He groaned, shoved his fingers into the watery hole until they found leather, then he pulled. There was a sucking sound and the shoe popped free so suddenly that he almost ended up on his back again. Once steadied, he held the shoe aloft and inspected it with mounting fury, until his chest hurt and his breath wheezed from his lungs as if they were filled with sand. *Damn and blast it all.* He grabbed his handkerchief from the breast pocket of his coat and coughed into it until his throat was raw and his eyes full of tears. Another hasty search revealed that whatever machinations had landed him in a field, they hadn't relieved him of his flask. For this much at least, he was grateful. He unscrewed the cap and drank until the flask was empty, then shoved it back into his pocket and set about the unpleasant ordeal of removing as much mud from the shoe as possible so it was wearable. He had no intention of trying to find his way home barefoot. Grimacing, he scooped the sludge from the shoe, then dropped it and wriggled his foot into it, groaning at the instant chill that oozed over his toes. At length, he began to walk, unsure of the direction, aware of the dangers of wandering on the moors—for that was certainly where he'd ended up—but too furious to stay still.

This latest development was just one of the many contrived to bring him down, he knew, to get him to concede to his own failures as a man, as a doctor...as a husband. God would have him lie in the earth until the cold killed him, or until tendrils erupted from the sodden grass to claim him. *You tried, you didn't succeed, it's time to give up. There can be nothing ahead of you but more disappointment, more pain. Your proper place is in the grave.*

Well, to hell with that, he thought, clenching his fists and craning his head forward as he tried to make out something, anything in the fog that might tell him where he was or in which direction he was heading. He surmised that the need to void his bladder had led him here before whatever had inspired consciousness to leave him. If so, then he couldn't be far from the road. Emboldened by this rationalization of his circumstances, he continued walking, taking small steps in case he suddenly found himself on the unstable edge of a mire.

Unfair, he decided. *My whole bloody life has been one unmitigated disaster after another.* Looking at the thick roiling fog only served to remind him of that morning, many moons ago, in which, yet again, someone else had dictated the direction his life was to take. On that occasion, it was his own friend—his *only* friend—and colleague, Jeremy Herbert, who'd broken the news to him that the chairman of the Royal London Hospital, where Campbell had worked for eight years, was letting him go. The board had cited allegations of morphine theft, drug dependency and patient neglect, none of which Campbell admitted to, but all of which were true.

He'd been forced out, ostracized and sent here to this godforsaken wasteland where a man was either measured in terms of how much money he had in the bank, or how many fox brushes he had strung over his mantel.

Campbell waved a hand through the fog, teeth gritted, a single tear rolling down his cheek. "*Bastards.*" His only friend had betrayed him, his employers had turned on him, his wife had treated the news as if it was expected, as if he'd taken the morphine in the hope of being relieved of his post. She'd never understood his need for it, how it had granted him a blissful escape from his demons. How it had made the world bearable. Or perhaps she had, and her demand that he give it up if he wanted to keep her was just another cruel ploy to prolong his misery. After all, she had accompanied him to this bleak, desolate nowhere, then promptly left him to wallow in despair. Since then, it had seemed as if every attempt he made to dig his way out of his misery only deepened the hole in which he'd found himself.

Now he was alone again and lost, with a monstrous headache, wet clothes and a dry mouth, trying to find his way back to a house that was just that, a house, not a home, for there was no warmth there. There was no warmth anywhere, but he would be damned if he would stand here and take whatever hateful gift fate had in store for him next.

Ahead of him, in the fog, something moved. Instinctively Campbell lurched toward it. "Hello?"

There was no answer. He paused, squinted and found himself trying to look *around* the fog. The damp clung to him like a second skin, the cold drawing a shiver from him. He wished he'd kept some of the whiskey, for he was not yet sure how far away from his house he might be and the chill was starting to make his back ache.

How long have I been out here?

He found himself wishing he knew someone who might look for him, someone who would care that he hadn't made it home. But he hadn't known anyone like that in a long time. It was a depressing thought, and one that almost sapped his will to keep moving. But then another glimpse of movement, this time to his left, made him lean in that direction. "Is someone there?" No answer, but for a faint shuffling sound. Slowly, he began to walk in that direction, his shoe squelching, the grass sinking beneath his feet. He cursed his stupidity, cursed the bandaged man—what had his name been?—cursed everything that had led him here to this ridiculous jaunt across the hostile moors.

Probably a bloody sheep.

"Is someone there?"

It was possible that someone *was* out here, he realized. One of the village youths, perhaps, already dressed for the October Dance and hoping to scare the wits out of someone. Disheveled and disorientated, Campbell would make the perfect target for such a scheme. He did not intend, however, to entertain it, and smiled grimly at the thought of what he would do if he managed to apprehend the rogue. Child or not, he would send them home with a bruised arse.

The fog swirled in front of him.

"This is Doctor Campbell," he said, mustering as much authority as the chill and his hoarse voice would allow. "If this is some kind of a trick, your parents will be hearing about it."

But just as quickly as his resolve had surfaced, it was contaminated by doubt. As lost as he was, should he really be threatening someone who might help him out of his predicament?

A figure began to emerge from the fog, and now he could see that it was most definitely not a sheep. He straightened. "Who's that?"

"A recent acquaintance," came the reply.

Campbell swallowed painfully, fresh thirst scorching his throat, even as the smell of seared flesh reached him. A pang of dread flared through him. *"You,"* he said, and saw the figure stop, just far enough away so that his silhouette, backlit by the opaque sunlight, was visible.

"You left in quite a hurry," Stephen said. "Just as our conversation was getting interesting, too."

Stephen's words shredded the temporary amnesia the alcohol had induced in the doctor and suddenly Campbell recalled Sarah's angry tone, the burned man's smug smirk, the farmers standing, silently challenging him. It filled him with a fresh wave of anger, but he kept it in check, for this was no mischievous youth, no trickster who would run giggling away from a confrontation, but a fully-grown man, larger than Campbell and twice as threatening. If there was retribution to be had, he decided, it would have to be later, and executed with more thought behind it. For now, it would be more beneficial to treat Stephen as an ally who'd simply had the misfortune to see him at his worst.

"I was very drunk earlier," he said, lightening his tone.

"Yes, you were, but you struck me as the type who can only count truthfulness and courage among his personal attributes when he's too inebriated to care about the consequences they might bring."

Campbell was shivering so bad he had to hug himself against the cold, a move that only pressed his sodden clothes closer to his skin. "Not at all," he said. "I just have a lot on my mind these days, and I'm sorry to say it has significantly shortened my tolerance for ambiguity."

"But there was nothing ambiguous about my words, Doctor Campbell."

Campbell frowned, as the fog momentarily obscured the man, then cleared again. "Then why? Why would you insult me like that? I've done nothing to you."

"Haven't you?"

"No, damn you, I haven't."

"Think, Doctor. Think hard."

"What is there to think about? I've already told you I don't know what the hell you're talking about!"

"Think of the last time this village had a fire."

Campbell did, and fear contracted his stomach. "But I had nothing to do with that." Questions buzzed through his mind. Had someone been in the house while it burned? "It's those others you should be after, not me."

"Oh, but you did something far worse than that, didn't you?"

"I don't understand."

"Of course you do. *Think*, you old fool. You took a life that day."

A face flashed through Campbell's mind and at last the wheels began to turn as it dawned on him what Stephen was talking about. But what on earth could this man have to do with *her*? "It wasn't my fault."

"Blood is blood, Doctor."

Campbell began to back away. "No, I tried to *save* her. If you know so much then surely you must know that."

"I know that your incompetence killed her, as I'm sure it has killed so many. I know that you suffered from a chemical dependency that made your nerves brittle. And I know that a better man would have been able to save her."

Campbell shook his head. This was madness. It couldn't be happening. "Who are you?" he asked.

"I'm the master of these moors."

"But all the masters are gone and have been for some time."

"Not all of them."

Suddenly, he was gone, as if someone had dropped a white curtain in front of him. The only sound was that of Campbell's labored breathing. "Why are you doing this?" he asked the swirling air. "I did *nothing* to you!"

For God's sake, run! he urged himself. His body obeyed a moment later, his flight not fast, or sure, but clumsy and dangerous. He felt as if he were blind, his arms outstretched to protect him against collision, his feet slipping in the grass. The strengthening smell of wet animal and decaying things drove him onward, and he prayed the gate to the village was close, willed it to emerge from the vaporous air.

The fog swept into his eyes like smoke, whipping around him as he lurched and staggered forward. "Somebody, help me!" He didn't care what the villagers might say about him in the morning if they heard the stark terror in his voice. Let them laugh at his cowardice. He knew any one of them would do the same thing in his place. Lost on the moors, antagonized by a disfigured man with an obvious, and utterly misguided vendetta against him—he was frightened, and not about to restrain a cry to save face. He ran the risk of losing more than that if Stephen, this self-proclaimed master of the moors, turned out to be some kind of raving madman.

In the corner of his eye, something long, low, and lithe crawled through the fog. Stricken with terror, Campbell was sure he'd glimpsed cerulean lights, like flaming orbs of marsh gas set deep in a dark flattened skull before the heavy veils occluded his view once more.

I don't believe in the Beast of Brent Prior, he told himself. *There's no such thing.*

Then a terrible rumbling growl shredded the last vestiges of his calm and he ran, but managed only a few feet before his legs were swiftly and cruelly torn from underneath him. He slammed down on the cold wet earth, an unvoiced cry becoming a whine in his throat as hot pain spread across his face. *I've broken my nose*, he thought with a strange but welcome sense of dislocation, and rolled over on his back. Blood, reassuringly warm, ran in rivulets into his mouth. He could taste that old penny taste on his tongue.

Dizziness made stars of the creature's eyes as it loomed over him.

I won't die here. Not at your *hands, bastard!*

Despite the crippling pain, he rolled, scrabbled to his feet and staggered blindly away, arms outstretched, the horrible burnt earth smell assailing his senses like extensions of the creature at his heels. He spluttered and wept with fear, glanced over his shoulder only to see the lumbering form of something wiry but enormous, its eyes blazing ice-white as it closed the short gap between them.

From hell. It must be something from—

A thousand needles stabbed his face and body as he came to an abrupt halt, his head jerking back. He gasped as something bit his fingers, the palms of his hands, drawing more blood from his trembling body as his legs collapsed from under him. Still he did not fall and despite the shock, he was aware of the sound of tearing as he was suspended in midair. The vision had been stabbed from his right eye. Curiously, there was no pain. There was, however, an abundance of debilitating panic.

Oh Jesus God help me...

His fingers twitched. Shuddering, he tried to swallow, wincing as the myriad spines dug painfully into his skin like the teeth of a thousand snakes. It felt as if he'd run into a wall of fishhooks. They tugged at him, tearing, scissoring open his flesh. Fluid ran slowly from his ruined eye.

Thorns, he realized, with a smile that split and bled. *I've only gone and run straight into the bloody brambles.*

Breath plumed over his shoulder, mixing with the fog. He went rigid with shock, which only aided the thorns in slicing him open. Painfully, he jerked his head away from the barbed black wall and felt the skin on his cheek stretch as the brambles tried to pull him back.

"What...are you?" he whispered. He hissed pain through his teeth, and ceased only when a hand, undoubtedly human, gripped his shoulder.

"I already told you who I am," said Stephen. "And I've come back for the hunt."

Through the haze and the gnarled mass of brambles, suffused yellow light began to materialize. The fog was lifting, and Campbell realized with grim resignation that those fuzzy oblongs were lights from the windows of the village houses. He'd found his way to the wall separating the village from the moors. He almost laughed at the irony, but the muffled sound of laughter brought tears instead. The farmers, he guessed, pouring out of The Fox & Mare, perhaps joking about the drunken doctor and his banishment from the tavern.

"Help me," he sobbed, but knew his brittle voice had not carried far enough to reach them. Sadness gave way to one final burst of bitter seething anger at this final stroke of unfairness.

"I hope you burn in hell, you miserable *bastard*," he hissed, hot tears stinging the wounds on his face.

"I already have," Stephen said, his face an indistinct shadow in the corner of Campbell's good eye. Fiery pain almost split the doctor in half and he convulsed, lurching deeper into the thorns. This time he felt nothing, and, as merciful unconsciousness swept its dark wings around him, the laughter from the villagers faded, until there was silence, broken only by the sound of flesh being rent asunder.

11

SHE FELL FROM HER PLACE ON THE CEILING. The rope went taut and snapped in the air, jerking her up and away from him, leaving her still-twitching feet to swing like Poe's pendulum through Mansfield's field of vision. The rope shuddered and bit against the rafters; she convulsed once, twice, and ceased her struggling as he screamed a horrified silent scream up at her swaying body, her toes just inches away from his face.

Creeeaaaaak.

The rope twisted, bringing her motionless body around to face him, to look down on him. Then, "He'll take the children," she whispered as her eyelids drifted open, revealing the swollen ruby red eyes beneath.

Another hallucination, Mansfield told himself. *She's not here. Cannot be here.*

He made a desperate silent plea that this cruel parody of Helen would vanish, dissuaded by his outright refusal to believe that she was here, now, swinging over his bed, a frail creature death had painted blue. But when he closed his eyes, the protection he'd hoped to find was corrupted by the sound of the rope.

"You must listen, Jack. You must heed."

He felt numb with horror, and it was a merciful reprieve from the pain. Not that it had left him. He could feel it lurking, waiting like an angry crowd behind a flimsy door, waiting to storm the castle of his body once more.

Go away...

He opened his eyes, and she was there.

"You must die," she whispered. "And you must die soon."

I wish I could, he thought then, and the admission disturbed him. Until this moment, he hadn't thought himself capable of such selfishness. It hurt, far worse than the agony that had taken him over. The children needed him. He was supposed to be there for them. That he could forget the most important part of his life—such as it was now—was a lapse he could not forgive himself for.

Why, he thought, meeting Helen's crimson gaze. *Why are you here?*

"If you live," she said. "The children will die."

I don't understand.

"He wants the boy, and he will take him when the time comes. But you are a threat the children don't expect. They love you, and that love will blind them to what the illness will do to you. Then, it will be too late."

He stared, terrified at the sight of her, willing her to leave, and yet her words nagged at him. Could it be possible that she was more than just a hallucination, a product of his feverish imaginings, a projection of the disease?

I would never hurt them.

Her colorless lips flickered a smile. "You won't love them anymore. It will make them little more than victims."

Never hurt them.

"Hold your breath. It will be so easy."

Never hurt...

"And in just a few moments the pain will go away forever." The rope creaked as she leaned forward to watch. "Save them, Jack. You couldn't save me, but you can save them if you hold your breath and wish..."

Never.

The silence then was so thick he was afraid the slightest movement would shatter it. He didn't dare believe she was gone. Only when the agony returned did he know without doubt that he was alone. He opened his eyes to a room blurred by tears, and wept quietly.

I'm so sorry, he thought and words flooded to his mouth. He wanted to speak, to tell this terrible representation—even if she was nothing more than a dream—that he was sorry for everything, for all the agony he'd caused her in those last few months, for no amount of physical suffering could ever compare to the memories that plagued his mind, of her smile, her laughter, the look of betrayal in her eyes when she'd found out what he'd done.

The look in her eyes the day he'd killed her.

He stared at the ceiling, pain raging within him, and clenched his teeth.

"Do it, Jack. Quickly."

Abruptly she was there again, and plummeting toward him, the rope swishing behind her, hair wild as the air whistled through lips frozen open by congealed blood. Her eyes were wide and seething blood he could feel pit-patting on his face.

"Do it," she said, and then her face was the world, her eyes twin furious red moons bearing down on him.

***

Kate sat on the windowsill in her room, gazing out at the moors. The fog was beginning to lift again, and for that she was thankful. It would make the walk to the village hall and the dance that much easier. Besides, after Grady's story, she didn't relish the idea of being so close to the moors without being able to see what might or might not be lurking there. In the fog, a bloodthirsty animal could kill them all and they'd never see it coming.

She shivered, her breath clouding the glass, and wiped away the condensation obscuring the view beyond.

On a clear day she had a perfect view of the moors, a vista that extended all the way from Merrivale to the Two Bridges over the glistening River Dart. But although the fog had dispersed, clouds had obscured the sun and darkened the valley, hazing the moors, so that only the village road was visible, a thin muddy strip that wound through the low huddled houses, the fields rolling away from it like green wings colored with patches of lichen and sphagnum and veined by rock fences. There had been times, she recalled, when she had thought she'd seen things out there, things she had told herself were horses, even though the shape of them suggested something different, something lower to the ground. On each occasion, she'd blamed the local storytellers and their wild fantasies for what was most likely an optical illusion. She'd listened to the village tales of the fabled Beast of Brent Prior and feigned belief, only because the old folk told their tales in a manner that suggested belief was the only polite response, that such yarns were sacred and ancient and foretold the doom that would befall those who refused to heed the warnings that accompanied them. So Kate had obliged, while secretly scoffing at the height of their tall tales.

Today, Grady's story had changed her mind for her. His tale, no matter how much he might have embellished it in the spirit of the season, proved that something was indeed out there and stalking the moors, or had been once. She doubted it was anything as ferocious or diabolical as the legendary Beast, or 'whist hound', as some of the storytellers called it, but it was certainly something dangerous, as the unfortunate Mr. Royle had discovered. What Grady hadn't told her was what had become of the other party, the members of the hunt that had continued without him. She knew something terrible had happened. That much she'd gleaned from a handful of nights spent listening to her father reliving his nightmare in the parlor with Grady and a bottle of brandy. But he had never been specific enough to satisfy her curiosity, almost as if, on some level he'd been aware that Grady's ears were not the only ones intent on the conversation.

There had, however, been mention of a shadow, a blindingly quick thing with white fire for eyes, and now that Grady had told her his side of events, she hungered to know more. But while sharing his account, the groundskeeper had seemed uncharacteristically subdued, almost reticent, as if he'd been sworn to secrecy, and that intrigued her. She was convinced he wasn't telling her the full story and though she'd heard tales aplenty, none appealed to her more than the one no one seemed willing to talk about. Mr. Fowler the shopkeeper bristled whenever she broached the subject. Mrs. Fletcher claimed ignorance. The teachers hushed her when she mentioned the scraps she'd heard from other overheard conversations. It seemed a black mark in the village's history, and her father had been a part of it, as had Grady.

She nodded slowly and traced a line through the condensation until she had drawn a dripping dog, its ears pointed, paws trickling into talons. Whatever had happened, she was convinced it was responsible for her father's illness. What she didn't know yet was how.

Finding out would be the next challenge.

***

Tabitha hesitated on the doorstep, a basket full of bed sheets clutched to her chest. Her mother had asked her to take them in before the rain but it was only as she was tugging the last of them from the washing line that she'd noticed the man standing by the fence her father had erected to keep the heather and brush of the moors from encroaching onto their property.

What is he doing?

He was tall, dressed in a tattered old overcoat that whipped around him at the behest of a rising wind, his hands resting atop the barbed wire but not enough to make it bend. At first, she thought he might be wearing a mask, for surely no skin was so pale, until she realized his face was bandaged, its loosened edges flapping at the sides. She considered hailing him, perhaps asking what he was doing on her father's property, but quickly decided against it. She wasn't sure why, but his unmoving presence there unnerved her.

Dark clouds spread across the sky, creeping up from behind the mountains like a hand cresting water, spreading its fingers wider as it passed overhead. Blue-white veins of lightning flickered silently. A storm was coming.

Tabitha looked away from the man and hurried inside.

She met Donald in the hall, his trademark sneer faltering only slightly at the concerned look on her face.

"Where's Mum?" she asked him.

He shrugged. "Why don't you go look?"

"Just tell me where she is."

"Why do you want to know?" He smiled, large teeth protruding just a little, a sign that he was prepared, and looking forward to, another opportunity to torment her.

"There's a man outside."

"Who?"

She set the basket of sheets down and folded her arms. "I don't know who. I've never seen him before. Strange looking fellow if ever I saw one."

In an instant, her brother's face lost all its smugness. An odd expression replaced it. "Bandages?"

"Yes."

He nodded. "Go to your room."

She almost laughed at that. "'Go to your room?' Have you been into Mum's sherry again?"

But Donald just stared at the door, as if the man at the fence had suddenly appeared there.

"Donald?" She put a hand on his arm, more than aware that the simple act of touching him could be dangerous if she'd caught him in the mood for violence. But he didn't even acknowledge it, and when she shook him, he absently removed her hand and walked to the door.

"Where are you going?" she asked.

"To talk to him."

Tabitha was confused. "You know him?"

"Yes."

"How?"

"We met earlier."

"He looks like a vagrant."

Donald opened the door. Dead leaves skittered into the hall. Thunder rumbled over the mountains.

"Donald?"

She stamped her foot in frustration and he looked over his shoulder at her.

"Who is he?" she asked.

Her brother smiled. "Someone who makes wishes come true," he said before stepping out and slamming the door behind him.

12

DONALD SPOTTED HIM IMMEDIATELY and hurried over to the fence. He wished he'd thought to put on his coat, but it was warm inside the house and he didn't imagine he'd be out here for too long. Not with Tabby being so bloody curious. It was only a matter of time before she went telling tales and had their mother standing at the door demanding to know what was going on. He would have to be quick and hope the bandaged man understood his urgency. Though he had only known Stephen a few hours, he had the horrible feeling that if his mother came storming out, the stranger wouldn't hesitate to hurt her for intruding upon their business.

As he drew to a halt, that unpleasant smell of moldy old earth and rotten things wafted to him from the man on the other side of the fence. "Hello," Donald said. "You get it, did you?"

From behind the mask of soiled bandages, dark eyes glittered. "Indeed I did, and your part of the bargain?"

Donald stuffed his hands into his pockets, the wind so cold it felt as if it was passing right through him. "My sister asked him to meet her at the dance tonight. She has no interest of course, but knows that little blind bastard does." He smiled, expecting approval. Instead, the bandaged man's left hand shot out and grabbed him by the throat. Donald's eyes bulged. "*What?*" he croaked, incredulous and more than a little frightened as the man's grip tightened.

Stephen's eyes blazed. "Watch your bloody mouth when speaking about the boy. If brains were my supper, I would harvest a bounty from his skull and mere crumbs from yours. So, the next time you feel compelled to cast aspersions on someone, look in the mirror, at the slow-witted, weasel-faced young imp you find staring back at you."

"*Sorry...*" Donald thought his head might burst, his eyes ready to pop from their sockets. Every breath felt like someone playing tug-a-war with his tongue.

After what felt like an eternity, long enough for the boy to convince himself he was going to die, strangled to death by a mummy in his own yard, the man released him. Donald massaged his throat and scowled. "What did you do that for?"

"I have little tolerance for sad, bitter little bullies."

"I'm not a bully."

"Really? I'd wager your sister, watching you from her bedroom window as we speak, would *strongly* disagree."

Slowly, Stephen's gaze drifted up over Donald's head, forcing him to turn to follow it. There were four windows spread evenly across the second floor of their home. On the far right, a pale shape lurked beneath the reflection of the leaden sky. Donald could just make out the scrawled shadows of his sister's concern, and immediately felt a rash of irritation.

"Busybody," he muttered.

"She angers you," Stephen observed.

"Yes. So what?"

"Tell me why."

"I don't know why. She's a prude, a smelly little cow."

"It's something more than that though, isn't it?"

"I don't know what you mean."

"You love her."

Donald shrugged. "Only because I have to."

Stephen nodded once. "Correct. You have to because the alternative is unattainable."

"What alternative?"

"You *desire* her."

Immediate, unbridled rage filled the boy and he dared step closer, his fists clenched by his sides. "You listen to me. I don't care who you think you are, but you'd better watch your mouth. My father could have you thrown in prison, or even an asylum, for what you just said to me."

The soiled bandages creased to allow for a smile. "Is it not true?"

"No! Of course it isn't! What kind of a vile thing is that to suggest? My own sister! You're off your bleedin' head!"

"You would turn her down if she offered to lie with you?"

No, he thought then, and felt the color rise to his cheeks. *No, I wouldn't, but damn you to hell you bastard get out of my HEAD!* He knew how disgusting such urges made him; he knew how the village would look upon him if it were ever revealed that he lusted after his own sister; he knew how badly his father would beat him, and yet none of it helped contain the flaring impulses that rose whenever she touched him. On such occasions, he lashed out at her, hurt her, to punish her for tempting him, and to punish himself for the feelings her touch had induced in him.

It was wrong, all of it. It made an anomaly of him, an aberration, a freak of nature, and he knew it. At night he whispered reassurances to himself that he was not mad, and promised himself he would grow out of it, find another woman who loved him and forget all about his uncontrollable illness. But then Tabitha would pass him by, or lay her hand on his arm and fire would spread from his loins to scorch his throat and he would hit, punch, kick to get away from the desperate need to be with her.

"You're a liar," he said at last, avoiding the man's eyes. "Take your horrible lies somewhere else."

"Donald," Christopher said, leaning over the fence to touch the boy's shoulder. The odor was noxious and Donald had to suppress an urge to recoil. "I count honesty among my many afflictions. It's my business to know people better than they know themselves. If I were you, I would not waste your time suffering because of a perfectly natural compulsion. There is no shame in it, and why shouldn't a fine young lad like you get what he deserves? Often the pariah becomes king and what woman wouldn't part her legs for a king?"

Donald frowned. "I don't know what you mean."

Stephen's crooked smiled widened. "You will soon. Here." From his pocket he produced a slim silver object and waggled it in the air between them. Liquid sloshed within. A faint smile crossed Donald's lips at the sight of it.

"Is that really his?"

"Oh yes."

"How did you get it?"

"I took it from him."

"I'm surprised he let you."

"What makes you think he had a choice? Now, take it."

Hesitantly, Donald did as he was told. "It's full?"

"Filled it myself."

"Who knew Doctor Campbell had a heart?"

"Oh, he had a good heart, Donald. A warm heart."

With a quick look over his shoulder at the watcher in the window, Donald slipped the flask down the front of his pants and covered the bulge with his shirt.

"I give it to you on the understanding that you complete your end of the bargain, or I'll come back for that flask, and anything else I deem worthy of taking."

Donald nodded. "It'll be done."

"I have no doubt. Once you've taken care of this for me, there will be something else in it for you too." Again, his eyes moved over Donald's shoulder, his smile widening as he looked directly at Tabitha.

Donald swallowed, but said nothing. He couldn't tell if it was excitement or fear that made his guts churn. His legs were shaking by the time Stephen's gaze found him again.

The man's eyes were dark as coals. "She'll beg for you," he said.

***

For supper, Mrs. Fletcher made rabbit stew, which she served with freshly baked bread. The jack o' lanterns watched with disapproving stares from the sink, Neil's turnip looking particularly appalled. Still, it looked a lot better now that Grady had surreptitiously pared off the rough edges. Of course, if Neil found out, he'd be furious, but if they were lucky he wouldn't.

"So, Mrs. Fletcher," Grady said, tearing the crust off a slice of bread and dipping it into his stew. "About that engagement of ours."

Mrs. Fletcher blushed and rolled her eyes in exasperation. Kate found herself wondering, not for the first time, if there was something more than just harmless joking going on between the charwoman and the groundskeeper. They had quite a bit in common, after all. They were about the same age. Mrs. Fletcher had lost her husband to consumption; Grady's wife had died in childbirth. They shared the scars of grief and had both been in Mansfield House long enough to see it pollute the hearts of others. And yet they shared a wicked wit and indomitable spirit, despite the melancholy that sometimes showed in their eyes. Kate liked to imagine them as husband and wife, in a different time perhaps, or under different circumstances. She thought they'd have made each other happy, just as they made each other happy now, even if Mrs. Fletcher liked to pretend it was torment.

"You're incorrigible," she said, closing her eyes and sighing.

"Well, when faced with such staggerin' beauty as yours, I often forget myself."

"Oh now, really," the charwoman protested with a smile. She waved her napkin at Grady as if it were a talisman to ward off evil. "Behave yourself in front of the children."

"It's quite all right," Kate said, drawing a glare from the old woman.

"I think they're in love," Neil murmured, his sly expression a far cry from the sullen one he'd shown earlier. Kate was glad to see his sour puss had lost some of its severity.

Mrs. Fletcher gasped. "Neil! I think Mr. Grady and I could forever go without hearin' another of your preposterous statements!" She began to fuss over the food, busying herself with the doling out of second helpings, even though no one wanted any. Grady, looking amused, touched her hand. She pulled away as if burned.

"Ah sure," he said wistfully, "the poor boy knows the value of speakin' the truth."

"Oh, go away," the charwoman scoffed. "All this mockery will have me in the madhouse."

"We'd visit you every day," Kate said, "and I'm sure Grady would bring you flowers every day to brighten up your cell."

"That's no laughin' matter," the charwoman said, "I've known people who've ended up without their wits, and those asylums are rumored to be awful places, like Hell without the heat."

"Well then..." Kate coaxed a chunk of meat from her bowl and popped it into her mouth. "We'd all better keep an eye on our wits!"

Grady chuckled, and glanced at the window over the sink. Occasionally, blue-white fractures broke the heavy dark as a furious wind buffeted the walls of the house.

"'Tis goin' to be some lark tryin' to get to the dance in this weather, and here we were worried about the fog," he said.

"You'll all wear your coats," Mrs. Fletcher cautioned. "There's enough sickness in this house without deliberately invitin' more of it."

Neil stifled a burp, then asked, "Is Campbell due to visit Daddy tonight?"

Mrs. Fletcher huffed. "He was supposed to have been here a half hour ago."

"Maybe the weather held him up," Grady offered.

"Could be, Mr. Grady, but I think we all know it's more likely the warmth of the spirits at The Fox & Mare that's held him up."

"We'll check in there on the way to the dance," Grady said.

"Will you sit with Daddy for a while tonight, while we're gone?" Kate asked the charwoman. "Just to make sure he doesn't wake again and find himself alone?"

Thunder crackled; the plates shuddered.

"Of course I will. Don't you worry about that. I'll be better than any nurse. In fact, with all of you gone, I may take my embroiderin' and sit with your father until you come home."

Kate smiled. "Thank you." She wondered if Mrs. Fletcher knew about the silver blood.

Mrs. Fletcher waved away her gratitude. "I was lookin' after that poor man before you two were born. It won't be anythin' strange for me to sit vigil by his bedside."

"Well I suppose I'll have to find myself a new dancin' partner then," said Grady with mock disappointment. "I daresay none of 'em will be as light on their feet as you though."

"You'll have a bowlful of jelly on your head for your troubles if you're not careful."

"You see," Grady said to Neil and Kate, "that's the kind of spirited woman I like!"

Neil laughed so hard he almost choked on his stew and it took a startled Kate a few hearty thumps on his back to get him over it. Even then he continued to giggle softly, until his mirth infected Kate, then Grady and Mrs. Fletcher, until they were all chuckling like fools.

Outside, the storm worsened.

***

Superstitious old man, Grady thought, with a smirk. *Yer bein' silly.* And yet, his own self-chastisement couldn't quell the persistent and aggravating feeling in his bones that something wasn't right. Even Neil's mood had seemed unusual. The boy hardly exuded good humor, but the dark mood earlier had been new to all who'd borne witness to it. Then, at supper, his old self had returned, ending in a fit of laughter Grady wouldn't have believed had he not been there to hear it himself. *The girl*, he thought. *The Newman girl has him excited.* But despite the light-hearted supper they'd all shared, it still felt almost as if it would be their last, like condemned men sharing a joke before being hanged.

Dear God, he thought, pinching the bridge of his nose and closing his eyes. *Stop thinkin' such bloody awful things or you'll wish 'em upon the lot of us.*

It was the storm, he supposed, the howling winds battering at the walls of their warm safe haven that had summoned his unease, making it a lot easier to feel the groundless threat of imminent danger than to relax and believe everything was fine. But the fact that he was not alone in his worry only fuelled it, for there was not a face at the supper table that did not exhibit the same signs of preoccupation and disquiet behind the laughter.

Above their heads, a man lay dying, and here they were laughing and preparing to go dancing. Perhaps that was it: guilt. But what alternative was there? He was not about to order them all confined—even assuming they'd obey, which was doubtful—and make them sit around thinking of their father while the rest of the village took advantage of the one night in the gloom of autumn when they didn't have to sit at home listening to the sounds of night and fretting over the future.

No.

Tonight, they would dance. The worry would wait. It would have to, for soon enough Kate would leave for a new life, Neil too would move on, the Master would die, and Mansfield House would stand in silence, overlooking a decaying village and waiting for time to bring it down.

Grady feared what the end of his life at the house would mean, and though he tried not to dwell on it, or ponder it enough for it to consume him, he couldn't help but think of his son, Conor, back in Ireland—a son who had a life of his own now and would not welcome the intrusion of a bad memory upon it, should Grady deign to show up on his doorstep.

The bad blood between them had come about because of politics.

Conor loathed the British for their attempts to Anglicize Ireland and frequently used his position as banker to fund the militant efforts of those who sought to oust them. Grady, who shared his son's belief, encouraged him to lend his aid in ways that might be less catastrophic in their implications. Incensed, Conor had accused him of sympathizing with the British, an accusation aided by the fact that Grady had many British friends. It was a ridiculous claim, of course, but Conor latched onto it, until it became clear that the divisiveness that had a stranglehold on their nation had succeeded in tearing them apart also.

Shortly afterward, Grady had accepted a post as groundskeeper for the mayor of Dublin, and two years later, had moved to London, where he learned of the available position at Mansfield House. It had seemed a place far enough away from the insanity of the world.

But the insanity awaited him, in the form of a mythical creature he, to this day, told himself he'd imagined. If so, however, then his imagination had killed half the men on the hunt that day, and he knew there was more to it than that. Something had been stalking them that day. Something had stalked them *with purpose*, almost as if obeying the commands of the man who had led them there.

And now, as he sat at the table forcing himself to laugh along with Mrs. Fletcher and the children, he worried that whatever it was had come back, that the uneasiness was a portent, telling him he needed to be careful. That he needed to protect the children against something the night was sending their way.

For the first time since that day on the moors, he was truly afraid.

13

MEMORY SPUN A WEB ACROSS THE ROOM so vivid Mansfield believed if he reached out a hand his fingers would sink into it and the images would shimmer beneath his touch.

I did it, he thought with equal parts wonder and terror. *I ended it.*

The darkness was no longer absolute. The cold empty hearth at the far end of the room now held a fire that licked and crackled around burning logs and cast out shadows that sprawled across the ceiling. The curtains were drawn, the cobwebs that had hung so familiarly like cradles in the corners of the room now gone. The room was as it had been, once, before his presence in the room became little more than a haunting.

It took him a moment to realize that the pain was gone, that he could move without sparking paroxysms of mind-numbing agony through his enfeebled body.

I'm dead.

It took him a further moment to realize he was not alone.

He turned his head and a woman lay beside him, the gentle slope of her face partly occluded by the fall of her dark hair across it. One hazel eye peered curiously at him, lips parted slightly to emit a breath that smelled of mint. She was trembling slightly, the sheet drawn to her chest, obscuring his view of her nakedness. Nevertheless, his gaze fell to the cleft of her breasts, the slender curves illustrated by the silken sheet, and as before, he longed for her.

"Sylvia," he whispered, with no fear at all, despite knowing that she was not really here, that she couldn't be, no more than his wife could have been here earlier. Both women were long in the grave.

"I should not be here," she said, in her strange accent. To him, her husky, but not unfeminine voice was merely the sweet sound of passion, a lure she used to draw him to the light in her eyes and the pleasure promised by her body.

"I want you to be here," he said, mimicking words he had used on the night this memory represented. "And you wouldn't have come if you didn't want it too."

"But what of your wife?"

"My wife is lost to me," he said, truthfully. "Every day she grows more distant. It's like living with a ghost. She cannot give me what I need."

"And what do you need?"

"To have someone love me as much as I love them."

"But if you truly loved her, would you be here?"

Annoyed, he shook his head, and raised himself up, his elbow dug into the pillow. "Why are you here? What of your *husband*?"

She looked away from him. "He has no love for me. I'm a trophy to him, something to be presented for the approval of his friends. Nothing more."

"Well...*I* love you," Mansfield told her, unsure whether or not that was actually the case. He did love his wife and he had exaggerated her distance from him a little, but his allegiances had buckled under the weight of his desire for the voluptuous woman lying beside him. He knew, with a degree of shame, that at that moment in time, he would have denounced God himself for the chance to touch her.

"Why?" she asked. "You don't even know me."

"I know you enough to know he doesn't deserve you. That you are rotting away in that cold house, kept like a prisoner. I want to show you what it's like to be loved, and wanted."

"But you don't know me," she repeated, her lower lip quivering as if she were about to cry.

"I think I do," he said, a trite response he nevertheless hoped was adequate enough to reassure her.

He reached out a hand and brushed the hair from her face. She was the most incredible creature he had ever seen and his need for her manifested itself as an almost physical ache in the pit of his stomach.

She turned her head, her lips brushing his fingers, as a single tear rolled down her cheek. "You don't know me at all," she whispered, closing her eyes and guiding his hand down over her chin, her neck, over her breast and its rapidly hardening nipple, and lower, until a shuddering sigh escaped her. He slid closer, licking the dryness from his lips; she released his hand and turned away from him. For one desperate moment, he feared she had changed her mind, a fear worsened when she slowly rolled out of bed and knelt on the floor, facing away from him. His hunger intensified at the sight of her, the soles of her feet white beneath the curves of her buttocks, jet-black hair almost long enough to shield her nakedness from him entirely.

"Sylvia?"

"I want you," she said.

He slid from the bed to kneel behind her and touched her shoulder lightly, urging her to turn and face him. She didn't.

"Please," he whispered. "I want to see your face."

Again, she did not comply, and when, finally. she moved, it was to slide forward, her arms braced on the floor, palms flat against the carpet, her back an inverted arch. He lowered his gaze to the dark mound she presented to him, the shadows leaping over her like jealous lovers. Slowly, she eased her knees apart.

"I want you," she said again and now she was weeping, her body trembling.

Mansfield knew he should stop, should console the grief that tormented her, but even as she wept on her hands and knees, she rubbed herself against him until he thought he would explode with desire.

"*Please...*"

The fire hissed and spat; the shadows lurched across the room.

Hands smoothing the flesh on her buttocks, Mansfield positioned himself and slowly, ever so slowly, eased himself into the warm, wet depths of her.

He moaned.

Sylvia wept as the shadows crawled along her spine.

He froze so suddenly his neck cracked.

Her skin was going cold, as if her blood had turned to ice in her veins. He watched, the horror escalating, as her hair turned silver and the shadows buried themselves beneath her flesh. She changed, nubs of bone crackling as she shook her head and forced herself back against him with a gasp that was not altogether natural. Her vagina felt like a tightening fist around his manhood. He could not withdraw.

"Sylvia, what's...?"

"Hush," she said in a voice that sounded vaguely masculine, and when she turned to look at him over her rippling shoulder, he saw that a feral grin had split her face almost completely in half, needle-sharp shards of bone glistening in the firelight. But her eyes...her eyes were the worst of all and one look at those stretched eyesockets leaking blue-white fire was enough to finally free him, to send him flailing backward into one of the bed's thick oaken legs. Pain exploded across his shoulders and he cried out. Fire raced down his back; it was as if someone unseen were flaying him, and delighting in their work.

"Hush," said Sylvia as she swung around to watch.

This isn't how it happened, Mansfield told himself. *It didn't happen like this at all.*

She approached him, her arms lengthening into lithe black stalks, her hooked nails digging into the floor, her beautiful breasts shriveling, darkening as the shadows consumed her, her face elongating but still smiling, still smiling...

He screamed.

***

Lightning stabbed the belly of the sky and fresh rain cascaded from the wound.

Grady, Neil, Kate and Mrs. Fletcher stood in the open doorway, the lamplight barely penetrating the turbulent dark, turning the rain into silver threads.

"Are ye sure this dance is worth it?" Grady asked, grunting as he hefted the burlap sack full of pumpkins, and Neil's turnip, over his shoulder.

Kate and Neil nodded. "It's not that long a walk. We should be there in ten minutes," Kate said. "Five, if we run."

Neil scowled. "And what will I do? Hitch a lift in Grady's sack?"

"You could wait and see if it calms down a bit," Mrs. Fletcher offered. "It probably won't last much longer."

"We're late as it is," Neil grumbled. "If we wait much longer there won't be much point in going."

Thunder roared, making them flinch. The rain hissed down even harder than before.

"We're goin' to get soaked," Grady said. "The lot of us will be laid up with colds in the morning."

Neil sighed. "We'd be halfway there in the amount of time it's taking us to debate the matter."

"All right, all right. Let's get on with it then."

"Fasten your raincoats tight," Mrs. Fletcher said. "And go as quick as you can."

"We will," Kate and Neil said in unison and moved off into the rain, their lanterns cutting short swaths from the dark.

Grady hesitated. Mrs. Fletcher touched his shoulder. "Are you all right?"

He nodded. "Sure I am. Just a feelin' is all."

"Well if it gets strong enough, you turn right around and come back."

"Them two'd love that."

"You're a grown man. The decision is yours if you don't feel right about somethin', and they'll have to like it or lump it, won't they?"

"I think in that respect, you're gifted with more courage than I am," he said. "There are few things worse than the wrath of two sulkin' children." He sighed heavily. "Besides, they're right.'Tisn't often they have any kind of a break from the boredom. I'd find it kinda hard to look at 'em if I denied 'em this one."

"You're an old softy." Mrs. Fletcher fastened the top button on his coat. "Now off with you before you lose them in the dark."

He nodded and glanced over his shoulder at her. "You'll keep an eye on the master?"

"I will."

"All right. Then do me one last favor."

"What's that?"

"Have a cup of your fabled life-restorin' tea waitin' for me when I get back, will ya? I'd say I'll need it."

"Just for bravin' a storm with those two terrors, I'll make a pot of it. Cake, too. And don't forget to check the tavern for that drunken doctor."

"Right." With a salute, Grady left the comfort of the doorway, the rain making a sound like fingernails tapping against his coat. As fast as he could manage with the burden of the pumpkins, he headed toward the dwindling lantern lights up ahead, their muted glow like the eyes of some night creature watching his approach.

***

Mrs. Fletcher waited until she could no longer see Grady's light before she closed the door and headed into the kitchen. She'd put a fruitcake in the oven earlier, and already the delicious, heady smell of it permeated the kitchen. She looked forward to helping herself to a slice when Grady and the children returned.

Children.

She sighed. Kate, and especially Neil, already bristled at the use of that word, and she supposed she couldn't blame them. Kate was sixteen now, with Neil only a year younger than her. They were no longer children, and the realization saddened her, just as it had saddened her to see her own children growing into young men and women. She supposed the death of her youngest had made her latch on to the others all that much more. Soon she'd be forced to say goodbye to Kate and Neil, and stand at the door waving them off on the respective paths to their new lives. Her heart ached at the thought. Sometimes it felt as if her only role in life was to witness and encourage the beginning of everyone else's journey, to ready young lives for the bold new world while in the process, guaranteeing she would be left alone again, and heartbroken.

But it was still her job and she had learned to accept it, no matter how heartbreaking the process might be. She was the matriarch, and despite the title she had worn in the Mansfield house for as long as she had been here—that of charwoman—she considered herself more a mother to Kate and Neil than anything else. Their own mother had died when Neil arrived, and since that awful dark day, Mrs. Fletcher had looked after the children, caring for them and tending to their needs as surely as any biological parent. All of it done, however, with the knowledge that, when they were grown and out on their own, they would remember her only as the kindly old charwoman of Mansfield House.

She quickly fetched a glass of water and filled it at the sink to distract her from the sorrow that was starting to bring tears to her eyes. This was her life, she reminded herself, and this was how things had always been. Mourning each child's passage into adulthood as if it equated to death was futile and unfair to them and to herself. She had scarcely given any consideration to her own parent's feelings when, as a young girl, she'd married a coal-miner and moved to Cornwall, visiting them only rarely. She'd felt no guilt at the time, and didn't now. No intentional neglect had been involved. She had just been too preoccupied with making her own life, and that was sometimes just how things went.

Sniffling and chuckling at her own foolishness, she set the filled glass of water on the kitchen table and took a small bowl from the cupboard, into which she scooped the still warm remains of the rabbit stew, careful to avoid the large chunks of meat the master would not be able to chew. Then she set the bowl, the glass of water, and a teaspoon on a small oval tray and made her way upstairs.

The wind played a discordant tune through the tin whistle eaves and bellowed down the flue. Rain sprayed against the windows.

Mrs. Fletcher felt alone. Despite the presence of the master in his bedroom, she couldn't remember the house ever feeling as empty as it did tonight. It seemed as if the weather was a cat pawing at a doll's house, with her the only doll still rattling around inside. Momentarily, she wished she'd accompanied Grady and the children to the dance. She would gladly have braved the weather in order to avoid being left on her own. *No, you're not alone*, she chastised herself, *and it's unchristian and uncharitable to think so.*

Perhaps it was not the loneliness she disliked but the amount of thinking and self-pity she allowed herself when there was no one around to distract her. With an irritated shake of her head, she reached the top of the stairs and turned, her eyes fixed on the tray as she carefully headed toward the master's room.

I'll feed him, she decided, *then I'll get my embroidery, or perhaps a good book, and I'll sit with him for a spell. It won't be so bad.* But she knew it would be. No matter what activity she engaged in to discourage her melancholy musings, the hollow wind and the tortured rasp of her master's breathing would be all she'd hear.

Despite the promise she'd made to Kate earlier, Mrs. Fletcher decided her vigil would have many reprieves.

She reached the room and, balancing the tray on one hand, eased open the door.

Inside, it was pitch dark, with only the occasional flash of lightning illuminating the huddled form on the bed. Mumbling a curse, Mrs. Fletcher realized she'd left the matches downstairs and gently set the tray down on the floor. On both sides of the upstairs landing, lanterns had been set, their low flames fluttering, the tulip-shaped glass blackened by smoke near the top. She went to the nearest one and adjusted the wick so the flame rose, brightening the hall. A branch whacked against the window in Kate's room and Mrs. Fletcher stifled a cry, one hand clutched to her chest, her grip on the lantern tightening reflexively. "Good Heavens," she whispered, taking a moment to let her thudding heartbeat slow, before she held the lantern out and, stepping over the tray on the threshold of the master's room, brought the light inside. She set it on a locker directly across from the door and once more adjusted the flame so that bright warm light flooded the room.

Still unnerved by the bang the branch had made against the window, she turned and went to retrieve the tray, her shadow soaring up the wall ahead of her. Sudden movement gave her pause.

"Master?" she whispered, looking in the direction of the rumpled sheets. "Are you awake?"

She stepped closer to the bed and gradually the master's pallid features resolved themselves from the gloom, his body little more than a wrinkle in the bed sheets. Dark eyes twinkled in a withered face. She felt a shudder ripple through her, immediately followed by shame that she should react with such revulsion at so decent and beleaguered a man, an employer who had never treated her with anything but kindness in all her years of service to him.

"Master?" she said again as she leaned over the foot of the bed.

"Florence..."

Her heart almost gave up the ghost right there and then. Of all the sounds she'd expected to hear in the solemn lonely house this night, her master's voice had not been one of them. It filled her with fear, hope, and horror in equal measures.

"Oh my God..."

"Florence," he said, his voice a grated whisper. "You must kill me."

14

"Grady!"

The alarm in Kate's voice stopped him in his tracks. He turned, raised the lantern and squinted into the rain to see her face. "What is it?"

The look of terror on her face filled him with the horrible notion that here, now, in the middle of the storm, his recent fears were about to be realized. No one would hear them cry for help, not with the thunder and the rain, even assuming anyone had stayed home from the dance.

She raised a trembling finger and pointed at his chest, prompting him to look down, but there was nothing there, nothing that he could make out at least. "What?"

"The sack," she shouted. "The sack of pumpkins."

"What about them?" he asked, already feeling the burlap turn to ice between his shoulder blades.

"It's moving!"

In an instant he dropped the sack and stepped back.

"What's in there?" Neil said, silver eyes moving back and forward in the lamplight.

Grady shrugged, momentarily forgetting that the boy couldn't see the gesture, and moved only close enough to the sack to nudge it with his foot. The material jerked in response.

"You're right," he told Kate, who had moved to stand by his side, her lantern upraised to cast more light on the twitching sack. It lay on the wet ground like a body struck down, moving faintly in the last throes of life.

"Maybe my turnip came to life," Neil suggested wryly. "Like in that story you told us when we were children, the one about 'Stingy Jack.' He choked to death on—"

"That's enough," Kate said. "And the turnip didn't come to life in that story. Neither has this one."

Grady slowly stepped around to the end of the sack. Looking up and blinking away the rain, he said, "You two might want to back up a bit. I don't know what's in here, but it's probably a rat or somethin'. You don't want to be standin' there if he comes flyin' out, do you?"

Both of them shook their heads and moved away.

Grady took a breath, leaned down and grabbed the sack by one of the corners. With a quick glance to make sure Kate and Neil were back far enough, he yanked on the sack and quickly moved away. The pumpkins rolled out onto the road, the turnip trundling after, until they came to rest a few feet away. Nothing moved.

"Did you see it?" Kate called.

"Was it a rat?" Neil said.

Grady, frowning, shook his head. "I didn't see anything." He picked up the empty sack by the same corner he'd used to tug on it and gave it a shake. Suddenly, there came a shrill shriek. The groundskeeper yelped and dropped the sack just as something wormy and black wriggled free. He watched it plop to the road and glare at him with baleful red eyes before it scurried away into the thicket.

"Good Jesus," he said breathlessly and bent over to catch his breath. Kate and Neil fell into fits of laughter, slapping each other on the back, their faces contorted with mirth.

"Oh, I see," said Grady. "I've been tricked. When do I get my treat?"

"I'm sorry," said Kate, still giggling. "Really, we didn't mean it."

"I'm sure."

"No, really! When you put the bag in the basement after supper, I saw a rat crawl inside it. I was going to tell you, really I was, but it just seemed like too much fun to let you find it for yourself." She erupted into hysterics. "Besides, *I* wasn't going to try and get it out of there!"

He waited for them to compose themselves, then draped the sodden empty sack over his shoulder. "Did you two jokers stop to think about the waste it would have been had I decided to do a jig on the sack rather than upendin' it? I'd have destroyed all the pumpkins Mrs. Fletcher worked so hard on and ye'd be arrivin' at the dance with yer hands hangin'."

They muttered half-hearted apologies, the smiles still on their faces. They weren't in the least bit sorry, and Grady couldn't blame them. Despite the fright he'd gotten, he had to admit it had been a damn good prank. Not quite as good as some of the ones he'd perpetrated in his youth, but a worthy effort. He made a mental note to tell them sometime about the day he'd set fire to a haystack his father had been carrying on his back for delivery to a local farmer. The old man had miraculously managed to walk almost half a mile before he smelled the smoke, and even then, someone had to point out that the hay was on fire. Grady had gotten himself whipped raw for that one, but it made for a hell of a yarn.

"Come now," he said, "let's get these things back in the sack or we'll be out here all night and yer costumes will be ruined."

"Oh, all right," Kate pouted. The folds of a red outfit showed above the neckline of her raincoat. She bent down and began to roll the pumpkins toward her brother, who aimed wild kicks at them.

"For Heaven's sake, pick them *up*," she told him.

Lightning flashed.

Grady's breath caught in his throat.

In the field, something moved. He had caught only a glimpse of it in the flare of lightning but he'd been left with the after-image of long lithe shadows, like giant charred lizards, only moving in a way no reptile ever could, bounding, loping, running across the moors. He waited, breath held, for the lightning to come again, but when it did, there was nothing to see but the empty plains. Whatever it was he'd thought he'd glimpsed was gone, assuming it had really been there in the first place. Perhaps he'd only seen costumed children cutting across the moors to reach the dance hall, but he knew that was a feeble attempt at rationalizing the images that still flickered in his mind.

Not children.

Animals.

Hunting.

It shook him so badly that when he whipped down his hood to give himself an unhampered view and the wind snatched his cap from his head, he made no move to retrieve it. Instead, he simply watched as it sailed away into the darkness beyond the hedge.

"Grady?" He snapped out of his thoughts to find Kate and Neil struggling with the weight of the refilled sack. He quickly relieved them of the burden and slung it over his shoulder.

"One of the pumpkins got a little split," Kate said. "His nose is part of his right eye now." She was clearly amused.

"Then you can have that one," Grady said, and lead the way into the dark on a wave of protests. Even as he laughed and cajoled with the children—*would you stop it, they're not children anymore*—he was on edge, the hair prickling all over his body. He felt watched, threatened...stalked. When he quickened his pace, Neil objected and Grady had to force himself to slow down, even as he waited for something to burst shrieking from the hedges on both sides of the narrow road. When they reached The Fox & Mare, he almost collapsed with relief. Even after learning that Campbell was not inside, he felt better knowing that the hall was only a little further. When Sarah Laws slid a tumbler of whiskey before him, he gladly took it to steady his nerves, and then ventured back out into the storm.

More than once along the way, he caught Kate staring at him, concern on her face, but each time he offered her a wink to appease her and bolstered his efforts to hide his fear from the girl. She was a perceptive one, however, and he found he had to struggle to make her believe he was not terrified to the core of his being.

"Is something the matter?" she asked him, as the raucous sounds of merriment flooded down from the long narrow building on Gallagher Hill. The hall lights rose like will-o'-the-wisps in the darkness ahead of them and shadows capered within the warm squares of the windows. Cheers went up only to be drowned out by the thunder.

"Not at all."

"You lost your cap."

Grady smiled. "I have another one at home," he said and quickly turned. "Neil, we've reached the hall."

"So I hear."

Grady led them up the short winding pumpkin-studded incline to the arched main door of the hall. A paper witch that had been fastened to a nearby oak tree was wrenched free of her moorings and carried away by the wind as they went inside. Before the heavy door closed behind them, Grady looked over his shoulder, waiting for the lightning to show him what he knew was prowling out there. Then he was inside and bathed in warmth and good cheer. It was almost enough to melt the chill he felt deep inside.

Almost.

***

The hall was filled with monsters. Grady shook his head in wonder at the array of painted skeletons and wild-haired demons masquerading as children, all convened beneath the hot spray of light from the lanterns mounted on the walls. He hadn't expected such a crowd. After all, there were hardly enough children left in the village to form one. But then he remembered hearing that the hall in Merrivale had been knocked flat by the last great storm to hit the moors, and the villagers had asked to share Brent Prior's for the night. As a result, a hearty, energetic mob had filled the place almost to bursting.

Shadows stretched up the walls and broke their necks on the ceiling. It was an unsettling effect, particularly when the projectors of those shadows leered and shrieked at each other before lumbering off into the crowd. Around the walls stood long rickety looking benches, orange heads of various shapes and sizes watching the proceedings with fiery flickering eyes. Before them, bored looking adults tried to make conversation with other chaperones, who looked just as unhappy to be here. At the front of the room, dusty old wooden pallets had been stacked three high to make a makeshift stage upon which sat a quartet of nonplussed men, who attacked their musical instruments with an almost psychotic fervor. Grady recognized them as four out of five members of a local group called The Grass Routes. They played every year at The Fox & Mare at Christmas and New Year's Eve, though Sarah Laws had hinted recently that she might not be able to afford them this year, or any year after that, unless business picked up, which Grady couldn't see happening. That saddened him. Although the music wasn't exactly to his taste, he looked forward to the sound of the instruments every Christmas. It helped break the monotony that was quick to descend on all the other dreary nights he spent in the tavern and reminded everyone gathered there that, for a time at least, they had a legitimate reason to drink like fools.

A portly man with graying hair approached them where they stood just inside the door. "Good Lord, look at you lot. You're like drowned rats."

At the mention of rats, Kate whipped down her hood and glanced slyly at Grady, who growled at her.

Neil raised his hand in greeting. "Hello, Mr. Fowler."

"Hello, Neil. Looks like you caught the worst of the storm, eh?"

"'Tis bad now all right," Grady told him. "Thought we weren't going to make it."

"Well, I'm glad you did. I need to talk to you." Although he was still smiling, it seemed forced.

Grady knew better than to ask what it was that Fowler wanted to talk about. It was clear by his forced composure that whatever it was couldn't be spoken about in front of the children. He nodded to indicate he understood and gently forced Kate a few steps ahead of him. "Go get those raincoats off," he said. "I know you're dyin' to show off yer costumes, and if you aren't, you damn well should be after havin' Mrs. Fletcher slave over them fer the past week. Go on, off with ye."

"You're just jealous because we couldn't find one to fit *you*," Kate teased.

Neil shrugged. "He didn't need one. He came as a scarecrow."

Grady felt his patience wearing thin, and Kate must have seen it on his face because she grabbed Neil by the arm, weathering his protests and threats of violence as she led him away. The worried look clouded her face once more. Grady tried to reassure her with a short wave, but she turned away and they vanished, two ordinary youths in a dancing, giggling mob of ghouls and goblins. He felt guilty for having been so unceremonious in his abandonment of them, and for using Mrs. Fletcher's labors against them yet again, but the nervousness he'd felt all day was plaguing him and he'd recognized the same fear in Fowler's eyes. Something was very wrong in the village, and when he looked around the room, at the parents milling around their hyperactive children, he saw an underlying note of worry beneath their bored expressions he couldn't remember seeing before.

They feel it too.

Doubt quickly followed. Maybe he was being too hasty in ascribing doom to what might just be a sequence of events with perfectly rational explanations. Couldn't it be the storm that had everyone looking so shaken, so uncertain, as if they feared that any moment now the wind would tear the roof off the hall as it had in Merrivale and spirit them all away?

Of course it could.

But the wind hadn't carved sleek black shadows from the moors, slender oily things that moved predatorily under the cover of dark. The storm couldn't be held accountable for that, or for the drawn look on Fowler's face that told him they'd shared a singular horror, just as they had all those years ago on the day of the search for Sylvia Callow.

"What's wrong?" Grady asked.

Fowler scratched his nose and looked around. "Can we step outside?"

"*What?* It's pissin' out of the Heavens out there. Look at me; I'm soaked to the skin! That steady flow of water you see tip-tappin' against my shoes isn't me takin' a sneaky leak you know."

"I know, I know." When Fowler raised his hands in a placating gesture, Grady noticed they were trembling. "But I'd rather talk about this in private."

Grady tugged down his hood and rubbed a damp hand over his face. "All right, but I can tell you now I'm not at all convinced I want to hear it." He dropped the sack of pumpkins. "Let me get rid of these fellas. Why don't you head down to The Fox and I'll meet you there as soon as I tell the children where I'm goin'. I'm assumin' this won't take long?"

Fowler looked relieved. "No, it shouldn't. I'll have a pint waiting for you."

"Make it a whiskey," Grady told him and, dragging the pumpkins behind him, made his way into the crowd of goblins.

***

In the cloakroom, Jack the Ripper was arguing with Little Red Riding Hood. Grady rolled his eyes as he stepped into the small damp room. Every hook held a dripping raincoat and by the glow of the single lantern suspended from the ceiling, they registered as a crowd of flaccid shadows in the corner of his eye. Again, he had to shake off the nagging feeling that somewhere a clock was winding down, ticking off the seconds to some unknown calamity. The most banal of objects seemed sinister, the gloom a blanket beneath which unknown horrors lurked. Since his glimpse of the things on the moors, his heartbeat had thundered furiously in his chest, as if he'd run a mile, and he found himself struggling to remain calm. He didn't believe in ghosts, ghouls or any of the horrors the children in the hall had come to imitate. But the strange loping things he'd seen tonight were not so easily dismissed. Those bounding figures had exuded a tangible threat, and worse, a threat tailored specifically toward him and the children. He didn't know how he could come to such a conclusion. That it was just a strong feeling somehow didn't seem adequate explanation for the paralyzing dread that crept unbound within him. There had to be something else. But did it really matter? Would a fuller explanation or a search for answers really make them any safer?

No. It wouldn't.

All he could think of was those scratch marks in Royle's saddle and what their attacker had done to the rider.

"There's nothing wrong with it. It's fine, and just as good as yours," Kate said, hands on hips, anger making her complexion the same hue as her Little Red Riding Hood costume. "You can't even see it for Heaven's sake, so how do you know it isn't?" She tugged up the velvet hood.

Mrs. Fletcher had made the costume for Kate from a pair of old curtains, and Grady found himself once more admiring the charwoman's talent. The hooded cape looked better than anything she might have purchased at a costume shop.

"Because it's not scary. You're supposed to dress in something scary for All Hallows. I told you that *last* year when you came as a swan!" Neil was dressed in a black sheet that Mrs. Fletcher had fashioned into a cloak, and one of the master's old dress shirts, the sleeves rolled up and pinned to fit. It still hung loose on the boy's wiry frame, but combined with the black pants, oversized top hat and the butter knife he brandished with wicked glee, the overall effect was appropriately sinister. Grady had even ringed Neil's eyes with shoe polish, while the charwoman had patted his face with flour the rain had all but washed away. Nevertheless, he looked just like the pictures Grady had shown Kate in some old copies of the *London Advertiser*—crude sketches of the fearsome maniac known as Jack the Ripper.

"Well I don't care what you think. I'm not going to listen to criticism from a blind old grouch like you."

At that, Grady had had enough. He pulled Kate aside, more roughly than he'd intended, but it communicated the message that she had gone too far. With a scowl she yanked free of him.

"I won't hear that kind of talk from you," he told her in a level tone. "And you," he said to Neil. "Leave her alone. Her costume is one of the best out there, and so is yours. Why the two of ye insist on gettin' on each other's nerves is beyond me, but we're callin' an end to it now, understood?"

They both nodded.

"Good. Now listen carefully to me. I'm goin' to leave ye two on yer own for a spell. I want you to stay out there in the hall where everyone can see you. Under *no circumstances* are ye to go outside."

Kate frowned. "Why? Where are you going?"

"I have to meet Greg Fowler down at the Fox. He needs to talk to me about somethin'."

"Drinking," Kate said in disgust.

"What does he want you for?" Neil said, no doubt wondering if his job was in danger.

"Well, I won't know until I get there, Neil. Now I want you to promise me ye'll stay in the hall."

"We will," Kate said, in a tone that suggested she would do what she liked and not be told different. She was a sensible, well-behaved girl, but she had a defiant streak a mile long, and knowing that made him feel even more nervous.

"Look," he said, running a hand over his hair. "This is important. I don't very often give orders, but I have to now, and I'm not leavin' until I get your solemn oath that ye'll follow 'em."

Neil took a step toward him, an expression of concentration on his face. "You're scared," he said. "I can hear it in your voice."

Grady smiled weakly. "That's the cold, boy. Wait 'till you get to be my age and you'll understand."

But Neil didn't look convinced and Grady silently cursed the boy's perceptiveness. He needed them to trust him, and the fear in his voice was betraying him. It would appeal to their curiosity, and might lead them to defy him.

"How long will you be?" Kate asked.

"Not long. Half an hour at the most. I'll be back in time fer the apple bobbin', I promise."

"All right." Kate went to Neil's side and took his arm. For once he didn't resist. The slow cautious quality of their movements made Grady feel guilty on top of everything else. He had scared them, and realized he should have known they would hear the unspoken fear in his words, sense the peeling edges on his mask of composure. They were not imbeciles, and now they would worry until he returned.

"I won't be long," he said again, watching them as Kate opened the door to the music and the babbling of the crowd.

"We'll be here," Kate said over her shoulder.

15

UNCOMFORTABLY HOT IN HER WITCH OUTFIT, Tabitha nibbled on a piece of fruitcake and forced herself to relax a little. The dance had started almost an hour ago and still she had seen no sign of Neil. She prayed the inclement weather had kept him and Kate indoors. If it had, then there could be no comeback from Donald. After all, she didn't control the weather, so she couldn't be blamed for his plan—whatever it was—failing.

Still, fear gnawed at her. Something felt odd about the night. Everything in the hall looked the same as it did every year, albeit with a lot more people present than ever before; there were dancing ghouls, giggling goblins, crepe paper on the walls, plastic devils on the doors, and people enjoying themselves, but the air felt different somehow. Up until now she'd blamed the storm. The air always changed before thunder and lightning, but deep down she knew that she had snatched that convenient explanation only to keep from examining more closely the ominous feeling she'd had all day long.

Just nerves, she told herself. Considering she had allowed herself to be manipulated by her brother into setting up an innocent blind boy, she had every right to feel uneasy. She had nothing against Neil Mansfield. He had never done anything to her to warrant reprisal, had not threatened her honor with his forced sullen responses. Worse, she realized that if she was completely honest with herself, a little part of her did like him, and yes, in a romantic way. She had, however, quelled those feelings in the past because of pity—which she knew was unfair but couldn't help—and a little fear of her own. Fear of what it would be like to court someone who couldn't see, and fear of what people would think of her for doing so. Her father would certainly react with disdain that his 'little princess' couldn't summon the resources to find a boyfriend with a less obvious handicap.

The fruitcake hung like a knot in her stomach and she quickly scanned the small tables set out around the hall for something to drink. At last she settled on a glass of punch from a confetti-filled bowl, but the knot remained, like a manifestation of guilt.

"You'll need a little something stronger than that if your boyfriend doesn't show up soon," said a voice behind her and she turned to find Donald standing uncomfortably close, the burlap sack he'd come to the party dressed in scratching against her fingertips.

"I can't believe you're wearing that," she said disdainfully, indicating the fabric stretched taught around his midriff.

"I'm a sack of potatoes," he proclaimed with obvious pride. "Besides, I only look half as ridiculous as the rest of these idiots, and that includes you. What are you supposed to be anyway? A granny?"

"Leave me alone," she said and turned back to the table. A moment later, her hat was gone, snatched deftly from her head. Slowly, she turned. "Give it back."

Donald propped the tall witch's hat on his head and spread his hands expansively. "How do I look? Better?"

She considered arguing, but then sighed in disgust. "Fine. Keep it."

Donald grinned. "So, where is he?"

"How am I supposed to know?"

"He's your boyfriend. You should know."

"He's not, and I don't. He mightn't even come."

Donald stepped so close she could smell the alcohol on his breath, and for a moment she thought he was going to kiss her. "You better hope he does," he said. His eyes moved briefly to her lips, reinforcing the peculiar fear. The pungent smell of alcohol wafted into her face and she grimaced. At length, his gaze met hers. "Because if he doesn't," he continued, teeth bared, "you're going to have to go get him and drag him here." His eyes were wide and bloodshot and now she knew what the silver item the bandaged man had given him earlier had been. A flask of alcohol.

"Why?" she asked then, "why do you want him so badly? What did he ever do to you?"

"'What did he ever do to you?'" Donald mimicked in a high voice. "Who says he did anything? I'm just sick of him getting special treatment because he's blind, that's all. He stumbles around the village like that old drunk Campbell and yet everyone treats him like he's royalty. Kick the feet out from under the little bastard and half the village is running after you with sticks. Pfft! That, and...well...let's just say a friend of mine has a special interest in him, all right?"

"Who is he?" Tabitha asked, aware even as she did so that she might be pushing Donald, forcing him to lose his temper and hurt her, but she couldn't help herself. She had to know, for it was growing ever more apparent that her brother, no matter how callous and cruel he could be sometimes, was not the sole instigator of whatever bit of unpleasantness was in store for Neil.

"None of your bloody business," Donald sneered. "Just—"

He was cut off by the sudden appearance of Little Red Riding Hood, who looked right past him to Tabitha, and smiled knowingly. "Hi Tabitha."

It was then that Donald, who'd been about to launch into an angry tirade at being interrupted and so brusquely shoved aside by, of all things, a *girl*, noticed who she was, and, more importantly, who she had on her arm.

Jack the Ripper.

Panic seized Tabitha as a wide grin creased her brother's lips.

***

Mrs. Fletcher had always considered herself a religious woman, though her faith had taken a considerable blow after the death of her husband and youngest son. She'd stopped going to church but hadn't abandoned her beliefs. Not entirely, at least. Tonight, that faith had returned in a wave, for what she had just witnessed could be nothing short of a miracle. A dying man had not only awakened, he had spoken to her, even if the words that had crept from his pale lips testified to little more than the extent of his agony. But then he had raised his hand and beckoned to her to help him sit up, dispelling all doubts she might have entertained that his apparent improvement had been an ephemeral thing, a brief misleading reprieve that portended his final moments. She was dumbfounded. Though she'd never have said so aloud, she had assumed he was not long for the world. His appearance, coupled with Doctor Campbell's grave pronouncements had led them all to believe they would soon be mourning him and comforting the children in their grief.

But now...

Now she couldn't wait for the children to come home, to see their father sitting up and speaking. They would not believe their eyes. Hope would be restored, and it would be as if the curtains had been opened at last on a dark and dusty house. A house she intended to invite Doctor Campbell to visit at his nearest convenience, if for no other reason than to see the proof that past accusations of his incompetence had been well-founded.

"My God," she said as she fluffed the pillows and set them behind the frail man's shoulders. She was weeping uncontrollably, her tears renewed each time he made a gesture on his own, displaying strength that had been denied him for so very long. He was still deathly pale, and frail, but in his eyes the life had begun to return, the white clouds dispersing, allowing the blue to peek through.

A miracle. A true miracle, and only the needs of the master kept her from running out of the house into the storm to find the children to break to them the news they'd been waiting an eternity to hear. *He has returned to us!*

Yet something about his demeanor, something she'd been quick to dismiss as the vagaries of his illness, bothered her greatly, damming the tide of her jubilation whenever she focused on it.

His hoarse whisper sent the thought fleeing from her mind.

"What is it, sir?" she asked.

"Water," he croaked.

"Of course." Concerned, she hurried for the tray she'd left in the doorway and carried it to the nightstand. In the glow from the lantern, the master looked cadaverous, prompting Mrs. Fletcher to wonder if she had been hasty in her assessment of events, if she had indeed been correct that his revival was simply a merciful gift before death came for him.

She watched him smooth the covers over his chest, a simple motion that had nevertheless become alien in this room; a gesture they'd never expected to see him make again, and was now all the more significant because of it, then she sat down on the edge of the bed. As she lowered the glass, preparing to bring it to his lips, he brought his hand up and took it from her. Again, she was astounded. Was it even possible to recover so quickly? What kind of strange ailment fled the body so fast and left a strengthened body in its wake?

He drank deeply until he'd drained the glass. Tentatively, she took it from him and set it on the nightstand.

"How are you feelin', sir?" she asked, voice quavering.

"As can be expected." The words dragged a cough from him that struck fear into the charwoman's heart. Would this be the moment in which all illusion of his recovery dissipated and once more left him a catatonic vessel?

A moment later, he recovered, on his reddened face an expression of steely resolve. One hand snaked out and latched itself around the charwoman's wrist.

"I have to get up," he said. "You have to help me."

"Oh," said Mrs. Fletcher, quickly rising as he started to hoist himself up. "I think you should stay in bed, sir. At least until Doctor Campbell has a chance to—"

"I've been in this damn bed long enough. Now I need to get up. Something's wrong. Something we must put right. Something *you* have to fix." When she looked at him dumbly, he added, "The children are in danger."

"Master, don't worry yourself now, I assure you, Kate and Neil are quite safe. They're at the dance, with Mr. Grady." She smiled but it cracked at the sight of him forcing back the sheets. The exposed legs were like pale sticks and she felt her heart miss a beat. "Sir, please..." He ignored her, his movements frantic, one arm outstretched, fingers splayed in a gesture that forbade intervention.

"They're not all right," he said, anger in his tone. "And won't be unless we do something about it."

He's delusional, Mrs. Fletcher thought, disappointment tainting her hope. *This is nothing more than another level of his sickness.*

He swung his legs over the edge of the bed, but there he paused, breathless, and looked at the floor as if it were the opening to an abyss. When he looked up, his resolve had faltered, replaced by fear. "I'm not sure I can stand," he said.

She sat next to him, took his hand and put his arm around her, even while mumbling her dismay that he should endeavor to rise before his body was prepared for the punishment. She stood, alarmed at the lack of weight in him; it was like lifting a sack of feathers. There she held him, again struck by how odd it was to see him standing by the bed instead of comatose within its folds. He removed his arm, and though not quite steady, he managed to stand on his own and gave a small satisfied nod.

Mrs. Fletcher shook her head at the sight of him. He looked like a scarecrow. "You're still weak, sir," she said. "This is foolish."

The glare he cast at her was another incongruity and the power of it hushed her.

"You don't understand," he said. "Someone is coming for the children. I should be the one to save them, but I'm afraid I have expended the limits of my usefulness. Now, I'm more of a threat than anything else."

She clenched her hands to her bosom. "But sir...you've been with fever. How could you know what's happenin' to anyone?"

"I don't know, but it's what's *going* to happen. Now, if you want to help me, you're first charge is to forget your concern for me. It's misplaced. Start worrying about the children."

Despite his words, Mrs. Fletcher shook her head, aware it would inflame his ire, but unable to indulge his febrile fantasies any longer. "Sir, you need to get back in bed. Let me fetch Doctor Campbell."

"I don't want him, Florence. If you summon him here I will kill him, do you understand me? This is not a situation that requires his involvement and if you persist in your nauseating maternal attitude, I'll be forced to do this on my own, and believe me—" His face darkened, "—I will."

Thunder exploded, rattling the windows.

Flustered and frightened, Mrs. Fletcher backed up until she was standing in the doorway, afraid that despite his weakened state he might somehow find the strength to throttle the life from her for refusing to aid him. The prolonged agony had obviously robbed him of his wits and she could only hope to entertain his ravings until Grady came home. Grady would know what to do. Despite their titles, the groundskeeper and the master had been steadfast friends for years.

"All right," she said softly. "What do you want me to do?"

He seemed to sag a little, and for one panicked moment, she thought he was going to collapse, but then he straightened and took a step toward her. "Help me downstairs," he said.

16

"I THINK THE BEAST HAS COME BACK."

They were sitting in the corner furthest away from the bar and nearest the door, the silence following Fowler's statement shattered by a peal of thunder that made them both jump. Behind the bar, Sarah continued wiping the mahogany counter with a soiled cloth, seemingly oblivious to the thunder even though it had rattled the glasses and the oval mirror on the wall behind her.

Aside from Grady, Fowler, and Sarah, the bar was empty, everyone else busy enjoying the festivities up at the hall.

Grady had already had two whiskeys, but tonight they weren't providing him with the comfort he'd hoped for. He clacked his glass on the small round table—an uncharacteristically impolite means of indicating to the barmaid that he wanted a refill—and, "I know," he said simply, avoiding the other man's eyes. "But up until now I was doin' a fine job of pretendin' it wasn't."

"You've seen it?"

"I've seen *them*."

Fowler paled. "More than one?"

Grady said nothing, but nodded slightly. "And you? What did you see?"

"I was closing up the shop to go for something to eat and there was one in the field right across the road. The fog had just begun to lift and at first I almost missed it." He paused for a sip of his whiskey. "It was like a big black dog, or a panther, only lower to the ground, like...like..."

"A lizard," Grady finished for him. "Like a lizard."

"Yes. Exactly like that."

"What did you do?"

"Ran like the clappers, what do you think I did?"

"I saw them tonight," Grady said. "On my way to the hall with the children. I can't be sure, but I think there were three of 'em. Just like you described: Black things, low to the ground. Like big lizards." He smiled bitterly then and covered his face with his hands. "Jesus, will you listen to us? Two grown men sittin' here tremblin' like little schoolboys and talkin' about giant lizards. We should be in the madhouse, Greg, there's no doubt about it."

Fowler shook his head. "No, we shouldn't. If I'd never been on that search I'd gladly agree with you. I'd say my eyes were playing tricks on me. But I was there. I saw something in the fog, something bloody big. I heard it growling and it wasn't a dog. You saw it too. You saw it kill..." He lowered his voice, "...Royle, and you saw it—*them*—again tonight. If we're mad, then so be it. I'll be only too glad to hold out my arms for the straightjacket if it means I don't have to lie awake every night wondering if one of those bloody things is going to come through my window to get me." He drained his whiskey and wiped his mouth on his sleeve. "But if we're not," he continued, "then you and me are in trouble."

Grady frowned and waved his hand in the air between them. "Right, right, so we know somethin' is prowlin' the moors, and the village, even if it only turns out to be a few man-eatin' panthers escaped from London Zoo, but what good does knowin' do us exactly?"

Fowler threw up his hands. "Haven't a clue, but I'll tell you there's not a day that goes by that I don't curse that bastard Callow for what he did."

Grady watched the pain cross his friend's face, then said, "You did all you could have you know."

Fowler shrugged, trying to be casual but the look in his eyes betrayed him. Grady imagined there had been a lot of sleepless nights for Fowler since that day on the moors.

"What he did to her..."

"You were there fer the woman, Greg. In her last moments I'm sure she appreciated that."

"I know, but..." He shook his head.

"What?"

"If I hadn't brought that gun..."

"You'd be dead, and so would Mansfield. You saved his life that day, and your own."

"Yes, but still." The guilt had added a lot of lines to the man's face over the years, and Grady had reassured him on more than one occasion that it was needless. Now, he had no words left with which to persuade his friend that picking up that pistol and shooting Callow dead had been the only option available to him at the time.

"What if it didn't end with that?" he said quietly.

Grady scoffed. "We tossed him into the Fox Tor Mire. Even if yer bullet hadn't killed him, he'd never have managed to crawl out of there."

"I'm not saying he did."

After a few minutes of thought, Grady realized what he was saying. "You're thinkin' it's his ghost?"

"I killed him. I stopped him from killing Mansfield, from feeding us to that monster he used to trap us. Now we're seeing those things again. What's to say we won't see *him* again too, walking the moors, herding those creatures? Back to finish what he started."

Grady shook his head. "Why would Callow wait almost this long to get his revenge?"

"That's what I've been trying to figure out," Fowler replied. "But if it turns out I'm correct, will the reason really matter?"

Grady had no response for that.

"Or...or maybe he hasn't come back," Fowler continued. "Maybe when he died his monsters just roamed the moors feeding on game and the occasional unlucky wanderer, but now they're no longer content with that. Maybe they've run out of rabbits. Maybe now they want *us*."

"I don't want to think about that."

Fowler sat back. "Well, you're going to have to."

When Grady looked questioningly at him, Fowler leaned forward in a conspiratorial manner. "I'm leaving tomorrow."

"For good?"

"Yes."

"That's ridiculous. What about the store?"

"I'll sell it when I get to Devon. Someone else can come run it. In the meantime, Neil can keep it going. You can help him divide the takings. He can keep half. Send the other half on to me. I'll leave the address in the store." His voice fluttered with nervous excitement, and in that moment Grady realized just how frightened Fowler was. He seemed to possess none of Grady's lingering doubt, only a steadfast certainty that something evil had set its sights on him.

"You're bein' a little hasty, aren't you?"

"No," said Fowler. "No, I don't think I am. I hear things out there, Grady, and I'm dreaming funny dreams. I was lucky the first time I walked into Callow's snare. I doubt I'm lucky enough to survive another round, and the way I see it is—if I'm not here, they can't get me." He sighed heavily. "I've never forgotten that day, Grady. Never. I've felt shadows across my back ever since, and now they've found me."

"But to leave yer home and everythin' you know because of somethin' that could be hunted down and killed with enough men and guns?"

Fowler didn't answer, and Grady quickly realized he didn't need to. The answer was already in both their minds, clear as day: What if bullets didn't stop them? Recalling the liquid, almost serpentine way the creatures had been moving toward the village under the cover of night made him think that something so unnatural could hardly be killed by human means.

The children.

The thought of them up there at the hall brought him back to himself and he rose so suddenly he banged his knees against the edge of the table. He restrained a howl of pain and grimacing, offered the still-seated Fowler his hand. "I don't think yer entirely right about these things, but I know why yer runnin'. In my head I'm doin' the same, but my heart isn't so easily won over. I have to stay, fer the children, and the master. He's been nothin' but fair to me in all the years I've looked after that house. I'm not about to desert him now." He reached for his cap before he remembered it wasn't there, that the wind had stolen it earlier and he'd most likely never retrieve it. That was fine too, he decided. If that ratty old cap was all he lost on the moors, he'd consider it a blessing.

"Glad to have known you, and I hope you find the peace you're lookin' fer in London," he added as Fowler shook his hand.

"Won't you stay for another one?"

"I'd love to, and maybe when you come back around the village I will, but right now I have to get back to the hall."

"You and I are the only ones left. I'm getting out, and if you have any sense you'll do the same," said Fowler, averting his gaze, as if he was certain Grady thought him a coward for fleeing. And if Grady was honest with himself, he *did* think that, but he also understood how fear could drive a man to do almost anything. Fowler was simply acting on survival instinct. He felt threatened; he ran. Another man might stand and fight, but different men made different choices.

Which man are you? he asked himself, and found, to his dismay, that he had no answer.

***

Tabitha was trapped. Whatever choice she made within the next few seconds would result in pain. If she interfered with Donald's plan and warned Neil, she would have to suffer his punishment. If she stayed quiet, she would forever suffer the consequences of having lured an innocent boy into a trap. The fact that Donald had yet to say anything disturbed her too. He simply stood there, a half-smile plastered to his face, his chest rising and falling rapidly as if at any moment he might explode from the excitement. She recognized the look in his eyes and it made her want to be sick. There could be no doubt now that her brother intended to hurt Neil. Armed with this certainty, she rushed forward and grabbed Neil's wrist.

"You promised me a dance," she said bravely, struggling to keep the tremor from her tone. "I think now is as good a time as any, wouldn't you say?"

Neil licked his lips. "Let go of me."

"Oh, don't be such a prude," Kate said, poking him in the back.

Tabitha didn't look at Donald. She didn't need to. Already she imagined she could feel the heat of his rage warming the air between them, but thankfully, he made no move to stop her, for which she was only slightly relieved. Whatever he was going to do, he would do it, no matter how much she attempted to delay the inevitable. She felt her chest constrict with sorrow and self-loathing that she had not been able to summon the courage to refuse her part in Donald's scheme.

Kate smiled at her as she led Neil away. "Don't be too long now," she teased. "He's not my favorite young man in the whole world, but I would like him back before he goes stale."

Tabitha offered her a wan smile and quickly moved away, still expecting at any moment to feel her brother's hand clamp down like a vice on her shoulder, his whiskey breath against her cheek—*I'll kill you for this, you little trollop*—but despite the phantom sensation of his strong fingers bruising the flesh on her shoulder, it didn't come, and then they were away, the crowd of monsters around them, the lamplight casting orgiastic shadows on the walls.

Neil looked nervous as the band began an unfamiliar ballad. Tabitha was trembling so badly she was sure he would feel it as they joined hands. He put his arm around her, holding her at a respectful, gentlemanly distance and they began to dance, slow rhythmic steps, keeping in time with the music, and Tabitha realized that under different circumstances, she would very much have enjoyed the closeness with Neil, the feel of him ever-so-slightly leading her, taking charge. Despite her fear, she smiled.

"I didn't know if you were going to come or not," she said, scowling as a laughing ape bumped against her shoulder and raised a furry hand in apology.

"We almost didn't. The prank we played on Grady slowed us down."

"What prank?"

"Kate put a rat in his bag. Well, not really, it went in there by itself. We just didn't tell him about it."

Tabitha grimaced. "That's awful!"

"He didn't get mad or anything. Not really, which was a shame actually."

"My father would have thrown a fit!"

"Grady's not my father."

Tabitha was surprised at the bitterness in Neil's voice, but any ideas she might have entertained about pursuing the topic vanished from her mind when, through a break in the crowd, she caught Donald's glare.

"I have something to tell you," she told Neil.

"I'm all ears. Not by choice, unfortunately."

Tabitha took a deep breath. *Cherish this*, she thought. *Cherish this final and brief moment in which he still believes you're someone worth wanting, before you tear his world apart and he comes to know you as worthy only of his hate.* She felt the tears welling and hurriedly blinked them away. "You're in danger," she said.

"What?"

The words felt like cold stones rolling off her tongue. "It's Donald."

"What about him?"

"I think he's going to hurt you."

Neil scoffed. "Let him try."

"No, listen to me. He's not in it alone."

"Really."

She knew Neil's blasé attitude was a form of defense, and it frustrated her.

"He's working with a stranger, a man who showed up at our house this morning."

"Stranger?" Their dancing slowed.

"Yes."

Neil tried to push her away, but she forced him to keep dancing, with the hissed caveat, "Stop it. If he sees we're done, he'll come after you."

"So what? If your ignorant sloth of a brother wants me, let him come. I'm not afraid of him."

"You should be. They intend to do you harm."

"Cowards," Neil mumbled. "Donald needs a partner to get the better of me, does he?"

"Neil, stop it," Tabitha demanded. "I know you're brave, but now's not the time. You don't need to prove it to me. I'm afraid they're going to do something awful to you. You have to leave."

"Why should I leave? I have as much a right to be here as your fat pig of a brother."

"What did you call me?"

Neil stumbled and stepped on Tabitha's toes. She winced, but quickly recovered and almost instinctively moved in front of Neil, whose odd silvery eyes were moving from side to side as if, despite his blindness, he was attempting to see the threat.

Donald stood before her, sneering. "Need a woman to defend you now, eh? You little sissy."

"Donald, please. Leave him alone."

Heads turned; dancers began to slow, though the music continued unabated. The fuss was being noticed. The ghouls were watching.

"Get out of the way, Tabby."

She was about to plead with him again, but a voice from behind her, Neil's voice, stopped her. "Do as he says."

"No," she whispered, knowing it would be lost to the music.

"Yes," Donald said, with visible glee. "Do as I say."

In her panic, she said the only thing she could think of that might save the situation. "I'll tell Mother." Too late she realized how infantile and hopeless a threat it was and by then Donald was almost doubled over with laughter. He wasn't the only one. The absurdity had inspired guffaws from some of the spectators, who had abandoned their own dances to watch the show.

Helpless, she had no choice but to be shoved aside by Neil as he stepped forward, his face streaked with shadow, blind eyes blazing. Donald composed himself and drew himself back up to his full height, fists clenched and ready.

The music was beginning to falter, allowing the muffled roar of thunder an uninterrupted audience.

"Neil!" It was Kate, rushing through the crowd, her face pallid, eyes wide with panic. "*Neil!* What's going on?"

He ignored her. Shadows slipped from the walls. The dancing ceased and the air grew thick with tension.

"You there!" someone said, as the chaperones broke away from the walls and started to infiltrate the crowd, but they were met with unyielding bodies and snorts of laughter. The threat of a fight had drawn the attention of everyone now and few of the onlookers seemed willing to see it interrupted.

Distracted by the plight of the chaperones, Tabitha didn't see Donald approaching her and she gasped as his hand knotted itself in her hair. Before she had time to struggle, her head was wrenched back so fast her neck cracked. "I'll have my fun with you later," her brother whispered into her ear and pushed her away. Her feet tangled and she fell, hands out to prevent her face from smashing against the hard floor.

Then Donald stepped close to Neil. "Come here, twat-face. I've been looking forward to this for ages."

Kate had reached them but suddenly found herself held back by the costumed bodies of some of the older boys from Merrivale, their skeleton masks leering at her as she tried to push through their human barricade.

"Leave it luv," one of them said cheerfully. "My money's on the big fella."

"Shouldn't take long," said another.

Kate felt her costume rip as she heaved herself against them and "Neil!" she screamed. But he didn't look at her.

"Someone wants to meet you," Donald said, bouncing slightly on the balls of his feet. "But he never said anything about bringing you to him in one piece."

Neil stood stock-still, shoulders thrust back, and raised his fists in front of his face. "Why don't you shut your mouth and do something, you fat idiot?"

Donald positively swelled with rage. "Oh, I will," he said, and drew back his fist.

"No! Don't!" Kate's struggles grew so fierce it drew grunts of effort from the Merrivale boys.

With a grin, Donald swung, the punch aimed squarely at Neil's jaw.

17

"I'M CLOSING," SARAH LAWS SAID in her usual cheerless drone.

Fowler raised his glass. "How about one for the road?"

"The road isn't thirsty, and you've had enough," the barmaid said, snatching the glass from his hand and giving the table a perfunctory wipe around his elbows. "You'd better go."

He offered her a sad smile, the amount of alcohol he'd consumed forcing melancholic thoughts to the forefront of his brain.

"I'm leaving, you know."

"Good," she said, making her way back to the bar.

"I mean, leaving the village."

She did not pause, her step did not falter, and he found that terribly disappointing. This night, of all nights, he could have used some good conversation, but as always, Sarah carried on about her business, as if he was no more remarkable than any of the other drunkards she had to listen to seven days a week. And he supposed that was the truth. He had never been remarkable. The years had filled his face with lines and loosened the skin where once it had been taut. His gut had swollen until it sagged over his belt and the accursed drink had brought broken capillaries to his cheeks and nose. His skin was starting to resemble corned beef, while above it all, his hair, once lush and blond, was starting to thin and turn gray.

"One more," he proclaimed aloud, embittered by his self-appraisal and willing to risk the ire of a woman he would never see again after tonight. "And I promise I'll be out of your way forever."

When Sarah didn't respond, he shrugged and muttered a curse.

Rain hammered against the windows, powered by a wind that made the walls shudder. The light behind the bar went out and when Fowler glanced that way, he saw Sarah's silhouette stooped over the lantern.

"So, who'll run the store?" she said then, her voice startling him.

"The young Mansfield boy," he told her, with another twinge of bitterness that that should be her only concern. There wasn't much in Brent Prior to keep a man there, nothing he'd mind leaving behind, but he had the distinct impression, aided by the barmaid's indifference, that no one here would miss him either. It was a depressing conclusion to have to accept.

Sarah said something then, her voice muffled, and when he looked up, she had her face pressed against the window, hands cupped around her eyes to see better.

"What?" he asked.

Her breath fogged the glass. "I said 'do you have dogs?'"

"No, why?"

She shrugged and moved away from the window. "Thought I saw a couple of them outside, that's all."

He watched her move to the lantern farthest away from the windows and felt his heart begin to race in trepidation. "Dogs?"

She nodded briefly and huffed out the flame. Shadows rushed in, painting the corner in darkness.

He swallowed his panic. "Please don't blow out the lights."

She ignored him, and moved to the lantern directly behind him, the only one remaining save the single light suspended above the inside of the tavern door.

"You're going to have to move," she said coldly. "I can't stay open all night."

"I know, I know." His vision was starting to blur, black dust pulsing in his eyes. "But just...just wait for a few more minutes. Please..."

She sighed and returned to the bar. He felt relief flood over him.

"Thank you. I promise you won't have to put up with me for much longer." He smiled, but soon realized she was standing by the window again, peering out, and the smile vanished. "Are they still out there?"

"I don't think so."

He wanted to stay here, in the warmth and safety of the tavern, but knew Sarah would brook no argument. And although it was a short walk home, he dreaded the thought of what might be out there waiting for him to brave the journey.

"I don't suppose," he began nervously, "there's any chance you'd let me stay here tonight."

Sarah straightened. "Just what are you suggesting?"

"Nothing ungentlemanly, I assure you. It's just that...well, it's hard to explain, but...I'm a little nervous tonight. Perhaps it's something to do with All Hallows, I don't know. All I *do* know is that the thought of braving the storm and what might turn out to be a pack of wild dogs doesn't appeal to me in the least."

"I'd say they're hardly wild. And where would you sleep?"

"Oh, the floor, the bar, anywhere would do me. I'm not at all fussy about that." He gave her his most charming smile, but then realized in the gloom she probably couldn't see it, not that he believed it would have made much of a difference anyway.

"I'm sorry," she said. "I can't have customers sleeping in here. If I started the practice at all, I'd have people expecting similar treatment, not to mention drawing all manner of unsavory conclusions about me, and *that* I can certainly live without."

"No, no," he protested, half rising from his chair. "I'll be leaving tomorrow, so no one need know anything!"

"And if you were to be seen in the morning they'd think Sarah Laws has a rather unique way of wishing her customers farewell." She waggled a hand in the air. "I'm sorry, you're going to have to go."

"But if—"

"Mr. Fowler..."

With a sigh, he eased the chair back and stepped clear of it. "I wouldn't be any trouble," he said.

"You're already being trouble by refusing to accept my answer," Sarah said, and strode across the room to the door.

"I didn't mean to," he said. "I'm sorry."

In silence, she put her hand on the latch and waited. Defeated, Fowler walked to the door and watched her reach up and unhook the lantern from the nail. Expecting her to extinguish it and shroud them in darkness, he was surprised when instead she handed it to him and cracked open the door. Wind whistled around the jamb.

"Thank you," he said.

"You can drop it off in the morning before you go."

He hesitated, met her eyes. "You're a good woman," he told her. "And I'm sorry you're not happy."

She gave him a curt nod. "Good night and good luck, Mr. Fowler. I'll miss your custom here."

He almost laughed.

"Good night, Sarah."

He stepped out into the violent night and hunched impulsively against the battering wind and rain. When he turned to see if Sarah was still watching, he saw that she'd already closed the door. He licked his lips and raised the lantern. The globe of light didn't reach very far, but it was infinitely better than the dark, even though it didn't help him determine what might be lurking on the fringes of it.

Do you have dogs?

He prayed she'd been mistaken; that the storm had whipped the night into such a frenzy it had only appeared as if hounds were roaming outside. Or perhaps there really had been dogs out here, scavenging. It was not impossible that some of the farmers had brought their collies with them to the hall and set them free before going inside. Maybe they'd gathered in the road outside the tavern hoping Sarah would toss them some scraps.

Maybe.

But he couldn't shake the memory of Grady's words to him earlier: *I think there were three of 'em.*

Them.

Until he'd heard that, he might not have given Sarah's words—

Do you have dogs?

—a second thought, and walked home with only self-pity and loneliness nagging at him. But now every shadow cast by the lantern was a hellish creature advancing on him, every illuminated raindrop was an eye glaring balefully at him, and every footstep was another move closer to his doom.

He began to walk, after coming to the remarkably sober conclusion that standing here sweeping his light around was more likely to draw whatever was out there to him than anything else.

Be calm now, he advised himself. *Just keep walking and don't look back. In a few minutes you'll be home, and safe, and tomorrow you'll never have to worry about—*

Something growled.

Despite the immediate, overwhelming impulse to run that exploded inside him upon hearing the sound, he froze, then spun with the lantern. The rain fell like a veil, a curtain trapping his light, allowing it to shine no further than he could reach with his own hand. Holding the lantern out in front of him, certain that was where the noise had come from, he slowly, slowly began to walk backwards, the wind aiding him with an invisible hand pressed to his chest.

It was nothing.

Another step back and something brushed against the backs of his knees. He screamed and whirled around, but in his attempt to lower the lantern to see what had touched him, it slid from his wet grasp and shattered on the ground, the candle fluttering briefly before the wind snuffed it out.

"Oh God..."

He was enclosed in total dark, with only his own heartbeat, the moan of the wind and the hissing of the rain against the road for company. Shivering, he took tentative steps forward, convinced that the only hope now was to get home as quick as possible and not to stand around waiting for what had just happened to happen again. He also retained the hope that because he could see nothing, maybe whatever was with him in the dark was equally blind.

A snarl and what felt like a light punch across his thighs sent him to his knees with a wail of terror. He swiveled until he was sitting down, his feet tucked beneath him and roared, "Sarah, help!" in the direction of the tavern. The fact that all the lights were out didn't discourage him. He had only just left her; she might still be awake.

The puddle in which he sat grew warm, and despite the paralyzing fear, he considered that most unusual. With an absurd surge of embarrassment, he wondered if he had urinated in his pants. He reached down. His pants were torn almost all the way open at the thighs.

So were his legs.

His probing hands had alighted on what he'd assumed was a strip of ragged material from his pants, drenched in warm liquid. But when he'd tugged on it, hot fiery pain lanced through him and he screamed. He released what he feared now was a strip of his own flesh and tentatively ran his hands over the wound. It was deep, and wide and he realized the warmth pumping from it was his own blood.

Oh Jesus I'm going to die!

Even though he knew he'd been hurt, and hurt badly, he attempted to rise and paid for it with a wave of pain that almost knocked him unconscious and briefly re-ignited the memory of the lantern-light in his eyes. He lay on the ground, motionless, and tried to summon the energy he would need to crawl back to the tavern, because despite his panic, he realized that was what he would need to do if he was to have any hope of surviving. It was closer than home, and once inside, Sarah could summon Doctor Campbell to come fix him up. Then, Fowler would tell them what he and Grady had seen and use Grady's advice that they get some men together at daybreak and hunt down these creatures once and for all. It was a plan, and it made him feel a little better. With great effort he flipped himself over until he was lying on his stomach and, teeth gritted, he began to crawl, the wet ground tearing at his open wounds.

He stopped when something heavy pressed against his back.

No...

A low rumbling growl that might have been the thunder had it not been so close to his ear signaled the application of more weight, this time on the backs of his legs, forcing his wounds to grind against the roughened surface of the road. He whined, the rain tapping hard against his skull. "Please *stop...*"

Sharp things pierced the flesh just below his shoulder blades. The creature was standing atop him, as if he were a pedestal. He could hear it's staggered breathing, and he turned his head, if only to catch of a glimpse of his killer, a glimpse of the Beast of Brent Prior.

What he saw was a thing of nightmare, a liquid shadow with white fire for eyes and sharpened bones for teeth, an image even the devil in all his madness could not have designed. As he watched, stricken with fear, it lowered its angular head toward him, nostrils flaring. Fowler was distantly aware of other sounds, other growls coming from all around him.

Grady was right, he thought and now his bladder did let go.

There were others, their eyes burning in the darkness like the eyes of jack o' lanterns, nails clicking on the road. He lowered his head and whispered a prayer into the sodden earth.

***

Tabitha, astride her brother's back, unleashed a scream of rage as she dug her nails into his neck. Even her assault, however, was not strong enough to divert the course of his punch, but at the last second, Neil leaned away from it. Donald cursed in frustration. The disappointed crowd began to jeer.

Kate managed to break through the fence of Merrivale boys, who were shaking their heads in disgust. "Can't even hit a blind boy," one of them called out and turned his back on the fight.

Donald grabbed his sister's wrists and wrenched her off his back, then, intercepting the blow she swung his way, gave her an openhanded slap across the face that sent her reeling. "You *mind* yourself," he roared, bringing a hand to his cheek then inspecting the blood her nails had drawn.

It was silver.

"What—?" he said, frowning, but before he got a chance to finish his sentence, a fist crashed into his mouth, mashing his lips against his teeth and cracking his nose. He gasped and staggered away, his mouth filling with something he dimly realized should have been blood but tasted like dirt. When he looked up, outraged, he saw Neil standing before him, absently massaging his knuckles as he prepared to strike again.

Word spread quickly and the crowd returned, but this time the chaperones were ahead of them.

Donald lunged for Neil and they went down in a tangle of fists and curses. Neil kicked and flailed and launched a volley of blows into the side of the bigger boy's head.

"Get him off the lad!" someone barked amidst the excited cries of the spectators.

"I'll kill you!" Donald said, and aimed another punch at Neil's face. The adult hands that locked themselves around his chest and hoisted him off the fallen boy foiled him. "Let me go, you bastards! Let me *go!*" But his request was ignored as the chaperones forced him through the crowd and toward the door.

Kate and Tabitha rushed to where Neil lay, blood streaming from his nose. Once more disappointed, the crowd began to disperse and after a few moments, the band recommenced their music. In seconds, it was as if the altercation had never happened.

"Are you all right?" Kate asked, as her brother rose. She watched him bring a tentative hand to his nose, and wince.

"I'm fine," he said and ran a hand through his hair. "I'm going home."

Tabitha glanced at Kate, who shook her head. The message was clear: *Better leave him alone for now.* She nodded and began to move away. Neil's words to Kate stopped her. "Is his tramp of a sister still here?"

Kate closed her eyes, and when she opened them again, they were filled with sympathy. "No," she said, looking at Tabitha. "She's gone."

A moment later, she was.

***

"Are you sure it's yours, lad?" asked the old man.

Neil nodded. "Yes. I was minding it for Grady and it must have fallen out of my pocket when I ran in out of the rain."

"Odd of him to give you something like this to look after."

"He trusts me."

A sigh. "Well, I suppose then I'll have to do the same."

The old man handed over the slim silver object and Neil accepted it with a smile he found difficult to maintain.

"Don't you go drinking any of it now," the old man cautioned, "Or that groundskeeper of yours will have my head on a pike."

"I won't," Neil told him and willed him away. He listened to the man's boots squelching in the mud and waited until the sound had faded to nothing before running his hands over the flask. The initials D.C. were engraved in the silver, but thankfully the old bugger hadn't seen it in the poor light.

Campbell. Kate had told him she'd seen the doctor in their parlor on several occasions sneaking illicit sips from a silver flask. But how had it ended up out here, left in the mud for an old man to find?

Neil had come out for a breath of fresh air, just in time to hear the old man mumbling about what he'd discovered. *Blimey, a flask,* he'd said. *Half full too!* Without knowing why, Neil had made his way over and staked his claim on the object.

Now, he intended to drink whatever it contained, even though he had never partaken of alcohol before and was a little concerned about the effect it might have on him. *I'll get blind drunk,* he thought and chuckled. He stopped when fresh red pain seared across the bridge of his nose and brought tears to his eyes. Rage followed at the thought of that worthless strumpet Tabitha and her equally worthless brother. They'd played him for a fool and he'd swaggered right into it with nary a blink of an eye. *Idiot!* But before the rage could swell to dangerous proportions, the hall door squeaked open behind him, the music suddenly irritatingly loud, and the familiar scent of Kate's perfume assailed his wounded nose. He quickly stashed the flask beneath his Jack the Ripper cape and sat down on the middle step leading to the main door.

"What do you want?" he asked coldly.

"You vanished. I didn't know where you'd gone."

"Well...now you found me, so you can go back to your dancing or whatever it is you're doing in there when you're not trying to embarrass me."

"*Embarrass* you? What are you talking about? When did I embarrass you?" She sat down beside him, her elbow brushing his. He moved, just enough so they were no longer touching.

"I don't need you to stand up for me. I can defend myself, Kate."

She sighed. "I know you can, I just...he's bigger than you, and it wasn't a fair fight. I didn't want you getting hurt."

"I can look after myself."

"I know, but maybe you shouldn't have to, at least, not all the time. There's no shame in admitting you need it sometimes."

"I don't need it," he snapped. "Especially not from you."

"I brought your cane."

She pressed the thin wooden shaft into his palm. Immediately, he tossed it aside. "And damn you, I don't need *this* either." He rose and began to walk.

"Where are you going?"

"Home, and don't bother following me."

"You know I will."

"I'm warning you."

"But I'll give you a head-start if you like." Playfulness had entered her tone and he knew nothing short of a miracle would keep her from trailing him back to the house. He cursed her, cursed everyone who had ever raised a hand to help him. He was *not* an invalid, *not* someone to be toyed with, and sooner or later he'd show them all as much.

Behind him the hall door squeaked again. "I'll get our coats," Kate called and he heard the door slam shut.

The rain was coming down in torrents, chilling his skin and he shivered. *Damn her*, he thought, miserable. *Damn her stubbornness, why can't she just do as I say for once?* Arms outstretched like antennae now that he knew Kate wasn't there to see it, he felt his way through the darkness.

The mud sucked at his feet.

I'll show them.

The rain needled his face. He coughed, and felt a tooth move against the probing of his tongue.

I'll show them all yet.

The thunder roared through the clouds; lightning seared the sky.

Then they'll be sorry.

Suddenly he stumbled, and someone was there to catch him, firm hands locking around his arms. *The old man?*

Donald! he thought then, and tried to yank himself free. His unknown savior didn't relinquish his hold. Then the smell crept up Neil's nose. Leaves, earth, fire, and rotten things, and he realized he'd have preferred to find himself confronting Tabitha's brother again, because at least Donald could be fought. At least he knew who and what Donald was.

No.

"It's time," said the voice. The blow that followed sent Neil plummeting down into the mud and the darkness beyond.

18

"WHAT DO YOU MEAN HE'S GONE?"

They were outside the hall. Kate was sobbing and gesturing impotently around her. Grady felt an awful urge come over him to shake her violently to force her to tell him what had happened and to punish her stupidity in letting Neil out of her sight, but he knew he would only be using her as a distraction from his own guilt. None of this would have happened had he stayed with his charges like he was supposed to.

Please God, let him be all right.

Though most of the crowd had stayed inside, or beneath the shelter of the hall eaves, many of them had clustered together on the steps, braving the weather either out of curiosity or a desire to help. Kate, though wearing her raincoat, was trembling uncontrollably.

"It was Donald," she said, "They brought him outside because he attacked Neil. He must have been hiding out there, waiting for him. I should have *known*." Her eyes flitted over the crowd, as if at any moment she might spot Neil in their midst. "He's gone. What have I done?"

Grady laid a hand on her shoulder. "Why did Newman start in on him?"

"Oh, why does that thug ever bother anyone? Because he enjoys it, that's why. He's a hateful, wicked bastard. He should be sent away somewhere where they could knock the evil out of him."

"Mind yer tongue. Where is he now?"

"He came back to get his coat. Can you believe that? Neil is probably out there right now bleeding in a ditch and he saunters back here to get his bloody coat!"

"Did you talk to him?"

"I tried, the chaperones wouldn't let me."

Grady nodded. "Come with me."

He led her back inside the hall, where groups of worried parents were conferring and muttering in the center of the floor, while others walked the room tossing papers, empty cups and decorations into empty potato bags. The festive mood so prevalent when they'd arrived had been shattered by Neil's disappearance, though Grady entertained the hope—because he had to—that the boy had simply headed home. But if Kate was telling the truth, and he had no reason to believe she wasn't, then he should have encountered the boy on his way back from The Fox & Mare. Though the darkness was thick and the storm violent, the road from there to the hall was not wide enough for him to have missed the boy staggering blindly home.

They found Newman and his sister in the cloakroom. Donald looked typically smug and defiant, while Tabitha appeared pale and defeated, her witch hat propped on the low bench beside her. Donald was slipping on his raincoat. Grady blocked the door.

"Where's Neil?" he asked.

Donald ignored him.

"I asked you a question, boy. Answer it." Grady was far from willing to prolong a conversation with this little blackguard when in all likelihood Neil was out there somewhere in the night, and possibly injured.

"How do I know where he went? I'm not his mother."

Grady took Kate by the shoulders and forced her to take his place in the doorway, fearing at any second she might explode and tear the head off the boy. He stepped close to Donald. Tabitha would not look at them; she simply stared at the soles of her shoes, tears glistening in her eyes. On closer inspection, Grady saw the pink ghost of a handprint fading from her left cheek. With a rueful nod, he reached out, grabbed Donald by the collars of his newly donned raincoat and shoved him against the wall. The boy howled in pain as the coat hooks dug into his back. He tried to wriggle free of Grady's grip, but the groundskeeper forced him back against the hooks, eliciting another obscenity laced howl from the boy.

"Watch yer bloody mouth," Grady said, his face inches from Donald's. He noticed the smudges of dirt on the boy's cheeks where, presumably, he had hit the ground when the chaperones tossed him out. A series of odd, vaguely metallic fissures were barely visible beneath the grime. A part of the boy's All Hallow's makeup, Grady assumed, and hoped he was right. He was briefly reminded of Doctor Campbell's queer vial of mercurial liquid.

Your father's blood...

"Let me go, you old Mick bastard," Donald protested, still struggling, dragging Grady from his thoughts and igniting white fire in his arthritic knuckles. The pain, the frustration and the fear of what might have happened to Neil, knowing there was something unnatural prowling out there, filled Grady with a dangerous anger, and before he knew he was going to do it, he brought his hand back and slapped the boy across the face so hard he had to restrain a wince himself.

The boy blanched and ceased struggling, eyes bulging with shock, and Grady supposed it was the first time in Donald's life that he'd been on the receiving end of the kind of violence with which he threatened everyone else. Secretly, Grady felt guilty for being the one to introduce him to it, but that guilt would have to wait.

"Why did you pick a fight with him?" he asked, and watched as a single line of spittle drooled from the boy's blubbering mouth. "Answer me!"

Donald flinched, as if he thought the old man was going to strike him again. This time he answered. "He made me do it."

"Who made you do it?"

"The man. With the bandages."

"What man? What are you talkin' about?"

Donald shook his head and began to sob, snot running from his nose as he held his hands up to his chest, palms out as if trying to discourage an attack.

"A tall man," Tabitha said then, her head still lowered. "He came to the house today and stood at the fence. He gave something to Donald. I think it was whiskey. It was payment. Payment for whatever he was supposed to do to Neil."

"Do you know this man?"

Tabitha shook her head. "No, but it wasn't the first time Donald met him."

Grady returned his attention to the sniveling boy. "Who is he?"

"I don't know, I swear I don't. I was hanging around outside The Fox last night and he walked up to me, asked why I was there. I told him I was hoping to get someone to buy me some ale. Asked him if he would do it. He laughed...said for the right price he could better than that. I told him I didn't have...have any money. He said he wasn't interested in money. Said he wanted me to arrange for Neil to be at the dance, to make sure he'd be here tonight and that I was to put the fear of God into him. For that he gave me Doctor Campbell's flask."

Grady frowned. "Campbell's flask? Do you still have it?"

Donald shook his head. "Lost it when those buggers threw me out of here earlier."

"This man you met—did he say why he wanted you to torment Neil?"

"No...just that if I didn't do it...if I failed, he'd come into my room at night and tear me to pieces."

Grady released him. Relief flooded over Donald's face as he straightened his collars.

"No one ever threatened me like he did," Donald added. "No one who looked like they really meant it, at least."

Grady felt dread twist his insides. "Did he mention what he was goin' to do with Neil if he caught him?"

"No."

Grady spun and hurried to the door. "Come on Kate."

"Where are we going?"

"Home, and on the way, pray like you never have before that we find him there."

"What if we don't?"

Grady opened his mouth to answer. Nothing emerged but a shaky sigh. He shook his head and quickened the pace.

Please God let him be there.

But in his heart and soul, he knew he wouldn't be.

19

THE HOUSE WAS LIKE AN OASIS IN THE DARK after their walk through the storm. While they were gone, Mrs. Fletcher had put lanterns in all the windows, giving it a homely, welcoming look it hadn't had in quite some time.

The charwoman greeted them at the door and both Kate and Grady hesitated at the threshold, despite the warmth that flooded out from the hallway. Mrs. Fletcher looked shocked and frightened, her face bleached of color. She wrung her hands nervously as she stepped back to let them in.

Whatever had upset her, Grady didn't give her a chance to say it. "Neil?" he asked, then ripped down his hood. "Is he here? Did he come home?"

Kate hadn't thought it possible that the woman could get any paler, but as the implications of what Grady was saying took hold, she looked as if she might faint.

"What's...what's happened?"

"Is he here?" Grady all but shouted, his impatience getting the better of him.

"No, he didn't, but—"

"I'll be back soon," Grady said, turning back toward the open door.

"But please..." Mrs. Fletcher pleaded, her voice brittle, "What's happened?"

Kate stepped aside to let Grady pass, unsure if she was supposed to follow, and then a voice, hollow and yet familiar, drifted out from the living room and froze them all where they stood.

"Grady."

He turned and looked from Kate to the charwoman, then past them to the door to the living room. "Is he...?" was all he managed before Kate broke into a run, almost tripping in her haste to reach the room. Mrs. Fletcher looked at Grady, who asked, "He's awake?"

She nodded, and stepped around him to close the front door.

"No," he said, putting his arm out to stop her. "Neil's gone...I have to try and find him."

"Not yet," the charwoman said softly. "Talk to the master first."

Confused, Grady nodded once and followed her to the living room.

Inside, they found Kate sitting on her father's lap, her face buried in his neck, weeping. Mansfield nodded in silent greeting at Grady, who moved as if he'd awoken to find himself in some bizarre alternate universe in which the air was made of glue. He practically had to feel his way to the sofa, where he sat and expelled a sigh that sounded like it had been locked inside him since birth.

Mansfield looked skeletal, his cheeks hollow and shadowed by stubble, deep gray circles ringing his eyes, but the eyes shone with life. Dark blue veins formed a network across his waxen forehead.

Mrs. Fletcher stood by the door, hands clasped beneath her bosom.

"My God...how do you feel?" Grady asked in amazement. Kate continued to sob, as her father gently stroked her hair.

"Much better," he replied, with a slight smile. "And by dawn it will be as if I'd never been sick at all."

Grady glanced at Mrs. Fletcher but there was no explanation in her eyes, only worry. "How?" he asked.

But Mansfield was looking at the door, a querulous expression on his face. "Where's Neil?"

Grady felt his stomach plummet at the thought of telling him what had happened. Would it trigger a decline in his newfound health? Ultimately, he decided that he had never before lied to the master and it would be irresponsible for him to start now. "I don't know."

"What do you *mean* you don't know?"

"The October Dance. Somethin' happened." Grady gestured futilely. "The Newman boy attacked him. Neil ran off somewhere."

"*Somewhere?*"

"I think someone took him," Grady admitted, and Kate looked up, her eyes puffy. "Newman mentioned a man, a bandaged man who came to the village and asked him to lure Neil outside."

Mansfield raised a trembling hand to his brow and sat so rigidly in his seat that Kate was forced to stand. Slowly, not taking her eyes from her father, she moved to Grady's side. When at last the master raised his head, there were tears in his eyes. "This is my fault."

"No," Grady told him. "'It isn't. The fault is mine. I should—"

"Listen to me," Mansfield interrupted. "There is a lot you don't yet know, but if you take a moment to cast your mind back, you'll realize this day has been a long time coming."

"Daddy?" Kate asked. "What do you mean? Is this about the search?"

Mansfield cast a tired glance at Mrs. Fletcher. "Florence...take Kate into the kitchen. Make her a cup of tea." Then to Kate, "We'll talk later, I promise. But for now, I need to speak to Grady alone."

"No. Don't. I know about the creatures on the moors. Grady told me. Now I want to know what *you* know."

"I know you do, but now is not the time."

"No," she said again, color rising in her cheeks, "You've been gone for so long, I don't want to leave you now. I—"

He glared at her. "*Now*, Kate. *Please*. We'll have time to talk in a while, but this is between me and Grady. I've been gone a long time, but I'm still your father and you need to do as you're told. "

She stared at him, the frustration evident in her eyes, as if she feared he'd be gone again when she returned. "What's going to happen?" she asked.

Mansfield nodded at Mrs. Fletcher, who hurried to Kate and put her arm around her. "C'mon, love," she said. "I'll make a nice brew and we can talk for a while."

"Kate," her father said. "Later. I promise."

Kate nodded, but it was clear she was not happy. Mrs. Fletcher led her into the hallway, and closed the door behind them. Mansfield stared after them for a moment, then looked at Grady. "Would you fetch us a drink? I fear we will both need it by the time I'm finished."

Grady obeyed, but it bothered him that Mansfield didn't appear more upset about Neil's disappearance. As he poured the drinks, he concluded that there had to be a valid reason for it; that perhaps Mansfield knew something about the bandaged man that might help in the search. He served the drinks and sat down.

"Are you sure alcohol's a good idea?" he asked.

Mansfield nodded. "Positive." There were a few moments of silence, then he said, "It's a virus."

"What is?"

"This illness."

"How do you know?"

He smiled, though it was little more than a brief pull of his lips. "I've had ample time to ponder it. Ample time to see the truth of it."

Grady sat forward. "Campbell thought it might be somethin' tropical."

"Campbell is and always was an idiot. I expect as we speak he has been distributed as spoor across the moors for his part in this nightmare."

"His part?" Though Grady couldn't help being interested, the need to find Neil nagged at him like an insolent child. He felt incomplete, hollow, as if he'd left a part of himself out in the storm.

"Oh yes." Mansfield stared at his glass. "He delivered Neil, and as such, had a hand in killing his mother. The birth was what finished her. A better man might have been able to save her life. Not Campbell though. The man is—*was*—an imbecile."

"How can you be sure somethin' has happened to him?" But even as he asked, Grady recalled Donald Newman's words at the dance hall—*he gave me Doctor Campbell's flask*—and wondered what, other than grave misfortune, could have made Campbell part with that cherished item and the elixir it held. But what Mansfield said next forced that memory to dissipate.

"Because I can feel them, Grady. I can almost, but not quite, see through their eyes, and let me tell you this—" He leaned forward, eyes narrowed, stick-like index finger jabbing at the air with every word, "—Brent Prior is done for. After tonight, it will be a place of echoes, nothing more."

Grady cleared his throat as a torrent of questions flooded his mind. At length, he settled on the most obvious one. "What's goin' to happen?"

Mansfield looked suddenly exhausted, and sat back again. "You remember that day, don't you Grady?"

"Of course. It's not somethin' that's easily forgotten."

"Only one person was responsible for Sylvia Callow's death, you know that don't you?"

Grady knew the direction the conversation had taken, but refused to follow it. "Her husband, sir. No one else."

Mansfield seemed amused. "Really? So, by your logic you would have me exonerated from all blame for the death of my *own* wife too, would you?"

"Why are you bringin' this up now?"

"Because it needs to be brought up. If you don't see the association here then you're not half as clever as I've always given you credit for. I fell in love with Sylvia and her husband killed her, no doubt because he discovered the affair. Then, shocked, I watched Campbell pluck a child from her dying womb, a child I claimed as my own, hoping it might aid in my atonement for a death I had most certainly caused. Proud, and anxious to introduce the babe into a marriage gone sterile, I brought it home despite my grievous injuries, only to find my beautiful wife hanging from her neck in the barn that same night. She knew, you see. She knew of my affair. She came with the villagers after the hunt, helped burn down Callow House, but she must have seen me in my grief over Sylvia. I lost both women that day. So, to whom, my dear Grady, would you assign the blame for their deaths if not me?" He waved a hand in disgust. "The virus wasn't punishment enough."

Grady felt a surge of guilt at the memories the words unearthed. He remembered the look on Mansfield's face that night, the utter devastation as he begged Grady to help him cut his wife down. And all the while, through his tears, he'd pleaded with him not to ever tell the children the truth. *"She must die in her bed, laid by the heels by some sudden malady. But not like this. Dear God, not like this..."* Grady had dedicated the next few months to erasing that night from his memory, but the image of Helen dangling from that old rope, her eyes filled with blood, still haunted him. But not nearly as much as he suspected it haunted Mansfield.

"It was not my business what you did with yer life, sir," he said. "And what came about was unfortunate, but not yer fault. A man can waste an entire lifetime thinkin' himself the villain, but that's a title I'd be hard-pressed to give you. You made some questionable judgments, I grant you that, but show me a man who hasn't?"

Mansfield drained his glass and held it out to Grady. "Another, please, to stave off the chill."

Grady nodded, and went to the decanter, but his thoughts were with Neil, who was likely somewhere out there in the violent night, wondering why no one had yet come for him. He shivered as he passed the drink to Mansfield. "We need to hurry, sir. Neil needs us."

"Yes, yes. I'm sorry. I've been alone with my own thoughts for so long, I suppose they've overwhelmed me, taken on more significance than might otherwise be the case. I do apologize."

Again, the groundskeeper was struck by Mansfield's casual tone. "There's no need."

"Indeed there is, Grady. There most certainly is a need to apologize and for more than we have time to discuss."

"I don't understand."

"I'm afraid my cowardice has damned us all."

Grady said nothing. In the wake of such a pronouncement, he could only wait for elaboration. The wait was not a long one.

"I believe those creatures are diseased. They carry within them something horrendous, a plague of some kind that attacks the body, and changes it."

Grady set his glass down on the floor. "What kind of a change?"

"I'm not sure, but I fear the metamorphosis might reduce—or perhaps the correct term would be *elevate*—a man to their level, force him to become a ravening animal."

"Men do not change into animals."

"I won't argue with you, my friend. But tell me, then, where do you think these things have come from? We both know they're out there; of that there can be no doubt, but where did they originate? Surely they haven't been roaming the moors forever or we'd have heard of them before that fateful search?"

"I don't know. Perhaps somethin' escaped from London Zoo."

Mansfield smiled. "And just how long have you been trying to convince yourself of that particular fantasy?"

"Quite a while," Grady replied with a sigh.

"While I was bedridden, I saw many things, most of which I would be willing to dismiss as delusion, but one thing is quite clear: In my illness I became a pawn stuck in the center of a board with my fate in the hands of opposing forces. On one side," he said, opening his right hand, "I saw Helen, telling me I needed to die in order to save the children." He transferred the glass to the open hand and repeated the gesture with his left. "On the other, I had visions, showing me what was to become of me if I lived. I saw Sylvia in a memory that corrupted itself and showed the true nature of my lover, the unspeakable thing that hid behind the immaculate mask of her face." He gave a small sad shake of his head. "I believe that is how I was infected, Grady. Sylvia Callow was one of them. In fact, I believe she was their mother."

20

"WHO ARE YOU?"

"My name is Stephen."

"Where are you taking me?" Neil shouted as rain lashed against his face, numbing his skin. All he had managed to deduce since waking was that his hands were bound and they were traveling across unsteady terrain on the back of a horse. His head pounded with echoes of the blow he'd been dealt. As the horse mounted an incline, he heard the man call out a single word: "Home."

"Why are you doing this?" Neil demanded, so cold he feared at any moment he would die from it. "I've done nothing to you."

"I don't recall ever saying you had."

"Then...why?"

For this, there was no reply, and the further they went, the more frightened he became. The storm roared around them, the rain like needles desperate to pierce his flesh. He wanted to lie down, to curl up in a ball in the wet grass and sleep. He was so very tired, but the uncertainty of what Stephen intended to do with him kept him alert and awake.

"They'll be looking for me!" he told his captor. "They're probably already out with the dogs."

"If there's one thing I can assure you, my child, it's that no one is looking for you."

Neil refused to believe that. Surely Grady would be searching for him the moment he realized what had happened. Unless...

Unless he was still at The Fox & Mare, getting drunk with his friends.

But surely Kate would have alerted him by now?

He remembered standing outside the hall, in the rain, waiting. It took a long time for her to come looking for him. She'd had ample time to come fetch him, and yet her arrival had been almost leisurely. She'd even tried to lessen his despair with humor.

He shook his head in anger. *No. They wouldn't give up on me that easily.*

He had to believe they were looking for him, that if he strained his ears enough, he'd hear their voices in the distance, penetrating night and storm, seeking him out.

"They *are* looking for me," he said defensively, more to convince himself than the man, who already seemed certain the opposite pertained, though Neil reassured himself with the realization that there was no way Stephen *could* know what Grady and Kate were doing.

In response, the man laughed. "I'm afraid you're entertaining false hope, Neil," he said, "and false hope is for the foolish, for those who crave disappointment and heartbreak. I would have thought with your intelligence and maturity you'd have given up on such things a long time ago."

"Well...why *wouldn't* they be looking for me? They wouldn't just leave me out here!"

"I'm afraid that's exactly what they did," Stephen said. "And if you think about it long and hard you'll realize you've given them something they've been hoping for all along."

"I don't understand."

"Of course you do. Would you disagree with me if I opined that Kate was always Grady's favorite? Always Mrs. Fletcher's and your father's favorite too?"

He didn't respond because he knew it was the truth. Kate had always been *everyone's* favorite, but he didn't see how that made much of a difference to anything. They still loved him and would never just forget about him if he got lost. Never.

"I'll take your silence as affirmation. You have always felt different from them and not just because you're blind, isn't that so?"

Alarmingly, Neil found himself drawn to Stephen's voice, only because it was warm and the night was so desperately, achingly cold. That voice was seductive; it promised relief from all of this, and though he was still frightened, he sensed the threat recede a little for now.

"There's a good reason for that, child, a very good reason why you've never truly felt a part of your family and why they in return, have never truly considered you one of them. Oh, I'm sure they didn't *intentionally* try to alienate you, to nudge you out of the nurturing warmth of the familial cocoon, but nature will always separate animals into their respective packs, just as it will divide man into the appropriate tribes. You never belonged to them, Neil. And they never belonged to *you.*"

Neil shivered, tried again to free himself, but the attempt was somewhat feebler than before. He felt the energy drain from him, the resistance buckle under the force of the stranger's words. It was true that he had always felt distanced from everyone else but he had blamed it on his handicap. Was it even remotely possible that his captor's claims had some basis in fact?

"I don't believe you," he said, without conviction, and though he thought the storm might have drowned out his words, Stephen said, "You will soon enough."

***

"You should stick to the road as far as you can," Mansfield said. "But it would be quicker to cross the moors. I know the danger but trust me, I doubt it's limited to just the fields now. If they want to find you, they will, no matter where you are. Your only hope is that Callow will want you to come to him, in which case those things won't bother you."

Things like you, Grady thought and shuddered.

"As I said before, if you don't want to go, I'll understand. The sensible thing to do would be to wait until morning, or at least until the storm clears up, but I'm not sure we have that much time."

Grady nodded dismissively. "Tell me somethin'," he said tonelessly. "Did you love her?"

"Sylvia?"

"Yes."

"I did," Mansfield replied without hesitation. "I believe at first it was only desire. You saw her yourself. You know what she did to men, and I dare say there wasn't a man in the village who wouldn't have done what I did given the opportunity. But I fell in love with her and—despite how terrible it sounds—I confess I would have left Helen, and the children, and this damned house if she'd asked me to. She was powerful, Grady, more powerful than any woman has any right to be. It scared and exhilarated me but so did it erase all thoughts of what I stood to lose while I was with her."

Grady chewed his lower lip until it hurt. He didn't want to admit the disgust he felt for Mansfield at that moment. It was perhaps, unfair. After all, he himself had kept the secret just as long. He had known about the affair, and what had come of it, and yet he had kept it locked away inside. And now everything was coming apart.

"I have to go," he said, opening the door and stepping out into the hall. Mansfield did not follow, but said, "One more thing, Grady."

"What is it?"

"Before you go, have Mrs. Fletcher lock this door from the outside."

Grady gave him a curt nod and, pulling the door closed on his haggard master's countenance, he sighed and headed into the kitchen.

***

When he returned with the rifle, Kate was waiting for him, arms folded, eyes blazing but still moist from crying. She had quickly towel-dried her hair and now it hung in damp clumps.

"I'm going with you," she said. "And don't you dare tell me I can't. I'm not a child."

Grady set the rifle down across the kitchen table and rubbed his eyes. "God forbid I should ever be allowed to forget that."

Mrs. Fletcher had just returned from locking the living room door. The ring of keys jingled in her trembling grip. "Grady," she said. "What on earth is goin' on?"

On the table, the lantern's flame dwindled, then soared up the glass bulb; shadows shrank away.

He shook his head. "I'm not entirely sure I know, love."

"But where's Neil?"

Grady looked at her and composed a grin. "I'll find him, Mrs. Fletcher, don't you worry."

"Well?" Kate asked him. "Aren't you going to answer me?"

"What good would it do? I don't *want* you to go. You'd be safer here but you've never listened to me before so why should I waste my breath now? And it certainly sounds as if you've made up yer mind."

"Yes, I have."

"But let me tell you *this*," he said, bringing a forefinger close to her face, "if you *do* come with me, you'll damn well do what I tell you to or I'll lock you in the cellar where you can scream and object to anythin' you want. Are we clear?"

She frowned, nodded slowly. "Yes."

"When I tell you to stay put, you do it. If I tell you to run, you'd better be prepared to run like the Dickens. If I tell you to go home, you'd bloody well better do that too. You'll do *everythin'* I tell you to do or you'll stay here, understood?"

"Stop *shouting* at me," she protested. "I already agreed with you."

"Good." He straightened and set about loading the master's rifle.

"Do I get a gun?" Kate asked, in a doubtful tone.

Grady looked at her, and was about to give her the answer she expected when he remembered how good a shot she was. How good a shot he had *taught* her to be, though she had never been that good with a Winchester. "Yer father's pistol is in the cellar. Fetch it, and hurry!"

With a smile, Kate did as she was told. Grady prayed she'd be as acquiescent for the rest of the night.

Whatever on earth it held for them.

21

THE GROUND CHANGED BENEATH NEIL'S FEET, each step resulting in a hollow thunking sound as he sensed himself rising, the rain no longer stippling his face. His fingers brushed against rough-edged brick and wood. Splinters punctured his skin; he pulled away, wincing.

"What is this place?" he asked, as Stephen tugged him forward, into what felt like a room, cold but dry. He was relieved to be out of the storm but only moments later the chill from his sodden clothes began to seep into him. He hugged himself with one arm. The room smelled like the man, but also of mildew and mold.

"Our home," Stephen replied, releasing him at last, and Neil said nothing further. Instead he listened to a series of what sounded like muffled gunshots, but which he supposed was wood being broken. *Good, a fire,* he thought, as he rubbed the numbness from his wrist. He heard the hasty crumpling of paper, then nothing for a few moments until the silence was broken by the hiss of a match.

"It will take a few moments to get warm," Stephen told him. "If you walk straight ahead for about five paces you'll be directly in front of the fire. Come, sit."

Neil hesitated. The thought of warmth drew him like a magnet, but he was still anxious and more than a little afraid of the man. "Why did you bring me here?" he asked.

"I told you we would have an opportunity to discuss our secrets, did I not?" He didn't wait for an answer. "Well, now is the perfect time."

A volley of thunder crashed overhead. It sounded almost on top of them, but despite the weight of the fresh rain that followed it, none came through into the room. "They'll hang you for this. It's kidnapping. If I were you, I'd bring me home while you still have the chance. Before they run you down like the dog you are."

There was amusement in Stephen's voice. "But you *are* home, Neil."

The fire crackled and spat. The acrid scent of treated wood burning filled the room, suggesting to Neil that the man had broken up furniture to light it. Still, he remained by the doorway. "My home is with my family."

"I am your family, as you are mine."

"My father and Kate are my family."

"Do you really think so?"

"Of course. Why wouldn't I?"

"Because you were adopted, or should I stay, *stolen* from your true parents."

Although Neil refused to believe what he was hearing, the shock of it still rippled through him, making him colder still. Again, he wondered why this man was saying these things, what he stood to gain by deceiving him. "You're a boldfaced liar," he said.

"Am I now? Why don't you come sit by the fire and we'll discuss it? I'm confident I can convince you of the truth once you've heard my story."

"No. It's a trick."

"Neil. I have no reason to want to trick you, or harm you in any way. I have brought you here to the remains of Callow House, to what should have been *your* house, to hear the truth. Once I've enlightened you, you'll be free to leave. I won't raise a hand to stop you."

"I don't believe you."

"Fine, then stay there by the door, but it's so much warmer here by the fire."

The tang of smoke was like a lure tugging at Neil's insides. He told himself that if Stephen wanted to hurt him, he'd have done so already, but even as he began to move, both hands outstretched, he realized that the desperate need for heat was blunting his suspicions and his good sense. Nevertheless, he continued forward, hands lowered and slowly sweeping through the air as it grew warmer and warmer still, until he could feel the heat on his face.

"Right there," the man said. "Sit. Do you need help?"

"No. And even if I did, I wouldn't accept it from *you*. You're nothing but a criminal and you'll pay for what you've done."

"Perhaps." Stephen didn't sound at all concerned that that might be the case.

Carefully, Neil lowered himself into a crouch, then straightened his legs out in front of him. Beneath his hands he felt slivers of wood and a dry dusty concrete floor.

"We're in the old kitchen," the stranger said almost wistfully.

"Are you Callow?"

"Not Edward Callow, no. He was the owner of this place. Him and his wife, Sylvia, before he died on a hunt. Before he was killed, I should say."

"But you said this house was yours."

"So I did, and for a time it *was* mine. I as good as owned it in all but name. I even laid claim to the mistress of the house."

"Who are you, then, if not Callow?"

"I already told you. My name is *Stephen*. Stephen Callow, child," he said. "Edward Callow was my brother."

***

Grady opened the front door to the violent night and looked warily at Kate, wrapped up in a raincoat that had scarcely been given time to dry. The pistol looked big and clumsy in her hand and he knew she was bravely trying not to show how the weight of it inconvenienced her.

"Yer sure you want to do this?" he asked, and called on every favor he imagined God, or Fate or Destiny might owe him for all the bad luck he'd endured in his lifetime that she would change her mind. But she was resolute.

"He's my brother," she said. "And I want to find him. I want to be the one to tell him that Daddy's awake. I want to be the one to bring him home."

"If he comes home in the meantime, you won't get the chance to tell him anythin'."

"He won't come home. We both know that."

Grady stared at her—a beautiful woman with an intensity to her that sometimes frightened him—and he knew he would never persuade her of the wisdom in staying behind, even though it scared him to think what might happen to her out there.

"Let's go, then," he said, tucking the breeched Winchester beneath his left arm. He raised the lantern and led them out into the rain.

***

Behind them, Mrs. Fletcher raised a trembling hand and covered her mouth. She was not the type of woman gifted with visions, or premonitory feelings, unlike some of the villagers, but at that moment, as she watched Grady and Kate huddled together under the barrage of rain, she was overcome with the awful certainty that she would never see them again.

Before the tears could come, she stepped back into the hall and closed the door on the storm. There she waited, her hands pressed against the door, her breathing shaky, until she had composed herself. She turned and glanced at the door to the living room at the end of the hall. She still could not believe the master was back, but she found herself almost wishing he'd stayed ill, for in waking it seemed he'd set in motion a nightmare that even now was rushing in to consume them all.

Why had he locked the door?

She didn't know, but she had overheard snippets of their conversation, enough to thrill her with terror, so she quickly crossed herself and went into the kitchen where she put the kettle on, and settled in for a long night.

22

Neil heard him rubbing his hands together over the fire.
"It started with the death of my uncle, a studious and wealthy man by the name of Arthur Callow. Arthur was a bumbling, tiresome old fool who liked to squander his money on silly things—charities, traveling to miasmic hovels around the world, spreading the word of God. I often wondered why he never became a priest, when in almost all respects he considered himself one."

Neil shivered despite the heat and inched closer to the fire. Stephen spoke in a monotone that he feared might lull him to sleep, but he daren't do so, for God only knew what this criminal might do to him then. He drew his knees up to his chin, cradled them with his arms, and silently offered up a prayer that everything the man said turned out to be obvious lies, designed to keep him here and nothing else.

"The last place he visited was a wretched village in Romania, and while in his letters he expressed a desire to see the rest of Europe, Calinesti was to be his last stop.

"Whatever it was that drew him to that village kept him there for almost six months, during which time he befriended the locals and drastically improved their lives. I imagine the worship they directed at him appealed to Arthur, making it harder still for him to leave. He built them a church after realizing to his disgust that they hadn't had one in over fifty years. Then, he paid a priest from Bucharest a staggering amount of money to perform monthly services there. Apparently, Calinesti had long been considered a cursed village, so even when the priest agreed to the monthly mass, he didn't dawdle there sharing niceties once it was done. No one who didn't have to be there stayed very long, aside from my fool of an uncle of course."

Neil sighed. "What does any of this have to do with me?"

"I'm getting to that," Stephen said. "You'll soon understand everything and, as I said before, once I'm done, you're free to go."

Neil felt a twinge of panic at the base of his skull. Something in the man's voice suggested he would not be returning Neil to where he'd found him, but would set him free upon the moors. Alone.

There was a long silence, then Stephen chuckled. Neil jumped as another chunk of wood was tossed on the fire with a loud *whoompf* followed by the firework crackle of sparks.

"My uncle died in Calinesti," Stephen continued, "no doubt spiritually at peace with all he'd accomplished for those *poor peasants*." He said this last with audible disgust. "And when he passed, my brother and I had not the slightest doubt that he had secured himself a place in Heaven. *Good for him*, we thought, but now our minds were set on what he might have left behind, what he might have left to help us improve *our* lives. I was a struggling artist, Edward, a musician, and only slightly better off than me. Neither of us would balk at whatever our uncle had decided to leave us in his will.

"Or so I thought." His tone was bitter. "He left almost everything to Edward, the house, the land, and most of the money. To me, he gave fifty pounds with instructions that I should use it to obtain a nobler profession. I was outraged, of course, but when I went to visit my brother to challenge him, I found him equally dismayed, despite his new fortune. It seemed even his inheritance had not been unconditional. To claim the house and the money, he was instructed to travel to that wretched place where my uncle had found such contentment, Calinesti, and continue the work Arthur had started. He was to build a school there, and hire a teacher, whatever the cost. He was to provide the villagers with whatever they needed to lead normal, healthy, and prosperous lives. A man named Petrica, a friend of Arthur's and one of the few English-speaking locals, would meet him there and aid him in completing Arthur's mission.

"Edward was, of course, disgusted. For weeks he ranted and raved about how no amount of money was worth such hard work and degradation. But in the end, with what little money he had slowly draining away, and with my deceased uncle's solicitor keeping a watchful eye on everything, he was forced to concede to the proviso.

"He left for Romania a week later."

A breeze ruffled through the flames, sending threads of smoke into Neil's face. He coughed. He was so tired, it was an effort to keep his eyes open, but he forced himself to stay alert, sure that at any moment he'd hear footsteps approaching the house. As soon as he did, he intended to run before Stephen had a chance to stop him. He knew from the sound of the wind and rain behind him that the exit was at his back and it helped that the man seemed lost in his own tale.

"I didn't see him for almost a year," Stephen said. "A year passed, and the man who returned to England was not the same one who had left it. In fact, if anything, he looked quite shaken, as if he had seen nothing but death and destruction in his time spent abroad. He was horribly thin, his face sunken, and he walked with a hesitant step, as if fearing bottomless holes riddled the path before him. Any satisfaction I may have derived from his appearance, however, was obliterated at the sight of the woman who accompanied him. Sylvia—an absolute vision, unlike anything I had ever seen before. A Greek goddess, a siren, the kind of creature that can make your heart melt just from the scent of her. A little like that pretty young thing you lust after, Neil."

Neil imagined reaching into the fire, plucking from it a blazing length of wood and hurling it in the direction of that mocking, hateful voice. Tabitha had betrayed him. She had lured him to the hall so her brother could ambush him—there had never been anything more to her seductive invitation. His burgeoning love for her had led him to follow her without question, to hope she felt the same, and in the end she'd made a fool of him. They had all made a fool of the poor little blind boy. Now he felt the anger compete with the heat from the fire, burning him from within, until he felt compelled to break something, to hurt something. Hurt *someone*.

"Months later, I learned the truth about Sylvia," Stephen continued. "That for some reason never revealed to us, the villagers had condemned her to death, but on the day she was scheduled to be executed, my brother fled with her back to England, sparing her a stoning, and gaining himself a wife.

"From the outset, it was clear she was no ordinary woman, no meek peasant driven to serve. Rather she was possessed of a fiery indomitable spirit and an incorrigible lust that drew men to her and reduced them to mindless sheep. For every day she was married to my brother, he grew weaker and more perturbed. His interest in Sylvia waned, except on those occasions when his demons drove him to use her as a target for his violent urges. In the end, she came to me. We became lovers, and I reveled in her Dionysian appetites. But outside of my bed, she became aloof and distant. When I quizzed her about her moods and about the past that seemed to weigh so heavily on her, she offered little more than tantalizing, maddening scraps of information about her village, superstitious nonsense about a centuries long cohabitation with what she called 'strigoi.' Then she would stop herself and leave me alone, with questions, and an insatiable need for her company. She became like a drug to me—opium in a beautiful sculpted vessel. I began to see her more and more until finally, she told me enough to at once strike fear into my heart and lead me to question the state of her mind. It was, she warned me, what she had confessed to my brother and slowly it was rotting his brain because of his refusal to believe it and, she said, because he had forced her to prove it to him.

"That night, in my room, which Edward had so graciously allowed me to keep in this very house, free of charge, she showed me the meaning of *strigoi*, and a new word, *strigoaica*, the females of those fabled creatures, which is what she claimed to be. She stood and disrobed, a move I assumed, as any man in my place would, that we were to make love. Instead, she changed. Before my very eyes her skin turned silver, as if she had frozen to death in an instant, and yet she moved. One blink and her hazel eyes glowed the color of sunlit brass. Her hair thickened, lengthened. I crammed my knuckles into my mouth to keep from screaming. If I tried to run, I can't remember, but I do recall desperately trying to convince myself that it was an illusion, something the gypsy folk had mastered as an art form, or as a weapon. I crawled backwards on the bed and tried not to look, but it was impossible. There, at the foot of the bed, stood not the Romanian beauty my brother had brought home, but a vile, hideous thing the color of a statue, its flesh cracking, birthing fissures that rippled with the hissing of air through them, its suddenly long face cradling a wide mouth full of long, bone-like teeth. Worst of all though, in the mottled countenance of that hideous thing, I could *still see Sylvia looking out at me*, gauging my reaction. I could feel my sanity threatening to sunder unless I forced myself to believe that what I was seeing was an illusion. But I couldn't. Witchcraft seemed more likely."

The urgency in Stephen's voice alarmed Neil. Whether or not this preposterous tale held even a modicum of truth, it was clear by the way he spoke that his captor believed it, and to Neil, that suggested utter insanity. As quietly and surreptitiously as he could, he placed his hands beneath him and slid back a few inches, stopping only when Stephen spoke again.

"Golden eyes," he said. "Like doubloons they were, fixed on me, penetrating me, searching my soul. And then, just as the horror threatened to drive me stark, raving mad, she hunched over and made a sound like someone choking, and when she straightened, she was herself again. Just Sylvia with the hazel eyes. No scales, no blue-white skin, no needle teeth. No *strigoaica*.

"I wept and curled into a ball, afraid that now that I knew what she was, she would kill me to keep her secret. But she didn't. Instead she sat on the edge of the bed with her back to me, and whispered, "This is what I am. I understand your fear and your revulsion, but there is something you need to know, something *you* need to understand."

"It was then I realized she was weeping, and to hear such a pitiful, mournful sound from something so monstrous lessened the fear a little. I no longer thought she meant me harm, but still the thought of having touched, caressed and *fornicated* with such a thing made me retch. But as it turned out, the repercussions of our union were more horrible than I dared imagine.

"'You are corrupted and poisoned now by your association with me,' she said. 'You'll become one of my kind once you acknowledge the disease that is, even now, reshaping you, redesigning you. Resist it, and it will kill you with a kind of agony that would make the devil himself take notice. Accept, and you'll be with me forever.'

"Almost immediately, as if it had been waiting for the truth to hit my brain, to be acknowledged, the pain began. It was small, no more troublesome than a headache, but immediately I believed her. I knew she spoke the truth, for I had seen her change and feared what our coupling might have transferred into me. I wailed into my pillow, rammed my fists against the sides of my head to jar the pain free, and writhed in the horror of what she had done.

"'Let it take you,' she said then and I braved a glance at her. She had turned to face me, one hand rubbing circles over her belly. She was smiling. 'And be the father to your child.'"

The wind soughed through the splintered roof. Neil raised his head and swallowed with an audible click. "I don't believe any of this," he said. "You're completely mad."

Another crash of wood into the fire.

"No," Stephen said. "I'm not. And I would never lie to my son."

Neil scrabbled backwards, his nails scooping up dust as he struggled to rise. It only took him a moment to find his feet but just as quickly, hands grabbed him. "No!" he screamed. "Let me *go!*" The man's arms were like tightly wound cords.

"I already told you I would," Stephen said sternly. "But first you must hear the whole story. Hear the truth. Then, and *only* then, do you get to leave. That is, assuming you'll still want to."

Neil continued to kick and struggle until he was shoved forcefully down onto the ground again. He landed hard and winced with the shock to his tailbone.

"We're almost done," Stephen said. "But it's important that you hear the rest. That you know who, and most importantly, *what*, you are."

23

GRADY THUMPED ON THE DOOR until his knuckles sang with pain. Fat heavy drops of rain from the eave above him tapped against his skull and he shuddered with the cold.

"What are we doing here?" Kate asked him, raising her lantern so she could see his face. Before he had a chance to answer, the door to the tavern opened just enough for his own light to reveal the eye peering out at him through the space between door and jamb.

"Sarah?"

"What do you want?" the barmaid asked. The stench of alcohol wafted out at them, and Grady suspected it wasn't all coming from the bar. Sarah regarded them with eyes at half-mast.

"I have a favor to ask you," Grady said, absently massaging his knuckles. "Neil's missin'. I want to ask if I can borrow yer horse."

"No," Sarah said and started to close the door. Grady quickly shoved his foot in the way. She looked at it as if it were a dead rat.

"Please. We think he's on the moors. If we walk it, it'll take us all night. On horseback, we'll cover more ground in half the time."

"Why don't you use your own horses?"

Grady sighed. "We got rid of them after the—" He'd been about to say 'hunt' but caught himself in time. Reminding Sarah of the day of her husband's death wasn't the best tactic to employ if he hoped to get her to loan them the horse. Then again, the change in the barmaid's demeanor ever since that day suggested she hadn't let go of the memory anyway. "We got rid of them ages ago," he said instead.

"Well I can't help you," she said and glared at his foot.

"Why can't you?" he asked, annoyed now. He knew all it would take would be for Sarah to give him the key to the back gate and he could manage the rest himself. There really wasn't any good reason that he could think of why she should refuse him, and yet she seemed intent on doing that very thing.

"Because it's my husband's horse," she said defensively, "And I don't want him coming back to find it missing."

Grady's mouth fell open. At first, he wasn't sure he'd heard her properly over the moan and sigh of the wind and the sizzling of the rain against the road, but as her words sank in, he realized the extent of the barmaid's grief, and what it had done to her. At a loss for words, he was relieved when Kate stepped forward and asked, "Can we borrow it for a short while, Mrs. Laws? Please? My brother is lost on the moors somewhere and I'm really worried something's going to happen to him. We won't be gone long, I promise you. We'll have your horse returned to the stable long before your husband comes back."

Sarah stared hard at her, and Grady feared even Kate's gentle tone hadn't worked, but then the barmaid's eyes softened and she nodded. "He's been gone ever so long," she said sadly. "So long I worry that something might have happened him too." She reached behind the door and there came the unmistakable sound of keys jingling. A moment later, she held a single rusty key out to Kate, who took it and nodded her thanks. "If you see him out there," she added, as they were preparing to make their way around the tavern to the stable. "Tell him to come home, that I'll be waiting up for him."

From the ashen hue of her face, Grady guessed that particular vigil was one she'd been keeping for quite some time.

Lightning cracked the sky, turning the world a ghostly white and momentarily freezing the rain in place.

Kate looked from Grady to Sarah, and gave her a pleasant smile. "I will, Mrs. Laws. I promise."

They said their goodbyes, then headed toward the stable. On the way, Grady expected Kate to bring up what had just happened, but she said nothing, even though the troubled look on her face had deepened. He had a feeling tonight would be the night when she'd learn everything there was to know about madness, in all its guises.

He prayed she'd live to appreciate the knowledge.

The gate shrieked as they swung it open. From the stable, the mare huffed and hoofed the floor. After a moment spared to calm her down, they saddled the horse and mounted it, Kate behind Grady, her lantern held in her lap, free hand gripping his raincoat. As they rode through the yard and back around the tavern, Sarah raced out to meet them. For one desperate moment, Grady thought she'd changed her mind and was going to demand they get off the mare and walk, but instead she thrust something at him he only barely managed to catch. He looked down at it—a bottle of Irish whiskey—and raised it to her in a salute. She nodded, and he chose to ignore what she cried after them. It didn't fit the warmth of the moment, and only further testified to the woman's madness.

Make sure you share it with him, she'd said.

***

They were not alone. A shuffling, slithering sound from above made Neil raise his head, ears cocked. "What's that?"

Stephen spoke, and there was pride in his voice. "We are an aberration, you and I, anomalies descended from what once were wolves until nature and cross-breeding with other mutated souls bred a whole new species. We are hunters, Neil. We exist for the specific purpose of taking our rightful place as the dominant species, to hunt men and kill them, or force them to become one of us, to join us as *gods*."

Neil, terrified beyond words, lowered his head to his crossed arms.

"Whatever we are, we are old and we will mold this world to suit us, starting here in this small pitiful little village. Contact is sufficient to perpetuate our kind, you see. If we inflict a non-fatal wound on a man or woman, our nails secrete an enzyme that contaminates the blood, immediately starting the change. The mechanics of that change however, remain a mystery to me. Even Sylvia could not explain why the effect is sometimes immediate, and other times protracted, sometimes by decades. Her supposition was that will alone can delay the process, an unfortunate choice for the subject, as resistance merely renders the enzyme unstable. Change becomes decay and over a period of years, the body slowly rots from the inside out. As was the case for the man who played your father for so long. Sylvia infected him too, but rather than accepting the change, he resisted, and the virus fed on him."

More shuffling and what might have been the scratching of claws on the ceiling. Neil tried to tell himself it was nothing more than field mice nesting, but Stephen's words had chilled him, making it difficult to believe anything even remotely natural was causing those sounds. He wished the man would stop talking, stop trying to fill his head with these bizarre and frightening fantasies. It proved he was insane and that frightened him even more, for it meant there could be no reasoning with him, and no escape.

"You would have liked your mother," Stephen said. "And she would have adored you. But things do not always work out as planned, do they? Her death was a mistake, an act of homicidal rage by my poor, misguided fool of a brother." He sighed. "Although I cannot claim innocence either. It was I who informed him of Mansfield's affair with Sylvia, hoping Edward would call upon his lifelong inability to face anything with a level head, and kill the man. The authorities would try him for murder, in which case the house, the land, and my beloved Sylvia would be mine for the taking."

Sadness entered his voice. "Even knowing how ill-tempered and unstable he was, I never dreamed he'd do what he did. It was my idea to arrange a hunt, during which he could kill Mansfield. Instead, enraged by her treachery, he beat and tortured my Sylvia to within an inch of her life and led the hunt to her, in an effort to prove his dominance over her and any man who attempted to steal her away from him.

"She tried, at the last, to change into her *strigoaica* form," he said. "But he'd cut off her hands and feet. Even changing would have done her no good." His voice wavered as if he were about to cry, a sound Neil found so undeniably genuine it was alarming. "I followed the hunt, content to observe my brother in action, until I saw what he'd done to Sylvia." There was a sound like fists thumping against the floor and when next the man spoke, he spoke with rage. "I lost control. Maddened, I lashed out with everything that was in me at those members of the hunt. I changed for the first time, and it was a wonderful, glorious thing. But while I ran them down, one of them shot and killed my brother. At the time I didn't care; the stupid old bastard deserved it for what he did. But before I could finish them off, the horror and the grief set in, overwhelming me with visions of my beloved Sylvia shuddering as her life's blood drained from her, and I began to revert to my human state. I couldn't stop it.

"Naked, exposed and vulnerable, I ran as fast as my pitiful feeble legs could carry me, back to the house, where I hid in the cellar and wept. I thought I'd be safe there, but I was confused. I should have known they would try to cleanse Callow House with fire, driven by preposterous and archaic beliefs that what had happened would never happen again if their enemy's home was obliterated.

"The cellar filled with smoke and when I tried to escape, I found myself trapped. Panicked, I ripped and tore at the walls, flung myself against the rapidly warming door until it splintered and I could unlock it by threading my hand through the gap.

"I made it as far as the hallway before the ceiling—a mass of burning plaster and wood—came down on me. And so, I burned, and screamed at the injustice that had led to my certain death. But I did not die. Someone pulled me free and dragged me from the house; someone I did not expect to see standing there with concern written across her ravaged face. A face I would have sundered had everything not come to ruin. A woman who wished for death at my hands, but took my advice instead and saw to it herself.

"A woman by the name of Mansfield."

***

Mrs. Fletcher was jolted from a doze by a sound from the hall. Blinking away the confusion of sleep, she sat up, her sewing falling to the floor unnoticed. She paused for a moment, listening.

Outside, the storm continued unabated, grumbling its way to unmerciful roars and filling the spaces between the curtains with white light as rain tapped incessantly against the glass.

But from within the house, there was silence.

"Mr. Grady?" she called, wondering if they'd come back and if it had been their arrival that had roused her. She rubbed her eyes and squinted at the clock above the mantel. It was close to midnight. She'd hoped they'd be back by now, safe and sound and with a shaken and sodden but unharmed Neil in tow.

"Kate?"

No answer. Sagging with disappointment, she settled back in her chair and joined her hands over her belly.

"Please God," she whispered in prayer, "Let them be all r—"

From the hallway, came the groan of stiffened hinges. Immediately she sat up, hands braced on the arms of the chair. "Master?"

A shuffling, then what might have been the sound of someone sliding along the wall that divided the hall from the kitchen. She waited a beat, then stood, grabbed the lamp from the mantel and quickly moved to the doorway. The flickering light from the lantern made the short passage to the living room seem impossibly long.

"Master?"

She took a step, then another, her scalp prickling as she drew to a halt a few feet from the living room door.

It was open.

With a nervous swallow, she held the lantern out and inspected the door. The jamb had splintered, leaving jagged spikes of wood poking out from the frame, and the lock had broken. It swung from a single screw like one of those 'Do Not Disturb' signs she'd seen them use in fancy London hotels. Cautiously, she leaned closer and brought her fingers to the paneled wood, realizing as she did so that the door would have had to have been pulled *inward* with great force to get it open, for it had been designed to open out onto the hall.

"Master?"

She edged into the room, lit by lanterns in all four corners. Still, the furniture looked sinister; hunched dark things that might at any moment rise to reveal themselves malevolent. Frowning, her gaze fell on the master's robe lying in a heap beside his chair.

"Hello?"

Where did he go? she wondered. And what kind of urgency had possessed him to almost tear the door from its hinges?

Despite the reassurances she whispered to herself, she felt as if lice were crawling all over her. Her skin positively buzzed with apprehension. Though she was still inclined to attribute the words she'd overheard earlier to derangement, the last echoes of fever, they haunted her now.

I saw Helen, telling me I needed to die in order to save the children.

There was broken glass in front of the chair. She set the lantern on the floor and began to pick up the pieces, each one wet and reeking of brandy. It wouldn't do to have the master return and step on the shards. The simple task made her feel a little less uneasy. Perhaps he'd desperately needed to use the bathroom and had thumped on the door until he couldn't stand it anymore. It was a reasonable theory, but one that didn't sit at all well. Given the state of him, she doubted he possessed the strength to all but yank the door out of its frame and she wasn't that heavy a sleeper. She would have woken at the sound of his summons, just as something had woken her now.

Carefully rising, her right hand full of glass, she picked up the lantern and looked around the room one last time, just in case he had fallen and the chair had concealed him from her sight. There was no one there. Clucking her tongue in irritation at her own inability to stay awake, to look after her ailing master, she turned, eyes fixed on the shards clustered atop her palm.

A hiss.

She froze, her gaze drawn by the shadow that slithered in the corner of her eye. Nothing there.

"Master?"

A scuttling from above her head.

Reluctantly, her skin crawling with fear, she looked up.

The man-sized shadow of the thing clinging to the ceiling leered at her, eyes burning with white fire, and she screamed, glass forgotten and falling in a shower to the floor.

With a horrible sucking sound, the thing released its grip on the ceiling and fell toward her.

24

"I WAS SCARED, YOU KNOW," KATE SHOUTED OVER THE WIND. "But I shouldn't have left him alone." A pause. "Daddy, I mean."

"He's not alone. Mrs. Fletcher is with him," Grady told her, but Mansfield's words weighed heavily on his mind, playing in an endless loop that made his head hurt. Everything about this night seemed predetermined, and destined to end badly.

I could turn around, he thought suddenly, his heart beating faster. *Go back, ride out of the village and keep ridin' till dawn. Take Kate away from this accursed place. At least I'll be savin' her life.*

And yer own, another, less charitable part of him said and he cursed under his breath. The prospect of avoiding a confrontation with these things and their master thrilled him, as did the idea of sparing Kate whatever consequences might come about as a result, but he knew he'd never be able to live with knowing that Neil might still have been alive, and waiting for him to come; that he had just abandoned him to his fate because...

Because I'm scared to death.

The horse staggered slightly as they trod across a marshy patch of grass and Grady quickly steered the mare away from the unstable ground. "Easy, girl," he said. The light from the lanterns illuminated little in the heavy rain, but he felt better having them. Plus, the frequent flares of lightning aided him in navigating the treacherous terrain. He couldn't begin to imagine what it would be like traveling across the moors in total dark, particularly knowing that there were creatures out here watching him—creatures that considered him prey.

"What's out here, Grady?" Kate asked, as if she'd read his thoughts. Frequently over the years he'd felt as if she had some crude ability to tap into the wavelengths of other people's musings, particularly his. He guessed it was nothing more remarkable than the kind of affinity shared by two people who have spent so much time together, and yet it never ceased to amaze him. On this occasion, however, he wished he'd guarded his thoughts more carefully.

"I'm not sure," he said.

"That thing you told me about," she said. "The thing that killed the man you were with that day. Do you really think it's the Beast of Brent Prior?"

He shook his head. "No, I don't."

"What is it then?"

Though he didn't want to scare her too much, he knew there was little to be gained by lying, and it wouldn't hurt to prepare her for whatever she might see out here. "Somethin' else," he replied. "Somethin' worse."

"Worse? What could be worse than a great big lumbering monster with fire for eyes?"

A pack of *them*, he thought, but did not say.

"Do you think it's out here now?"

He forced a chuckle and reached a hand back to pat her thigh. "Unlikely," he said, "but even if they are, this gun'll scatter 'em right quick and in a hurry." Even though he'd silently agreed with Fowler that guns might prove useless against whatever these things resolved themselves to be, he couldn't think of any other way to defend Kate if they ended up facing them.

"They?"

Damn it. "I wouldn't worry yerself about it, Kate. We're just goin' to have a little chat with this man the Newman young fella was talkin' about. See if he's seen Neil."

It was a lot more than that, of course, and he knew Kate knew it too.

They rode on in the silence and he was thankful that so far at least, he had not seen any sign of those slinking shadows. While that didn't mean they weren't there, it made it easier for him to hope that they might make it to Callow House unchallenged.

The slate gray face of the Fox Tor rose in the lamplight.

They were getting closer.

***

Kate's dream had turned to nightmare in the blink of an eye. When she'd come home to find her father sitting there waiting for her, she'd only been permitted a fraction of the elation she'd always imagined she would feel when he awoke from his torturous slumber, before the horror that had clung to her since Neil's disappearance from the October Dance reasserted itself. She'd hugged her father and kissed his cheek, but she hadn't been with him. Not really. In her mind she'd been battling with the guilt of not having stayed with her brother. But would she have vanished too? It didn't matter. Neil was gone, and maybe gone forever, and the thought of never seeing him again made it difficult to draw breath.

She closed her eyes and willed Neil to be all right. To reinforce her hope, she pictured him waiting for them at that house, cold and scared but relieved that they had come. Only then, once they knew he was safe, would they truly be able to celebrate their father's return. They'd be one big happy family once more, and everything would return to normal.

She smiled feebly. It was a beautiful thought.

But one she suspected would only ever be realized in her dreams.

Worse, she could feel the fear radiating from Grady in waves. She had never known him to be so afraid and it added fuel to the fire of her own terror. Until this moment, she hadn't understood how much she had depended on him all these years, how much she loved him as if he were her father. He had certainly slipped into the role during Father's illness without any of them really realizing it. The fact that this was the first time she had sensed such terror in him made her feel as if the world itself might end tonight.

***

The room was alive. Neil curled himself into a ball, hugging his knees so tightly his chest hurt, his sightless eyes darting from side to side.

They were here; he could sense them, could feel the passage of air as they circled him, and smelled their foulness.

Monsters.

Another *whump* and a crackle of sparks.

The room had grown crowded. It was no longer just the two of them, Neil was sure of it. He could sense them moving around the room, could hear the tick-tick-ticking of their nails against the floor. Petrified, he drew himself in further and struggled to block out the debate that raged within him.

Grady, where are you?

—*They left you.*

No, they didn't. They wouldn't.

—*Of course they would. They left you. Stephen is right. No one cares. No one ever cared about you. Why would they? What good are you for* anything?

The voice was like an extension of the vile things he could feel watching him from all sides.

They wouldn't leave me. They wouldn't. Grady will come. Any minute now, I'll hear him coming.

—*You're a fool to believe that. You're alone because all you've ever done is strive to be left alone, and now you'd better get to like it or accept these creatures as your kin, just like your new Daddy says...*

No, these are not—

"Your brothers," Stephen said. "Come to witness your rebirth. Each and every one of them once a man, flawed and vulnerable, lovelorn or heartbroken, until the day of that fateful hunt. Now they're your brothers, your family, all gathered here to see if the myth is true, if in dying Sylvia provided them with the key to their future."

Neil shook his head, though he had no idea what he was denying—the insanity of it all, perhaps. He should be dancing with the girl of his dreams, a girl who in his heart would never betray him, not sitting in the ruins of some old house listening to a madman grandstanding to shadows.

Shadows that hissed, and scrabbled at the walls.

"The Strigoi with Silver Eyes," Stephen said. "Sylvia's last words, and I believe she was telling us how to survive, how to find a king who would herald the end of mankind's reign and the beginning of ours."

Something heavy shifted against the wall behind the boy. He felt the hair rise on the nape of his neck. Elsewhere, a mouth snapped shut, as if in the aftermath of a yawn.

"You'll recall," the man continued, undaunted, "that I asked you if you'd accept your sight if I offered it to you."

Neil said nothing, but of course he remembered. It had been a cruel taunt, an impossible offer he had turned down only because it was clear there was no worth to it. There couldn't be, unless the man worked miracles, and while there was no doubt in Neil's mind that this lunatic *believed* he could work miracles, there had been no evidence to substantiate such a claim.

"Well...now I offer it to you again. It does, however, come with a price."

He's the devil, Neil thought. *I'm alone with the devil and he's attempting to take my soul. Just like Faust.*

A snapping hiss, a low grumble and a growl from close to Neil's ear and he jerked away with a startled yelp. "Go *away!*" *Dogs*, he thought with increasing panic. *He's got wild dogs here. The hounds of hell in the flesh!*

"Leave him be," Stephen said, and Neil sensed their obeisance. Breathing heavily, he looked in the direction of the man's voice. "I want to be away from here. I want to go back to them."

"I want you to *see*," Stephen told him. "I want you to be what you were always *meant* to be. I want you to regain your place in this family, to lead your brethren on the hunt. I want you to be my son, your mother's son."

Neil squeezed his eyes shut. Behind him, the dogs circled impatiently. He could hear the ticking of their unclipped nails against the flagstone by the entrance, the whuff of their frenzied breath. "I'm *not* your son."

"Yes...you are." His voice was getting closer. Neil stiffened. The heat from the flames was cut off as the man stepped before them. "And once you see again, you'll realize that." The voice was in his face now; he could smell the sour breath. "I promise."

Then Neil screamed as thick-fingered hands clamped the sides of his head, the thumbs moving to rest beneath his eyes. He thrashed, his fists connecting with damp bandages, pulling, tearing away swaths of sodden material. He lashed out with his feet, felt the satisfying thud as his blows connected. The dogs, hounds, creatures, monsters—whatever they were—roared in orgiastic delight, the sound like a thousand saws cutting rotten wood. Rage and fear erupted within Neil, pushing against his skin from the inside, whirling through him until he felt as if he might explode, and with a yell, he let go, releasing all the hate, pain, and frustration he'd ever felt in his life. He snapped with his mouth, tore flesh with his teeth, bucked and flailed and screamed bloody murder. Yet the thumbs remained, pressing gently against the lower rims of his eye sockets, as the rest of the fingers cradled Neil's jaw, throbbing as if some mysterious energy pulsed through the stranger's hands.

"Let me *go*, damn you!" He balled his fists and pummeled the sides of the man's head, aching to hear the sound of skull caving in, not caring that even if he managed to get the upper hand, Stephen still had the hounds on his side. The room was filled with the stink of them. But then, suddenly he was on his back, fuming, raging against empty air, the source of his fury gone, the fingers removed. "*Where are you, you bastard?*" he seethed, breath hissing through his teeth. "Where did you go?"

"Open your eyes and see for yourself."

"You know I can't."

"Try."

"I told you, *I can't!*"

"Try!"

Neil did...

I can't—

...and screamed in utter agony as his eyeballs split open with a faint zipping sound like a knife slicing through pumpkin hide. Fluid wept from the wounds and the boy halted his shaking hands just before them, terrified to touch them but desperate to feel the damage, to know what the man had done to him. "*Oh God!*"

"Go on," Stephen said, amusement in his voice. "*See.*"

"You cut them open!" Neil shrieked in horror. "You cut my eyes open! Oh God, help me!"

"*See*," Stephen repeated, as if it were a chant.

The hounds growled.

"Oh God," Neil said again, and felt as if he was going to vomit. He doubled over, bile filling his mouth and saw his hands floating before his face, wet hands, soaked by the—

He froze.

His hands. Soft white blurred things, the fingers moving with a dreamlike, submarine quality.

His hands. He flexed them, felt and *saw* them respond, albeit with a slight delay between action and result.

My God...It's a trick. The Devil's trick...it's got to be...

But if it was, already he knew he would do anything to keep it. No matter how selfish, or dangerous, no matter what the cost, he would never relinquish the miracle that had just been granted him.

Not a miracle.

A gift.

He looked up in amazement, momentarily unable to breathe, and saw the fire, the flames silver tongues, the tendrils of smoke like dark arms swimming upward.

The world was black and white and silver, and above the flames floated a face, a bleached orb with dark smudges for eyes and a black crescent moon for a smile. Neil blinked, felt the jelly-like liquid ooze down his cheeks, and stick to his eyelids, making his gorge rise again, but now he thought of it as something that had been occluding his vision, the release of some viscous long pent-up poison responsible for his blindness.

A current of disbelief buzzed through him.

"I..."

He swiveled round and saw dust rise from the floor, a haze of black stars. He smiled. "I can *see*..." And he rose on unsteady legs, studying the explosion of colors wrought by every move he made. Ahead of him, beyond the door, the night was a white square, black insect-legs of lightning occasionally piercing the veil.

And guarding the door, were the dogs. Only, now he could see they were not dogs at all, nor did they intend to do him harm. Rather, they stared at him in awe with eyes as silver as the fire.

"Welcome to the world," said Stephen, coming around to join him. When he reached out a hand, Neil saw it writhe through the air between them.

"How is this possible?"

"It's who you are," Stephen told him. "Who you've always been."

Neil waited to wake up and find he was dreaming. Although he could see clearly enough to find his way outside, he took the hand Stephen offered and slowly moved toward the door.

"How?" he asked, feeling everything change, feeling the confines of his dark world shred beneath the weight of this bold new power, this miraculous *gift*. The walls seethed with strange shapes and mysterious shadows that streaked across their surfaces. Sometimes he fancied he saw faces, but when he looked upon them directly, they were gone. The room pulsed, vibrated with color like veins beneath the monochrome veil.

"It's all yours," Stephen said, gesturing expansively at the moors. "All of it, and anything foolish enough to walk it is your prey."

"What about my father? And Grady? Kate? What about them?"

"That, my child, is up to you to decide, but think of them no longer as your family. He tilted the boy's face up to look at him. "We're your family now."

Suddenly, there was light and fire and an explosion of pain he felt sure would tear him to pieces. He shrieked and fell to his knees, only vaguely aware that the crowd in the room was standing, shifting, changing, their necks craned forward, watching his agony. His spine crackled and he sprawled on the floor, his lungs in flames, every breath scorching the roof of his mouth, his tears like acid burning trails down his cheeks. He pleaded for the pain to end, for one of those silently watching shadows to kill him and end the misery. He convulsed and invisible hands spun him over on his back. His heels drummed against the floor; he gasped and felt the skin on his body tighten.

He cried out behind teeth clenched so hard they must surely shatter. His muscles spasmed, every bone in his body splintering, as his newfound vision wavered, darkened, then settled into focus as the agony abruptly left him and his back slammed against the hard floor.

Neil coughed, but the sound was horribly wrong. Breath returned and emerged in staggered hisses from all the wrong places. He lay still and listened, mesmerized by the alien sound of his respiration. *Sss-k-k-k-sss. Sss-k-k-k-sss. Sss-k-k-k-sss.* It sounded more machine than man—like steam escaping from a ruptured funnel—or the amplified sound of an insect.

His skin felt heavy, like armor.

He sat up, his vision even clearer than it had before the merciless pain had erupted in him. Stephen, a figure of radiant silver and drifting shadow stepped close. Other figures moved into view behind him.

"Now," Stephen said. "We are ready to hunt."

25

IT LANDED BEFORE HER, WHITE EYES GLOWING, mouthful of needle-teeth bared, and Mrs. Fletcher, terrified, and with no consideration for the consequences of such an act, did the only thing she could think of, and kicked it. Hard. Her heel connected sharply with the creature's jaw and it recoiled with a grunt, its head whipping to the side and spraying the wall with translucent slime, and in the few seconds it took for the thing to recover, the charwoman dodged past and ran screaming into the hall.

There was no time to wonder what the hellish creature might be or where it had come from but she was sure it was responsible for her master's disappearance. However it had gained entry into the house, it had done so stealthily, and probably while she'd dozed, then ripped the door to the living room open and—

She didn't want to think what it might have done to her employer, and there was no time to grieve. Already she cursed the precious moments she'd wasted watching the bizarre creature's hypnotic descent from the ceiling to the floor.

She reached the front door and risked a glance over her shoulder. The creature was following, albeit with a languid crawl that suggested it was in no hurry to run her down, that it would catch her no matter how fast she ran, and that this was a part of the hunt it enjoyed. It moved like a huge cat, its shoulders rolling, narrow head lowered, but had no fur, rather a dark hide that seemed to absorb the light rather than reflect it. Thick white claws clacked against the parquet floor as it casually made its way toward her.

She tugged the door open and raced out into the storm, her heart thudding so hard and fast she feared she might drop dead of a heart attack. Only the thought of the slavering beast feeding on her cooling body propelled her onward.

The icy wind and rain blasted against her, slowing her flight and freezing the skin on her face. A short distance ahead, the low stables waited, each stall a mass of shadows. For a moment she hesitated, struck by the awful notion that the monster might not have come alone. A whole pack of those things might be watching her from the dark. A low rumbling growl from behind her forced her to dispense with the fear, and she ran on, to where she knew there were more places to hide, and plenty of weapons to defend herself with.

Behind her, the open doorway of the house showed the silhouette of the beast, slowly, ever so slowly descending the steps. She prayed it wasn't taking its time because it knew she was about to run straight into the claws of its brethren. Holding her breath, she reached the stables and hurried inside. The air smelled of hay and old manure never quite washed away. Quickly, she felt her way in the gloom to the back wall until her hands brushed a wooden handle. She grabbed it and tugged, until it came free of the copper bracket, then felt along the handle until wood became thin steel tines that curved away from her.

A pitchfork.

Perfect.

Lightning lit the world, thunder pounding at the black skin of the sky a heartbeat later, and she spun around to face the open stable door. She gripped the pitchfork and held it out, business end aimed at the liquid shadow that swung around the corner and into the pen, baleful eyes alight with pale fire.

"*Florrrencccccce,*" it hissed then and the shock of hearing it speak weakened her. The fact that such a terrible, unnatural thing could *know her by name*, was almost enough to prompt her to drop the weapon and concede to her fate, for surely such a diabolical evil could not be defeated by man or anything fashioned by his hand. But just as quickly she forced herself to recover, to call on every ounce of her Christian faith and believe that she could best, or at the very least deter this horrible, devilish thing. After all, if she simply let it take her and do its worst, who would be here to warn Grady and the children when they returned, unsuspecting, to see their father?

But that thought led to another and the first inexorable twinge of sadness rose in her as she pictured the children's faces when she told them what had happened, what had become of their father after all their years of waiting for him to return from his catalepsy. They would posit that a demon had come to take him away and she would have to struggle to dispel the theory as nonsense, for secretly she thought that perhaps it *was* a demon that had taken their father and now stood in the stable doorway, waiting to take her.

It watched her, jaws split in a semblance of a grin.

"Get away," she said, forcing authority into her tone. "Go on, get away from here or I'll skewer you, I swear I will!"

It didn't move.

"Go on," she said again, jabbing the pitchfork at the air in front of its nose. "Get away!"

The air smelled of damp earth, a scent that grew stronger as the creature took a hesitant step forward.

"Damn you, get *away* from here!"

It didn't comply, but lowered its head, the queer phosphorescent light from its eyes casting shadows on the earthen floor of the stable. Mrs. Fletcher jabbed at it with the pitchfork and it casually shifted its head to avoid the strike.

Devoid of other options, Mrs. Fletcher knew what she had to do. This standoff could continue all night, until her strength and will gave out, or until the creature dismissed the pitchfork as a threat and rushed her, so she slowly moved to the right, her intention to keep the thing at bay as she circled it and reached the door. The stable doors were swinging open; perhaps if she was fast enough she could lock it inside. It was risky and more than likely she'd fail, but it was all she could think to do. If it tried to pounce in the meantime, she would stick it like a pig and leave it bleed to death on the stable floor.

Good, she thought, bolstered a little, *a miserable plan, but a plan at least. Better than standin' here waitin' for it to figure out that it's faster than I am.* Adrenaline pulsed through her, bringing a coppery taste to her mouth not unlike blood. She spat and continued to move, the creature moving in the opposite direction, clearly infuriated at being forced to move against its will when all it wanted to do was savage her.

"That's it," she mumbled, almost at the open door. "Thaaaat's...it..."

She glanced to her right to gauge the distance she would have to cover and realized too late that it was exactly what the dog-thing had been waiting for. Apparently deciding to disregard the tines held inches from its throat, it lunged at her, and the pitchfork did nothing but graze its underbelly. With a roar, it soared into the air, eyes like moons. With a cry of panic, Mrs. Fletcher tried to back away and thudded against the wall hard enough to set the tools on the far wall rattling. Her legs skidded from under her and she fell heavily, the pitchfork slipping from her grasp.

"No," she whined and saw those dreadful white lights descend on her. Without thinking, she rolled. The beast landed in a crouch where she'd lain only moments before and snapped its head in her direction, mouth wide open, tongue like a worm uncovered in its lair. Mrs. Fletcher scrabbled backward, her joints protesting with fiery bolts of pain as she whimpered and pawed the floor for the pitchfork.

The creature tensed, ready to spring, and at this distance, there was no hope that she could avoid it.

Oh God, no!

Her hand touched rounded wood still warm and clammy from her grip and she snatched at it.

The white fire narrowed, the beast's ears flattened against its skull and it shrieked at her as it sprang.

In an instant, she brought the pitchfork up so that the handle was braced against the floor, the tines raised toward the ceiling. Her hands were so sweaty she feared it would not be long before it slipped from her grasp. *Please, please, please God...*

Already in the air, the creature could not change the direction of its leap, but it tried, wriggling like a cat being held over a fire but it was too late. Mrs. Fletcher steeled herself, eyes wide, heart pounding painfully, as the creature slammed into the pitchfork, the momentum carrying it over the charwoman's head and tearing the weapon from her hands. She cried out, ducked and covered her head, sure the beast would land on her, crushing her beneath its weight. Instead it thumped down on the floor next to the stable entrance and thrashed. Mrs. Fletcher scooted aside and turned. In an instant she was on her feet. To her dismay she saw that although the pitchfork had pierced the animal, the thing's last-minute efforts to avoid it had paid off and only two of the four steel spikes had penetrated its flesh, catching it in the ribs rather than the underbelly. But any satisfaction she might have felt at the sight of the creature's struggling was quelled by the realization that even now, it was slowly shuddering free of the tines, and when it did, she had no doubt that it would be possessed of a fury she would be helpless against.

And so she dashed forward, yelping as she dodged the claw it swiped across the gap between where it lay and the doorway. Then she was past it, and out into the cold rain once more, hurriedly slamming the stable door closed and fumbling with the bolt, even as the thing inside pounded weakly against it. Then, the bolt slid home and Mrs. Fletcher crumpled to the ground, relieved, but all too well aware that the wood behind which the creature was contained was old, and would not hold for very long.

She quickly rose and in a stumbling run, made her way back to the house.

***

The wind sent rain streaking across the glass. Tabitha listened to the animal howl of the storm and shivered, though her bedroom was warm. Inside the house, all was quiet. As she lay on her side in bed, she thought of Neil out there somewhere, possibly in the clutches of a maniac who might be doing untold things to him, and she felt a cold jab of guilt in her stomach. She realized that her part in this nightmare was much more than she'd allowed herself to believe up until now. Donald might have engineered a trap for Neil by himself, but it would undoubtedly have been something crude and clumsy, and therefore destined to fail. His total incapacity to be discreet would have guaranteed that. In short, only her involvement had made his plan work, and even then, it hadn't been a complete success. Donald had hoped to humiliate Neil in front of everyone. Wear the poor boy down. But it hadn't turned out that way, not exactly, though the end result had been achieved. Neil was gone, presumed taken by the man with the bandaged face and, while she had no doubt that Donald would sleep easy tonight (aided in no small part by the alcohol the stranger had given him as a reward for his services), Tabitha feared she might never sleep again, not with the knowledge of what she had done.

Then why did you do it? she asked herself—a question for which she had no answer. That the situation had, from the very beginning, seemed unbelievable, and unlikely to ever spiral into the nightmare it had become, was a feeble defense, and she knew it. At most, she had feared Donald would terrorize Neil for a while until he got bored, or until Grady came knocking at their door demanding he find a new focus for his ill-bred cravings.

Abruptly she sat up, her legs dangling off the side of the bed. The rain lashed against the window, as if disputing her burgeoning resolve.

She tried to tell herself that it was entirely reasonable to assume that Neil was fine, that even now he was safe and warm at home after being rescued by Grady. The groundskeeper was a kind, gentle sort, but tonight in the cloakroom she'd seen a side of him she'd never seen before. He'd seemed lit by an inner fire, a dangerous flame that threatened to spill out and consume everyone within reach if it wasn't satisfied. His eyes had been like pools of oil, cold and filled with threat, the kind of look one might expect from an animal whose young have been threatened. She knew he would stop at nothing to find Neil. But none of them knew anything about the bandaged man, or what he might be capable of. Would an old man like Grady be able to reason with him? And if that failed, would he be able to defend himself against a man obviously demented?

She didn't think so.

In the meantime, then, was she to sit and wait, enshrouded in blankets that reeked of guilt, for confirmation that all was well, that ultimately, she hadn't doomed an innocent boy to unthinkable horrors?

No. She knew the waiting would drive her mad.

She had to know for herself.

Decided, she sat up.

And had one foot on the floor when something scratched at her bedroom door.

***

Neil ran, the night seething with life around him in a phantasmagoria of silver and black. The ground sounded like the beating of a drum beneath his clawed hands and feet as he loped with the others, their breathing echoing the sound of his own. Wet earth sank and flew in his wake, the sensation like the splitting of the skin he craved so badly. Hunger infected him and it was the most natural thing in the world, despite the lingering confusion that scintillated across his brain that he had not always felt so hungry, or so desperate to be sated. The cold scythed over him, making the faintest whistling sound as it sliced over his fissured skin. He felt as if in an instant the weak flesh he'd languished beneath all these years had hardened, become impenetrable. Become armor. He opened his mouth, his *jaws* and laughed with delight, and the sound was not at all like laughter. For a moment it unnerved him, but the sheer power that rippled through him soon dispelled it. He was alive. Dear God, he had never felt so alive in his life. There was nothing that could hurt him now.

But there was plenty *he* could hurt, and intended to.

The night, the storm, was like a curtain, billowing in the wind to reveal the strange new world beyond, a world full of prey, a world he had been born to rule. A world he'd been blinded to until he was ready for it. Until it was ready for *him*.

He raced on, dizzy with the euphoria of this strange new life, drunk on the implications of his new form and its implications.

And eventually, inevitably, when vague, foggy thoughts of his old life leaked back into his brain, bringing with it images of the people who had shared it with him, he was most relieved and encouraged that they did not inspire love within him, but disgust.

26

A FLICKERING ORANGE-RED RECTANGLE OF LIGHT FLOATED through the storm. At first Grady thought it might be a lantern, but after a few moments spent squinting into the rain, he straightened and quickly urged Kate to dismount.

"What is it?" she asked, obeying his prompt with more than a little irritation. He had all but pushed her off the horse.

"A fire," he told her and descended, with obvious difficulty, from the mare. "Inside the Callow House."

"Are you all right?"

He nodded curtly. "Fine. Old bones."

She watched him brush an open hand across the horse's flank, study his boots and tend to the lantern. He was looking everywhere but at her, and clearly delaying.

"What's wrong with you?" she said, raising her light to study him.

"Nothin'."

"You're lying."

"I shouldn't have brought you out here." He sounded pained and the expression on his face when he turned around confirmed it.

"I wanted to come."

"I know, but I still should have made you stay at home."

She shrugged indignantly. "I'm sixteen, Grady. You can't *make* me do anything."

He gave her a weary smile. "Don't I know it, but perhaps if there'd been time to tell you everythin' you'd have volunteered to stay behind and watch yer father. Only thing is..."

"What?"

He avoided looking at her. "I'm not so sure you'd have been any safer there. In fact, the more I think about it, the more I'm startin' to believe that this might be the last night any of us will see."

Anger and fear brought her closer to him, the raised lantern all that stopped their faces from touching. "Why would you say such a thing?" she demanded, eyes wide in the light.

"Because it's true, that's why. I don't know what the hell was runnin' through my mind when I agreed to bring you out here, but there you are. We've left poor 'oul Mrs. Fletcher back home with yer father, who, as we speak, could be tryin' to kill her—"

Alarmed, Kate said, "Why would he try to kill her?"

"Because he's not right. Whatever relief you felt at seein' him up and around, forget about it. Put it back in that big dark box you've been keepin' yer hope in up until now, because the disease that's been keepin' him down hasn't magically vanished, only let him up on his feet with a scrambled mind and God only knows what else." His face seemed to age the longer she looked upon it, as if it were merely a painting, the artist unsatisfied and adding lines and shadowy creases in an effort to save it. "He says he's a creature, that he was wounded by one of them the day of the hunt, that he's infected, and that by the time we get back home, he'll have changed." Rambling now, the speed of his words perfectly timed to the beating of Kate's heart and the soaring of her panic. "I left him there because I couldn't believe him, and didn't know what the hell to do with him even if I did. So if it turns out he was right, I might as well have killed Mrs. Fletcher myself." Frantic, he spun around and yanked the bottle of whiskey Sarah Laws had given him to share with her dead husband out of a pouch on the saddle. As he opened it, he continued, "That alone would be enough to make any man feel like lyin' down and dyin' but no, for me it gets worse, which means for you it does too. I took you away from that house—and who knows, you might have died there too, or maybe the sight of you would have been enough to knock some sense into yer father—and I brought you out here, into the playin' field of a bunch of monsters I'm still not sure I believe exist, despite havin' seen 'em with my own two feckin' eyes!"

"Grady..."

The wind tugged at his silver hair as he wiped the back of his hand across his eyes and took a lengthy pull on the whiskey. When he was done, he hissed air through his teeth and looked at her where she stood trembling. "Neil is probably dead," he said, "and it's my fault for lettin' him slip into that man's hands."

"Grady, no. You don't know what you're saying," Kate pleaded, tears filling her eyes. She couldn't absorb all that he was telling her. Didn't want to, and wanted less to think about what he feared still awaited them.

"I'm afraid," he said, with a rueful smile and a quaver in his voice. "I've made plenty of mistakes in my lifetime, Kate, but none as bad as this one. I alienated my own son and now he hates me. I'm already dead to him. I knew somethin' was wrong with Callow the day of the hunt, and I let it go, and people died. I kept secrets people deserved to know. And now look what's happened. We're walkin' into the dark with guns that may turn out to be as useful as a blade of grass against a cannon ball. Everythin' I have left to live fer is in danger and I don't know what to do to...stop it." He spoke the last two words so quietly the wind all but obliterated them, but Kate saw his quivering lips struggle to shape them. The sight of Grady crying made her want to scream, for up until the tears had moistened his eyes, she was willing to believe that he'd simply had too much to drink with Fowler earlier, or that he was overwhelmed by guilt because someone had taken Neil. But now, all the strength she'd associated with the groundskeeper had vanished, leaving behind a frail-looking shell completely robbed of hope, a rickety semblance of a man whose purpose had been reduced to harbinger of doom, a shuddering signpost pointing the way to disaster.

"You can't just give up," she said. "We're almost there. If something has happened to Neil, if he's...if he's dead, which I know he isn't, then who cares what might happen to us? But we need to know. We can't just *leave* him there! You know that Grady." She reached out a hand and grabbed the collar of his coat and tugged, as if by doing so she could pull the defeat from him. "I know you do!"

He looked at her hand on his coat and for a moment she was afraid he'd ask her to remove it, and then she'd know she'd lost him. But instead he raised his face and regarded her with desolate eyes, and nodded. "You're right," he said and took one last swig from the bottle, capped it, and tossed it into the dark.

The mare whinnied.

Kate stepped back as Grady turned to calm it. "Easy," he said, "Yer goin' home."

Kate frowned. "What?"

When Grady turned back to her, she saw, with mixed relief, that a little of his old self had crept back into his face. But not much, and his expression worried her. "I was an eejit bringin' you here," he said firmly. "But there's still a chance to rectify things."

Automatically, she moved away from him. "What are you going to do?"

"What I should have done earlier." She watched him unhook the Winchester from the saddle. Next, he breeched the chamber, checking to ensure it was loaded. With haunted eyes, he snapped it closed and raised it. "Goodbye, love," he said, cocking the gun and leveling it at her chest.

***

"Tabby?"

She sighed, relieved that the voice from the shadow standing in the doorway was a familiar one. Still, it prompted her to get back under the sheets to hide her undress, and a flush rose to her cheeks. "What is it?"

Donald, his features blackened by the gloom in the hallway, said nothing. At length, Tabitha frowned, irritated by his staring, for she could feel his eyes on her.

"Did you want something?"

For a moment, she entertained the wonderful notion that maybe he had come to apologize. Maybe his run-in with Grady had finally knocked some sense into him. Maybe the same guilt keeping her awake had at last caught up with her brother.

Then he jerked, as if pulled by a puppeteer's hand from above before slouching back into his natural posture. Then he slowly straightened. And when he spoke his voice had deepened, like it did when he had just awakened from sleep. "...Said you would beg for me..."

All hope diminished at that, and Tabitha rolled her eyes. "What on earth are you talking about?"

"...Hurts..."

She squinted, hoping to see his face so she could read the intent there, but it was too dark. "Donald, please go away unless you have something imp—"

"He said you would *beg* for me."

Tabitha's skin went cold. She had heard anger in Donald's voice more times than she could count, but this was different, devoid of the hysterics that usually accompanied his outbursts. He hadn't even raised his voice. He'd just spoken, but the malevolence in his tone was like a slap across the face.

"Donald, what's wrong?"

He took a clumsy step into the room.

He's drunk, Tabitha realized, and quickly lunged for the lamp beside her bed. It had been turned down low enough to reveal the shapes of furniture hunkered in her bedroom, and the menacing form of her brother at the door, but little else. Now she turned up the flame and warm light washed across the room.

"You hurt me," Donald said and Tabitha felt the breath leave her at the sight of him.

Thick black veins like leafless tree branches stood out on his face and throat, pushing against the skin as if at any moment they would break free and tear it apart. Donald's lips were drawn back in pain, revealing all his teeth in a hideous frozen grin. But his eyes...his eyes were the worst of all. White fire had filled them, silver fluid leaking from the burned, ragged sockets.

Tabitha wanted to scream, but instead she pulled the covers up so only her eyes and the top of her head was exposed. "Go away," she mumbled. "Please. There's something wrong with you."

"I know," Donald said, his breathing growing tortured the more he tried to speak. "I can't stop it. Help me."

"I don't know what to do."

He shook his head and the muscles creaked. He gasped and a shudder ran through him. There came the sound of something splitting, tearing, but Tabitha saw no new wounds on his face or throat. "You must..." he said. "I want you to help me."

"How?" She was more terrified than she'd ever been in her life, but there was nothing she could do. He was blocking her way out of the room should she dare try and escape him, and the window led to nothing but a long drop to the yard below. All she could do for the moment was pray, and hope that if a merciful caring cell had ever existed in her brother, he would call upon it now.

"What happened to you?" she asked, as she burst into frightened tears.

He stared, the white fire fading for seconds at a time, then blossoming again and casting odd twitching shadows around the room. "*He* did it to me," Donald said, the rage back in his voice. He looked up at the ceiling and touched a bruised and blackened hand to his throat where the awful black veins were thickest. "He grabbed me by the throat. Sss...scratched me."

"Maybe you should go get Mum. Get her to fetch Doctor Campbell." It felt odd to be making such rational suggestions, given that not a single part of her felt capable of it. Surely her brother had become possessed by the devil, for she could not imagine anything remotely human looking like Donald did as he struggled to breathe before her.

He began to move, in slow, unsteady steps until he was standing at the foot of her bed, towering over her, his face a terrible mask that at any moment she fully expected to see slipping off. She fancied she could see his skull, charred and blackened beneath translucent skin and it made her ill, while an inner voice screamed at her to flee.

"Donald..." she whimpered, pulling the blankets tight across her face. "I'm scared."

He stood there watching her, in his blue and white striped pajamas, silver ichor dribbling down his throat, hair stuck up in tufts from restless sleeping, and a look of uncertainty wrenched tight the skin on his face. She stared back in horror, knowing she should avert her eyes but unable to tear them away from the monstrosity her brother had become, and she saw him smile.

"Tabby..." he said, the light in his eyes brighter now, his voice surer. "He said you would beg for me."

"I don't—"

"Will you?"

"Donald...stop."

"Will you beg for me?" He started to move around the bed, but this time his steps did not look hindered by whatever ailment had done this to him, rather they were slow, deliberate...teasing movements. "Will you let me lie with you?"

"Oh God." Tabitha scooted herself up, making herself smaller, her back pressed hard against the headboard. "Please, Donald, don't hurt me."

"I won't," He told her, trailing one broken-looking finger over the blankets where barely a moment before, her legs had been. In a sing-song voice, he announced, "I never meant to hurt you, Tabby. Not at all. But I had to do something to satisfy the urge. The fire inside me that wanted to *do* wicked things to you."

Tabitha would not believe him. His voice was no longer his own, and that made it easier for her to look upon this thing, this devilish representation of her brother, as something out to trick her, to influence her, to weaken her resistance by hitting her where it knew she was already sore. Donald would never have thought such awful impure things about her, even as badly as he sometimes treated her. Of this she was certain.

But he was still coming, ever so slowly.

"I want to see what you've been hiding from me." His fingers ceased their exploring and clutched a bundle of blanket. He tugged. "I want to see your tits, Tabby, and all the rest of that delicious meat you've kept beneath your stuffy clothes."

Now she drew her feet beneath her bottom until she was half-sitting on the pillow, the blankets forgotten and bundled next to her. "Donald, please, listen to what you're saying. These are not your words. This is not you!"

He continued to advance, and now she could smell him, a horrible, diseased, earthy smell.

"Please...let me try to get help."

He stopped, and something changed in his face. It might have been a look of confusion, or sorrow, the flames burning brightly in his eyes made it hard to tell. He lifted one hand from the bed and brought it close to his face. He studied it, as if it were something new to him. And in a way, it was, for long thin bone-like nails had jutted forth from them. His smile returned, and he peered at Tabitha through his fingers. "I'm going to eat you all up," he said and lunged for her.

She screamed, and without thinking slid diagonally across the bed, her outstretched hand grasping for whatever it could find to use as a weapon.

It found the lamp.

"Give it to me," Donald roared as he tore at her nightdress. Fabric ripped and nails found her skin. She screamed again and wrenched the lamp off the nightstand. It almost fell, slipping from a palm made moist by terror, but she tightened her grip and swiveled around.

With a gasp of excitement, Donald tore open her nightdress, exposing her nakedness. Instinctively she was mortified, but her embarrassment was quickly dismissed by the awareness that soon he would hurt her, and badly. In the state he was in, he might even kill her. As his mouth opened wider than any mouth was supposed to, revealing a set of serrated and pointed teeth, and his head ducked low to meet her small breast, she brought the lamp over her head in a two-handed grip.

"I'm sorry," she whispered.

"There she is," Donald said, a black tongue worming its way toward her right nipple.

The hot glass burning her hands, she brought the lamp down in as vicious an arc as she could manage given the limited space. It connected and shattered on impact, the flame guttering once before oil soaked the bed, and Donald's hair. It ignited. Blue-white fire rushed over her brother's face and he jerked away from her, away from the bed until he was standing and slapping at his face. The white flames of his eyes reached up toward his brow as if eager to meet its kindred spirit, and then Donald was running, screaming, howling in agony toward the window.

Tabitha didn't want to watch what happened next. She couldn't. All she knew was that the threat was gone, and had quickly been replaced by another.

The bed was on fire.

But as she tumbled out of bed, kicking in a panic at the blankets, she almost collided with Donald as he dove headfirst through her bedroom window. She saw the flames, blue and white and yellow, sailing back from his head as he crashed through the glass and descended in a hail of screams to the ground below.

***

"Get on the horse."

Kate stared at him, mouth agape.

He shifted his stance. Swallowed. "Kate...I'm not foolin'. I said get on the bloody *horse*."

"No."

"If yer thinkin' I love you too much to shoot you, yer right, but I also love you too much to let those things get you and I'd rather you died by my hand than theirs, so *get on the blasted horse* and get *out* of here!"

"Grady, *please*."

"*Now!*"

"Where am I supposed to go?"

"I don't know. Not the house. Get as far from Brent Prior as you can. Stop at the next village and tell them what's happened. Get them to send all the constables and hardy men they have. They'll need them. Only a fool would come out here on his own." He paused, and smiled humorlessly. "Or with a young girl."

"But I can *help* you." She glanced pointedly at the pistol in her hand and for one appalling moment, considered using it.

"Yer right. You can. You can get on that horse right now and ride away. That's how you can help me."

"Grady," she sobbed, still making no move to comply with his demand. She couldn't believe this was happening, that a man she had loved her whole life, as much if not more than her father, simply because he had been there for her more, was pointing a rifle at her and threatening to kill her if she didn't leave. "I want to stay with you."

"Kate..." The gun shook in his hand. "Please." The wind slapped at his raincoat. "*Please.*"

"You'll have to shoot me," she said, the remnants of the rain, now stopped, dripping from the tip of her nose.

He paused, the rifle stock nestled against his jaw, and he was weeping. Or perhaps it was just rainwater dripping down his cheek, Kate couldn't be sure. His face was ghost-white in the lamplight, eyes wide and glassy with terror.

Kate braced herself as sudden determination seized the old man's face, his eyes widening. Again she became conscious of the weight of the pistol in her clammy hand. Wondered if she could ever live with herself if she used it.

"Don't..." she pleaded, one last time, slowly bringing the pistol up.

Then, with a muffled choking sound, Grady pulled the trigger.

27

IN THE MANSFIELD'S YARD, TABITHA SCREAMED as a section of wood the size of her fist tore through the stable door in front of her. Instinctively, she ducked, arms crossed over her face. Her eyes were ringing and the coppery taste of blood filled her mouth. She fell to her knees into a puddle, the icy water instantly soaking through her skirts.

Despite her confusion, she knew she had been shot at. She had grown up around huntsmen and the thunderous report of a rifle had been unmistakable. Worse still, something inside the stable had *growled* in response to the shot. Any other night, she might have concluded that the Mansfield family was keeping some kind of a dog in there. But after what had happened with Donald, she knew better. Something terrible had been set loose in Brent Prior and it seemed now that she was not the only one who knew about it.

In a low crouch, she hurried away from the stable door across the yard toward the darkness that encroached upon the house from the moors, her feet splashing through puddles that sent more water up her legs, eliciting a gasp from her at the coldness of it.

"Wait!" said a voice and Tabitha froze, aware even in her terror that disobeying the command might mean her death. Shivering, she slowly turned around to face the speaker. Her fear lessened only slightly at the sight of the rotund charwoman standing in the doorway, framed by the light from the hall. To her relief, she saw that though the woman was still holding the rifle, she had lowered it to her side. "Who are you?"

"It's me, Tabitha. Tabitha Newman."

For a moment the woman said nothing, then she stepped aside, allowing the light from inside the house to spread out into the yard. "You'd better come inside," she said. "And quickly."

"What's going on?" Tabitha asked as she hurried to the door. "Why did you try to shoot me?"

"I was trying to stop you from openin' that door, lass. If you had, you'd be dead now, and not from any bullet. Now get inside. *Quickly!*"

Tabitha rushed inside and watched as Mrs. Fletcher slammed the door closed and bolted it behind her.

"What's happening? Did Neil come home?"

The charwoman turned, a haunted look on her face. "No. There's no one here but us. And that thing in the stable."

"What is it?"

"I don't know what it is," the old woman replied, gesturing at the stairs. "But we're goin' to have to hide. Now that I think about it, weakenin' that door with a shot wasn't very wise at all, but I panicked when I saw you tryin' to open it."

"Well if it's locked up, shouldn't we try and get into town?"

"It won't be locked up for long, and once it's out, it'll come lookin' for me. I stabbed it with a pitchfork." She smiled wearily. "Made it mad, I expect. It's a fast bugger. Lightnin' fast. We'd never make it into town before it got a hold of us, and we wouldn't see it comin'. It's the color of night, that thing. We're better off here, where we can see it."

Tabitha's mind raced. She had come here hoping to find that the nightmare, which had begun with Neil's disappearance, had been resolved, but now it seemed as if she'd walked into another battleground. It led her to wonder how many more houses around the village were trying to fight off monsters.

Mansfield House, like her own, was solid brick, a veritable fortress built to withstand the harsh moorland weather but that hadn't prevented them from infiltrating her room in the guise of her brother. "I've seen them," she said. When the charwoman looked questioningly at her, she continued. "They did something to my brother, changed him somehow, and...and my mother's gone. I found blood in her bed but I can't find her. I thought she might be here. I thought maybe she had come to see if Neil had been found. I came here to see if I could find *either* of them."

Mrs. Fletcher shook her head. "I'm sorry, pet. No one has been back here. Except for that thing, of course and I think it did my master in."

Tabitha nodded. This had to be some sort of cruel nightmare. In the real world, people didn't turn into monsters, and loved ones didn't die. And though a tiny ounce of hope remained in her, she feared her mother was dead, if not changed like Donald had been. She didn't know which was worse. But while she knew there was grieving to be done, it would have to wait. If not, it could distract her and make her another casualty of this horrific night.

"It's not anythin' I've ever seen before," Mrs. Fletcher said. "The more I try and understand it, the more I think that the Beast of Brent Prior *itself* is locked up in that stable." She moved to the stairs and motioned for Tabitha to do likewise. "Let's move. We'll hide upstairs."

The Beast of Brent Prior. Tabitha swallowed. *It's supposed to be just a myth.* But so were all monsters, and the reality of them had already been proven to her.

"But what if someone comes home in the meantime?" she asked.

"We can keep watch from the upstairs window. When we see them coming, we'll shout a warning."

Tabitha looked dubious. "I don't like this."

Mrs. Fletcher took her by the elbow and led the way upstairs. "Nor do I, child but we're hardly spoiled for options."

They had just reached the landing when they heard a sharp cracking sound like dry wood being broken across a knee.

"Go!" Mrs. Fletcher said, shoving Tabitha in the direction of the master's bedroom.

More wood splintering, then a furious crash as the stable door was destroyed.

In the bedroom, Tabitha parted the curtains. She quickly snapped the latch and pushed the window open. Hands braced on the sill, she peered out. In a voice wracked with terror at the monstrosity she saw below, she said, "Mrs. Fletcher...it's free!" The stable door was in ruins, fragments of wood scattered halfway across the yard. "Oh my God," she breathed. "What *is* it?"

The creature below was much different than the corrupted version of her brother. He at least had retained a human shape. The thing in the yard didn't look even remotely human.

The charwoman raised the rifle. "Close that door," she said. "And lock it."

This time Tabitha ignored the old woman's command, for the thing she saw lumbering across the yard paralyzed her with fear. It was an abomination, an unnatural thing woven from shadows, with white fire for eyes.

Donald's eyes...

It was the kind of monster she had once feared might dwell in the darkness beneath her bed, waiting to grab her ankle. As she watched, terror-struck, the creature landed in a crouch directly below the window and raised its queerly shaped head.

"Tabitha!" Mrs. Fletcher shouted. "Where is it now?"

Tabitha couldn't speak; her thoughts were leaves in an electrified stream of panic. She wanted to tell the charwoman—knew she *had* to tell the charwoman—that the creature was at the door, but even if she found her tongue, she knew she'd be lying.

Because the creature was not at the door. It was *on* it, hugging the wood with the ease of a drunken man sprawled across a table, and slowly, ever so slowly, creeping up the wall toward the window.

***

The scent of gun smoke wafted on the air.

Kate sat on the sodden earth, trembling.

The horse had bolted at the explosive burst from Grady's rifle and now the two of them stared at one another, ears ringing, but not deaf to the sound of grass crunching all around them.

He wasn't shooting at me, Kate realized with a twinge of relief that was a mere scratch of light in the painted-over window of her panic. Grady's shot had missed her by inches, but it hadn't missed whatever he'd been aiming at. As she'd dropped to a defensive crouch, she'd heard the bullet thud into flesh, followed by the agonized roar of something as it thrashed in the darkness. She'd been afraid to look, paralyzed by fear, as the night became a wild, unbridled thing that smelled of blood and smoke.

But now she had to look, because the roar had faded to a pitiful keening sound that called to every ounce of sympathy in her. And when her eyes fell upon the dying thing lying on the grass only a few feet away, she saw that it was not the ravening beast her mind had imagined it would be. It was a man, and half his head was gone.

She stood, the lantern forgotten at her feet, the pistol in danger of slipping from her rain and sweat-moistened grip.

The footsteps grew louder. Loud enough that she knew if she raised the lantern she would see who was making them, but found she was unable to move. She looked over her shoulder at Grady, who looked as if someone had crept up behind him and stolen his spine. He was hunched over, and wheezing, his gaze dark but defeated, and staring straight ahead. He held his lantern by his side, illuminating little but adding thick ugly shadows to the valleys in his face. Following the rain, the wind had died too, and now the night was still, stars appearing through the clouds like the glint in the eyes of cold angels. Smoke still leaked from the barrel of the rifle.

Kate looked down at the man in the grass. He was naked she saw, his skin wrinkled and loose, but any shame she might have felt at seeing him in such a state was overruled by the shuddering that passed through him. *Death throes.* She suddenly felt ill. The man groaned and Kate found her feet. She went to Grady, her eyes still searching for the source of the crunching sound. Whoever was out there, they were close enough to touch. For a moment, Kate imagined they were men from the village, summoned by Mrs. Fletcher perhaps, to come assist them in their search. But if that were true, she realized, then Grady had just killed one of them. *Just like he almost killed me.*

But somehow, she knew these people weren't villagers.

They were the embodiment of Grady's fears—the reason he'd suddenly faltered and let his terror overcome him, the reason he now looked a hundred years old, a tired old man with a rifle for a cane.

"Tell me," said a voice directly in front of her and Kate jolted with the fright, "Do you always kill friends of yours with nary a cry of warning? What if that had been Neil? Wouldn't you now feel a little silly, a trifle inadequate, if it was he who was lying there with the life draining out of him?"

Grady straightened, but despite it, he still looked defeated, and tired, incapable of defending himself against anything that required effort to conquer it. He looked as though all he wanted was to sleep, for however long. As a result, Kate suddenly felt alone, completely abandoned, and surrounded. She quickly thumbed back the hammer on the old pistol, praying it would work if it became necessary to use it.

***

Grady cocked his head at the sound of the grinding click, but his face remained impassive.

The men stepped into the light.

"Jesus Christ," he breathed, and heard Kate gasp.

Grady shook his head, denying the truth about what he was seeing before his very eyes. It had to be witchery, some diabolical hoax.

There were five of them, including the man he'd shot, and the bandaged man, who was wearing Grady's cap. The significance of this mockery was not lost on him. It meant the man had been there, with the creatures, when the wind had whipped it over the fence and onto the moors. The thought of him standing there, hidden by the dark and the thicket, watching, as Grady fussed over the spilled pumpkins, made a shiver dance up his spine.

The last of them stepped into the feeble light and Kate stiffened.

It was Neil.

"Oh my God, you're all right," she said, her voice wavering, uncertain. She made to go to him but Grady held her back, drawing a look from her that could have razed the moors. He shook his head and gave her shoulder a reassuring squeeze. "Wait," he said softly. She didn't respond, but her resistance waned.

Other than his nakedness, there was something wrong with the boy, something the groundskeeper couldn't quite place.

Grady swallowed and licked his lips. The cold had infected him and it took every ounce of restraint to keep from collapsing in a heap. Only the thought of leaving Kate out here alone with ghosts and monsters kept him standing. But he didn't think he'd be able to do much more than that. The strength and the will to fight had flown from him like the cap he'd lost to them earlier.

We're going to die out here, he thought with glum certainty, reinforced now by the ragged semicircle of friends and former acquaintances who glared at him with undisguised malevolence. Doctor Campbell was there, his face stark white, his eyes jet-black, like the carapaces of beetles. His hair was tousled, as always, but in the gloom, it seemed stuck together by dark clots of something. He was naked, as were they all, except for the bandaged man. None of them, however, seemed affected by the bitter cold. Next to him stood Fowler, and Grady felt a wave of sorrow that his old friend hadn't made it out of the village before the bandaged man recruited him. Or rather, *infected* him, for no amount of conditioning could force a man as generally benign as Greg Fowler to turn against his friend so completely.

The man on the grass was faceless thanks to Grady's bullet. Which left only Neil, incongruous among the death squad because his smile was the only one that appeared to hold no malice. But Grady was bothered by his expression all the same, for while the boy didn't share the wicked look the rest of them wore, neither did he look concerned by the situation in which he had found himself.

Beneath his grip, Kate was like a coiled spring, waiting to be released. He understood her impatience, but didn't yet want to let go. It was clear this monstrous gathering had plans for them and he intended to keep her close until he knew what it was.

"The man you've killed is Arnold Williams," said their leader, reaching up, with deliberately exaggerated movements, to unravel his bandages. "You remember him, don't you?"

Grady did. Williams had once been the local priest, unfortunately given to evening walks upon the moors. He'd vanished eight months ago. Memories of the benevolent octogenarian's cheerful and often witty toasts at wedding receptions and Sunday picnics tried to push themselves to the fore, but Grady willed them away. What he had killed was *not* the priest the community had known and loved. But the thoughts brought in to replace those unwanted memories were just as disturbing. *They're going to kill us We need to get away I've got to save Kate They'll run us down before we get two steps Think of something How can this be happenin' What did they do to Neil Think of somethin' damn you!*

He looked from Neil, who did not react, to their leader, who was still busy tearing mildewed-looking strips of bandage from his face.

"Some of these men died," he said, in a voice barely above a whisper.

"Not quite," the man replied. "They were dying, yes, but it only takes a scratch, or a bite, or the ingestion of a fleck of saliva to halt it. Then they get a second chance at life."

"A better life," Campbell added jovially.

"Reverend Williams might beg to differ," Grady said.

The man chuckled. "Williams, for all his theological wisdom, was not nearly as spiritually pure as you like to think. He was a failure in both lives, and we can do without the contamination he'd introduce to our breed."

"Why are you doin' this?" Grady asked him.

"Because I want to," the man replied simply. "And because it's what I know. We're the dominant species, Grady, and our reign begins here, in this desolate wasteland. It will be our lair, the nest from which we'll spread our tendrils and convert the masses."

"Into what?"

"Into superior beings, just like we are. I don't expect you to understand. I didn't, in the beginning. It's like trying to tell someone the sky is actually black, not blue, the sun silver, not gold. Unless you're there beneath the skin, you can't possibly begin to imagine what this world has to offer. My companions," he said, gesturing at the men flanking him, "resisted at first, until they saw this life through their own eyes. Now they can't imagine anything else. The change means power. There are none of the pitiful worries, frailties and concerns that corrupt the life of humans. For our kind, the waters are never tainted. We rule; we dominate. Everything else is prey."

Grady felt Kate's muscles contract and knew she was ready to fight, despite the overwhelming odds. A small mote of admiration at her courage drifted down through the seething dark within him, searching for sunlight. He reminded himself of his duty: to protect her, to make sure she and Neil made it home to safety, and yet the thought of resisting these creatures, ghosts, demons, whatever they were, exhausted him. He was so godawful tired he just wanted to lie down and be done with the whole damn mess. But he couldn't, and Kate's resistance added a spark to the dwindling fire of his resolve.

We can't give up, he thought. *I won't let them kill her.*

And then: *Not without a fight.* He had, after all, let Neil out of sight long enough for the bandaged man to take him, and had then allowed his own secret fear to govern his decision in bringing Kate along to find him. He owed it to them both to at least try to save them. And if it cost him his life in the process, then so be it. He'd lived about as much as he was going to.

He raised the gun, broke it and produced a shell from his raincoat pocket, and loaded the weapon. None of the men moved. Grady found it disconcerting that despite the damage a bullet had done to Williams, they were making no attempt to stop him from reloading.

And then he realized why.

The rifle only held one bullet at a time, and one bullet would not stop all of them if they rushed him. He'd be dead before he had a chance to reload. It astounded him that they hadn't already charged. But then he concluded that they were merely toying with him, as a cat will toy with a mouse before ending its misery.

The man tore the last of the bandages from his face with a grunt and let them fall in a heap to the ground. The exposed flesh was a dark color, the skin ridged and knotted, as if the man's face had been melted, stirred, and allowed to set again.

"Who are you?" Kate asked, and the man smiled.

"Stephen Callow. My brother led your friend Grady and his chums on a hunt many years ago. A hunt that cost Edgar, and my beloved, their lives."

Callow's brother. Grady had to struggle to absorb this new information, to try to see if it could be used to his advantage, but came up empty. There was nothing natural about the man, or any of his new 'friends'—they emanated threat, and there would be no reasoning with them. But if there was one thing Stephen had in common with his brother, it was that they were both utterly mad.

"Yer brother cost us the lives of our friends," Grady argued. "We did nothin' to him, and he led us out here to die."

"Your master was sleeping with his *wife*," Stephen said. "It was hard enough to bear the thought of my own brother touching the woman I loved without having to learn that your pious bastard of a master was violating her too. They both got what they deserved. You just be thankful that I spared him, that even now he's repaying his debt to me by tearing your fat old cow of a charwoman to shreds."

Mrs. Fletcher. A debilitating wave of sorrow washed over Grady at the thought of her lying bleeding on the flagstone floor of the kitchen. *Her* kitchen, the scene of countless exchanges between them, the trading of well-intentioned barbs and affectionate smiles. A woman he could have loved, and perhaps, for it was high time he was honest with himself, a woman he *had* loved.

Kate was looking at him now, but he couldn't meet her eyes, couldn't bear to see the demand for answers in them. There were things she was better off not knowing, and in realizing that, he realized also that he had been too hard on himself for a long time. That he had forever been punishing himself for failings he could not have prevented. He could not have stopped his wife from dying, nor his son from turning against him. He could not have influenced Mansfield's decision to have an affair, no more than he could have voluntarily ruined the children's lives by telling them something their young minds might not have understood. Had he forced Kate to stay at home tonight, or forbidden Neil to attend the dance, it was clear now that this man, this wicked inhuman being, would have gotten to them anyway. Maybe not tonight, but some other night, as sure as a fox will wait with the patience of the devil for the coop to go unguarded.

There was no Beast of Brent Prior, only men infected with some shape-shifting, body-altering virus that maddened the sane, corrupted the virtuous, and set them after the ones they loved.

"It was yer brother who killed yer woman, not the hunt," he told Callow. "He cut off her hands and feet. Doctor Campbell—" He cast the pallid physician a glance. Campbell, his bare hollow chest tattooed with bruises, sneered back at him. Grady continued, "Campbell might have been able to save her, had she not gone into labor.

The fact remains, she was bleedin' to death when we found her. It was a miracle she was able to give birth."

It was only as the words tripped from his lips that he remembered Kate was standing with him. Now she whirled around to face him, her eyes wide. "Give birth? What are you all talking about?" The pistol trembled in her hand.

Grady raised a hand to placate her, but she was possessed now by the need to know the truth. Before he could stop her, she rushed forth, pistol hanging limp by her side, and stopped before Neil.

"Are you not cold?" she asked him. "Why are you undressed? Please tell me what's happening, Neil?"

Around her, the men watched with interest but again, none of them moved.

Neil stared.

Grady cleared his throat. "It's all right, boy," he said reassuringly, "we're here to take you home, and that's exactly what we're goin' to do."

It was only then it dawned on him what had been bothering him about the boy, apart from his obvious imperviousness to the chill air. Though the light was faint, Neil was staring straight at his sister, and the silver clouds were gone from his eyes.

Oh Jesus...

Kate, weeping, reached a hand out to touch Neil's cheek. "Did they hurt you? Please say they didn't."

"Kate!" Grady said suddenly, and began to move toward her. The men watched him, and he sensed the sudden tension in their postures. He saw Kate frown, and knew she'd finally, through the veil of her concern, seen Neil's eyes and felt the directness of his gaze.

Neil leaned away from Kate's touch as if she had mud on her fingers, then looked up at Stephen.

What he said in that moment brought Grady to a halt and sucked the breath from his lungs.

"May I kill her now, Father?"

28

IT HURLED ITSELF THROUGH THE OPEN WINDOW, its chest narrowing like a mouse trying to squeeze through a crack half its size, and slithered into the room.

Tabitha stumbled backward, her hand frozen in front of her face as if it might at any moment sweep aside this cruel mimicry of reality and restore the world to normal. Her lips moved in silent denial as the oily creature gathered itself into a crouch, its angular head cocked, watching her with feral interest.

"Get *down*, child!" Mrs. Fletcher yelled from the doorway, but Tabitha did not obey. Couldn't, for what she was looking at filled her with so much dread she felt it entirely possible that her body might freeze and shatter into a million pieces. It was the devil, she knew, sent up from Hell to claim her for betraying a blind boy's trust, and it would not be at all tidy or careful in wrenching her soul from her body. From the look on its dark face, she guessed it would enjoy it too.

She continued to back away, breath locked in her throat, until she collided with the edge of the bed hard enough to send a hot lance of pain down her left leg. Discomfort flickered over her face, but with it came clarity.

"Jesus Christ in Heaven, girl, will you *move?*"

The command registered. She broke from her paralysis and ducked. Beneath the window, there was a faint creaking sound as the creature's joints tensed. The white mist of its eyes burned and coiled and licked against the thing's blackened cheeks.

It sprang.

Instantly, Tabitha found herself tugged out of her crouch and off her feet as the creature's hind claws snatched at her. She crashed into the bed and hit the floor, her nose slamming against the floorboards hard enough to send dazzling fireworks of pain into her brain. She whimpered and crawled toward the door, expecting at any moment to feel wickedly sharp teeth piercing the flesh on her back, puncturing the organs inside with torturous delight. She was bleeding, the warmth of it trailing down over skin made cold by fear.

"You *bastard*," a voice said and Tabitha flopped over on her back. Mrs. Fletcher stood by the bed, the creature weaving on the floor like a charmed snake in front of her, the malicious smile still spread across its black hide face. It looked like the embodiment of sinful glee.

Mrs. Fletcher pulled the trigger. The creature flung itself to the side with a victorious, crackling laugh, avoiding the bullet and mounting the wall opposite the bed. The window shattered in its frame, the report deafening in the small room and a moment later, they heard the tinkling of glass in the courtyard. "Get out of here!" Mrs. Fletcher shouted at Tabitha, as she quickly reloaded, the smell of fear and gunpowder thick in the air. Tabitha moaned and tried to ignore the stinging pain in her ribs as she scrambled to her feet. The creature readied itself to pounce.

Tabitha ran.

The seething shadow roared and leapt from the wall.

Mrs. Fletcher cursed, snapped the rifle closed and swiveled on her heel, gun raised in a desperate attempt to track the flight of the creature as it closed in on the wailing girl.

Tabitha put her hands over her head as she crossed the room, tantalizingly close now to where the charwoman waited, gun poised.

The rifle roared; there was the thud of a bullet striking thick hide and Tabitha looked up just as the falling creature snapped to the left, slamming into the wall, but still falling. She lurched out of the way with a frightened wail, but not fast enough. It landed heavily, crushing her feet and she screamed, her nails clawing at the floor. The monster thrashed, blood spurting from the shilling sized hole in its back. From between its snapping spittle-flecked jaws, a black tongue flickered, as if tasting the floor.

"Help me!" Tabitha shrieked, now slamming her fists against the floor and jerking her legs in an attempt to be free of the hideous thing that had her pinned. Hard, moist, scaly hide rubbed against her exposed skin. "Quickly!" she pleaded, uncertain how long its own agony would preoccupy it, how long before it realized its prey was caught beneath it and those nails found her flesh again. And then the memory of her brother's words came to her,

He *did it to me. He scratched me.*

Mrs. Fletcher deftly chambered another cartridge and rushed to where Tabitha lay. She seemed uncertain whether to put another bullet into the raging creature first, or help the girl. To Tabitha's relief, she opted for the latter, and, rifle clenched in her right hand, held out her left. "C'mon, grab hold" she said, face flushed, as Tabitha reached out.

Their fingers touched. Tabitha gasped in exasperation. "Come closer. I-I can't reach. Hurry!" It was clear that the charwoman was trying to keep her distance from the creature, but her reluctance only frustrated Tabitha, who could already feel phantom claws shredding her flesh.

Mrs. Fletcher eased forward, and Tabitha's hand slid into hers. The charwoman tugged, and instantly Tabitha was free. Her relief was brief, and quickly became confusion, then finally dread. Mrs. Fletcher hadn't pulled hard enough to move her that quickly. Which meant that...

The creature had moved.

Mrs. Fletcher released her hand and back-stepped, fumbling with the rifle as she went, her eyes raised to the top of the wall, which still bore the dark smear of blood where the creature had smacked into it.

"Now, child," Mrs. Fletcher said in a low voice. "Go now while the door is clear."

"What about you?"

"Just *go!*"

Tabitha didn't wait to be told again. On her knees, she turned, all too conscious of the swollen black shadow hanging over her. Got her feet beneath her, one hand braced on the floor for balance.

Behind her, she heard the click of the rifle being cocked.

"Now!" Mrs. Fletcher cried, and Tabitha ran.

The gun banged; the creature shrieked again, and blood flew.

Tabitha crossed the threshold, and Mrs. Fletcher's tremulous sigh filled the vacuous silence left by the report.

29

"LISTEN CAREFULLY," SHE TOLD THE GIRL. "I want you to run, get out of this house and find someplace safe, though God knows I can't say if there's such a place left in Brent Prior tonight. Stay off the moors, lock yourself in somewhere until dawn. Now go!"

The girl did as she was told, gone down the stairs in an instant. Mrs. Fletcher gave her time to clear the house, then, and only then, did she allow the bile to rush into her mouth, and the fear to caper down her spine. But it didn't last long. She knew there was no time to entertain the revolt of her stomach. The creature still clung to the ceiling, almost above her head now, a steady patter of its blood dripping down to tap like a metronome against the floorboards. Its movements were sluggish now.

Mrs. Fletcher sighed shakily, and struggled to keep her mind off the girl. She should have sent her running as soon as she saw her by the stable door, but in her panic, she had suggested the first thing to come to mind, and it was only through luck that she hadn't been killed. *I didn't want to be alone.*

But there was no time for such regrets, and it had worked out all right in the end.

For Tabitha, at least. And for now.

The creature was not yet dead, and the danger was close. Mrs. Fletcher reached into her pocket and found to her dismay that there was only one cartridge left. A single bullet. Her heart sank. She had already skewered it with a pitchfork and shot it twice. If the final shot didn't kill it, or if she missed, she was as good as dead.

Watching the shadow overhead, she loaded the rifle, and whispered a hurried request to God, if he was watching, to please help her, to guide the final bullet home, to end this horror once and for all.

She raised the rifle, and the creature turned its eyes on her. The white light had faded to a storm cloud gray that swirled within sockets too wide for its head. It was dying, shriveling, wasting away of its injuries. Strings of blood drooled from its upside-down maw, its tongue floundering in a wheezing mouth.

"Good," Mrs. Fletcher said, with a surge of hope.

The creature released its grip from the ceiling, tearing chunks of plaster with it as it spun around in the air so that it was right side up again. Grainy dust plumed. As it fell, and the charwoman tracked it, finger tensing on the trigger, it began to change.

And when it hit the floor, it did so with human feet.

Mrs. Fletcher's mouth fell open, and, without realizing she was doing so, lowered the gun slightly. She wanted to scream, to wake up, to weep, to die, anything but stand here feeling her sanity break away like pond ice in the springtime. Indeed, for a split-second, she imagined she could hear it crackling.

He shuffled closer on broken limbs, his skin suppurating and leaking blood.

It was Master Mansfield.

"Florence," he said, weakly. He was naked, and his bare legs wobbled as he stopped in front of her, the bones beneath making sounds like broken glass being crunched in a fist. "Help me."

Stunned, and uncertain, sure now more than ever that this was nothing more than an intensely vivid nightmare, or witchcraft at work, she kept the gun raised, the muzzle mere inches from her master's throat.

"You're not real," she said. "It's a trick of the devil. Away with you!"

She started to pull the trigger, but the man-thing cowered away from her, his blood-streaked arms crossed protectively over his head like a child anticipating a blow from an irate father, and she hesitated, listening, as a peculiar sound drifted from beneath the cradle he had made around his head.

Sobbing.

Yet, she kept the gun trained on him, too afraid to give in to the ache inside her that told her *yes, this is the master, and you need to help him. He's sick*, because she had seen what he had tried to do to the girl, what he wanted to do to *her*.

Teeth clenched, but with her resolve trembling like leaves in a gale, she swallowed and sidestepped, moving around the master just as she had in the stable earlier. She brought the rifle back up and aimed at his head.

"What's become of you?" she asked, softly, still moving around him, waiting for the slightest sign that he was reverting back to his animal form, in which case, guilt or no guilt, doubt or no doubt, she would pull the trigger and send him to his grave, or the hell that might roar beneath it. But he continued to weep, his hands slowly floating away from a bowed head, the features streaked with shadow.

"It was *him*," he said, snot dripping from his nose. "*He* did this to me."

"Who?"

"Callow."

"Edgar Callow? He's dead. Everyone knows that."

"No, Florence. He's not."

She kept moving. "What kind of a man has the power to come back to life? To do somethin' like this to anyone?"

"There was a woman," he said. "Edgar's wife. He brought her here from abroad and she was poisoned, Florence. But we...we both loved her, as I'm sure every foolish man who ever got close enough to look in her eyes loved her. She was a witch, a harridan of the worst kind because she delivered her evil into the hearts of men with mere glances, moistened lips and night whispers, not spells and potions and hexes. She was the mother of what I've become, the carrier of this terrible disease that courses through me." He winced, and clutched a hand to his chest, and when he bent over, fresh blood flowed from the bullet hole on his back, just below his shoulder.

Instinct almost drove Mrs. Fletcher to him then, but she resisted, using the image of the monster he had been only moments before to give her strength. Instead she took advantage of his pain and hurried around so she was facing him and had her back to the door, exactly where she wanted to be. Three steps and she would be out on the landing.

"My dear Florence..."

She could only hope the pain meant he'd conceded, that it had forced him to embrace his humanity again.

She only hoped she'd be fast enough if it hadn't.

A chance, however, was something she was not willing to take. She had served the master in this house for decades. She had tended to his children when business or illness had spirited him away. She had always been loyal and yes, would gladly have given her life for him.

But this was not the man she had served, and when it came down to it, the children would always come first, those innocents who even now could be traipsing across the dark moors, drawn only by the light of this house and the comfort they knew resided within, the security they had grown to know in her embrace. Despite its misfortunes, she and Mr. Grady had made Mansfield House a haven, from all the bad things that existed in the outside world, the things they would not yet need to know about. The things their father had brought down upon them. In his foolishness, he had become the embodiment of life's cruelty, of everything that would shadow the children's steps as they made their way through life, Mansfield House forgotten and crumbling at their backs. All the trials and obstacles that would arise to foil their happiness throughout their years stood bleeding before her. He was a manifestation of her own loss and despair, all rolled up and seasoned with the fear that she had failed her own children, let them wander into the woods where unknown horrors waited to gobble them up and reduce them to the sad, wistful thing she had herself become.

Neil and Kate could not come home to this.

To a father they worshiped and prayed for with every whisper.

To a father now a ravenous beast that might rend them to pieces with his teeth because his own unfaithfulness had seen him cursed.

"Florence..." he said again, and slowly turned around, his eyes catching the light. They were dark red and swollen, like the eyes of a crushed rabbit. "Florence..." A chastising tone had entered his voice. "Listen to me. I'm dying. You have to help me. You know me, you know I—"

"You've become something from Hell," she said, flatly, still tugged by the need to forgive him, to help him, but she realized that in all his years of sleeping, her love for him had gathered dust. He was more a stranger now, and that made it easier to say what she had to. "And I can't say if I trust you not to hurt your own children."

"But Florence..." he implored, trembling hands held out to her, close enough for his fingertips to brush the barrel of the gun, forcing her to move back another step lest he attempt to snatch the weapon from her. "Surely you must know that wasn't the real *me*? It's this damned *disease!* And if I must die because of it, then so be it, but it is of utmost importance that *you* accept the truth of the matter. Accept what your own two eyes have beheld."

"They've beheld a monster," she told him. "No matter what the costume. A man's heart stays pure unless he lets it be tainted and I believe that's what you've done." She nodded. "The world can't pay for your mistakes, no more than I should expect it to pay for mine. I'm sorry. We all pay for our sins eventually, whether here or in Heaven."

He made a sound that might have been a laugh, or a sob. She couldn't be sure, but the muscles in his neck tensed, stuck out like ropes beneath a silk sheet. "Heaven," he scoffed. "So you're judging me, in the absence of God, is that it? I look after you. I give you a home, wages and my children to fawn over, and now you're standing there *judging me?* How *dare* you!"

"I'm sorry," she replied, her own body steeling itself for violence. "Truly I am. You were good to me, but by the look of you that goodness has run out, and I can't let you hurt the children."

He straightened, his blood tap-tapping on the floor, his skin so pale he looked made of moonlight. "I would never *ever* hurt my children," he said, "No more than I would hurt *you* for suggesting it."

He took a step toward her and the air changed as if some unseen laborer had strung invisible filaments from wall to ceiling and made a harp of the room. Even the light seemed to have to strain to penetrate it.

"I believe my master is gone," Mrs. Fletcher said. "And you are merely an echo of his good self, a shadow he left behind."

She took a deep breath, held it and released it slowly, then moved back a few more feet to the door, her eyes registering every ripple and twitch in his body, waiting for the beast to forsake its costume and lunge at her.

"Give me the rifle, you whore," Mansfield said, a snarl, all too human, contorting his face. Mrs. Fletcher closed one eye, checked her aim, and, satisfied that he would not survive the shot, said, "Please forgive me," before she fired, the blast obliterating that snarl and everything above it.

***

Like curious children, wisps of ground fog curled out from behind the tors and hunkered mounds of craggy rock and hurried across the moors. Starlight limned the rain-soaked sprawls of fern and induced in the sphagnum moss an almost ethereal glow. The moon had wrenched a shroud of lightning-bruised clouds across its face denying the naked birch their proud dominating silhouettes.

Grady shook his head in frightened awe. Kate slowly backed away from the boy she had once called her brother, the shock draining all life from her face.

The naked men in the semicircle exchanged delighted grins at her reaction.

Then Stephen shook his head. "Neil, it would appear you are still ignorant of your position. You're the leader now, so all decisions are yours to make. If you wish to kill the girl, that is up to you, but if I may offer a piece of advice..."

Neil nodded.

"I would consider keeping her alive and using her as a breeder."

Grady went to Kate and put his arms on her shoulders.

Neil looked appalled. "A breeder? But she's...she was, my sister."

"Precisely. She *was* your sister. Such relations mean little now. But even then she was not your kin. A female is a breeder; man is the hunter and sower of seeds. That's the way of things."

Despite the explanation, the boy still looked disgusted. He turned his *seeing* eyes toward Kate and a look of disgust contorted his features. "I'd rather kill her."

"Then that is your choice. But a rather poor one, given our needs."

Neil hesitated, the eyes of the gathering on him, and Grady took the opportunity to delay. "Neil...why are you doin' this?"

The disgusted expression held on the boy's face, making it clear that whatever had happened to him, whatever had possessed him, it hadn't elevated Grady above the contempt with which he'd viewed his sister.

"Stephen gave me my eyes. He gave me my life, and all the power it brings with it. You heard what he said: I'm a *leader* now, not a follower like I've been all my life. I won't have to listen to the pity in everyone's voice when they talk to me. I won't have to depend on anyone but myself from now on. And most importantly, I won't have to pretend to care about people I *hate*."

"Why do you hate me?" Grady asked. "I was never anythin' but good to you."

"Good to me?" Neil took a step forward, fists clenched and teeth bared. Grady still found it unnerving that the boy was *looking* at him, the burnished cast gone, leaving behind focused and *seeing* eyes. Seeing eyes that were filled with malice. "You kept the truth from me. You let me grow up in the care of people who were not my kin. You carved out a hollow life for me, old man, and filled it with lies. You kept me trapped in a miserable house for years, talking down to me as if I was a whipped cur, convincing me I was nothing more than a poor blind boy. Well, look at me now, Grady. I'm not that boy any more. My *real* father has given me everything I've ever wanted: my sight and my freedom, and I intend to use both to tear you apart for what you've done to me."

Grady was stunned. That the boy could see was a miracle, but the words he spat from that sneering mouth suggested possession, corruption, and he refused to believe there was any sincerity to them.

Not again.

Not from another young man who should have loved him.

He glared at Stephen. "What have you done to him?"

"Oh my, foolish fellow," Stephen replied cheerfully, "I've done nothing to him. He did it all himself. It was in his genes, don't you see, a little something he inherited from his mother and me. All that was required was a scratch of my nails on his eyes and a choice. He could embrace or resist, and as you can plainly see, he chose the former. If you had seen the speed with which he converted, it would take your breath away. He's truly of our blood. And now he'll lead our army into the world until your kind are reduced to mere legends we'll tell around campfires."

Grady tapped Kate on the shoulder. She looked up at him and he whispered, "When I shoot, I want you to run, fast as you can toward the village. Bring the pistol with you."

She looked about to argue, to protest in silence, but to his surprise, she nodded, and he realized he should have expected it, despite her usual stubbornness. After all, what she had come for was gone. The boy standing across from her with the hungry, hateful gaze was no one she knew. Grady hoped the distance the boy had always shown her would lessen the blow of his betrayal, but doubted it somehow. Kate had never been one to love only as much as she was loved in return, and if she survived this night, Grady imagined that quality would mean much heartbreak in the days ahead.

He raised his head and addressed the boy. "Kate is an innocent in all of this. I want to ask you to please let her go."

"No one is innocent," Neil said flatly.

"She never did anything but help and love you, Neil. Fer God's sake, no matter how much this man has poisoned you, you must still *see* that."

Neil said nothing for a moment, but stared at Grady. The old man felt as if invisible fingers were digging their nails into his skull. The gathering seemed to thrum with impatience, until finally Neil smirked and said, "I won't kill her. Yet. I'll take you in her place and while we're feeding on you, she can run. Call it a head start. She won't get very far, but perhaps during those few precious moments of freedom she can reflect on all the times she was cruel to me over the years."

When Kate spoke, her enraged voice cracked with sorrow, "I was *never* cruel to you. No more than you asked for, you spoiled little bastard."

The gathering began to move.

Neil smiled. "You'd better run, sister. As fast as your feet can carry you, because you're nothing but *meat* to me now."

In that instant, Grady shoved Kate aside and "Go! Now!" he roared, as he brought up the rifle and fired without pausing to aim. There was a *thunk!* like an arrow slamming into tree bark and Campbell spun around in a circle, then staggered, blood jetting from the side of his neck.

Kate ran, and quickly cleared the circle of light. In an instant she was gone, the ringing in Grady's ears from the gun blast giving her flight a soundless, curiously dreamlike quality. *That's my girl*, he thought, struggling to reload as the group of men looked from him to the stumbling figure of their brother Campbell trying to stem the flow of blood from a wide dark hole in his neck.

And then they changed. The effect was like someone pouring scalding hot water over ice sculptures. One moment they were standing stock-still, pale figures in the half-light, tendrils of fog coiling at their feet; the next they had fallen forward, shriveled while lengthening, blazing with light while darkening, until they were crouched before him, then moving with the eerie synchronicity of tigers stalking prey.

All except Stephen, who stood, arms crossed, studying him.

Grady's hands were trembling uncontrollably and he watched in dismay as the first cartridge bounced across his fingers and vanished at his feet. He quickly procured another, eyes flicking from the stock to the sleek dark figures pouring like oil toward where he stood by the lantern.

"C'mon, c'mon," he urged himself and slammed the bullet into the chamber. It stuck. "Damn it!"

Claws found his legs, and the air filled with a chorus of clicking hisses.

He winced and restrained a gasp of pain as those nails punctured his right ankle and drove deeper and deeper until they scratched bone. Warmth flooded his shins and it felt as if a river of his strength was leaving him. A moment later, they found his left ankle.

He rammed the heel of his palm against the cartridge and it went in with a sharp clack. With a triumphant nod, he raised the rifle and aimed it down.

It was like standing in a river of tar. Sinewy black limbs flashed and tore at him; blazing white eyes rose, cresting the mist and gone again. Frantic, he adjusted his aim. They swarmed around him. Another razor-sharp pain, followed by a tugging and something ripped away, setting his leg on fire. He muffled a scream and tried to pull away.

He couldn't move.

They had him anchored where he stood, a tree waiting to be razed by saws of bone. And in a moment, he would fall.

They're going to do it slowly.

He thought of his son, of Kate, and of the boy he'd loved so much now tearing at him like a maddened animal, and tears filled his eyes.

One of the creatures rose from the mist, claw raised and aimed at Grady's face. Suddenly, something sailed over its head and hit Grady's cheek softly before rolling and landing in the crook of his arm.

It was his cap. He looked questioningly at Stephen, who said, "It will be cold where you're going."

Grady took the cap and donned it, tugging on the brim until it fit snugly. Oddly enough, he felt more secure with the cap than he did with the rifle. Habits were like a pair of comfortable old shoes, he supposed.

The creature before him leaned in and in the second before it sliced open his belly, he found himself wondering if it was Neil. He hoped not, hoped that none of the claws ripping at him belonged to the boy, that perhaps he was watching, with sorrow and regret, from somewhere in the fog.

"I have one last thing to say to you," he said to Stephen. "A little mistake I'm sure yer unaware of."

"Is that so? Do tell."

Grady did, and then, with a smile, swung the rifle around so the muzzle was a dark eye staring him in the face. With a whisper of "God forgive me," he gripped the barrel with one hand, brought it up under his chin, then reached down and depressed the trigger with his thumb.

He was sung into oblivion by Stephen's outraged cry.

30

KATE STUMBLED, FELL AND QUICKLY GOT TO HER FEET, then ran on, sweat beading her brow, her breath adding to the rising mist as she wept in hitching sobs that threatened to suck the air from her. On she went, over the stony mounds and down into the valleys, through the network of drooping dying trees and across babbling streams that would soon become ice. She slipped and fell again, jarring her elbow against a rock and howling with pain, cursing with frustration as she rose, the pistol heavy and useless in her hand.

I should have stayed with him, she thought miserably, but knew she would have been unable to help him if she had. The gun was for show, meant to scare, not kill. Grady had trained her how to use it and she had been quite adept at pegging old cans and bottles from a considerable distance. But cans and bottles were not men. They didn't have eyes that looked back at you and watched you preparing to cross that tumultuous river between good and evil into the realm of murderers. She would never have been able to kill one of them. They could have shot Grady before her very eyes and she would have aimed, cocked the gun and yes, maybe even squeezed off a shot, but it would have gone astray because she would have ensured it would. Killing was not a part of her design, but because of that, she was quite certain she had left Grady for dead. Now her own brother and his new brethren were hunting her down, and even if she somehow managed to avoid them, the guilt would find her wherever she went.

A shot splintered the night behind her. She half-turned, then sobbed and kept going, her heart racing, pulse tapping in her throat.

A chorus of shrieks flayed the air and this time she did stop, uncertainty keeping her still—and oh how good it felt not to be running. She listened. Had that been a sound of creatures in pain? She'd only heard one shot though, so how would Grady have managed to hurt the rest of them? The lanterns were like the gleam in the eyes of a mouse from where she stood, and yet she considered going back. She shivered, and waited, watching those lights, half-imagining she could hear Grady's victorious summons. *Got the bastards, Kate. Come on! Killing their master killed them all, by God!*

But the cry didn't come, and after what felt like hours of waiting, the lanterns went out.

Allowing her to see the white eyes burning through the mist as the creatures closed in on her.

***

Sarah opened the door, her eyes narrowed against the fluttering flame of Mrs. Fletcher's torch. "Do you know what time it is?"

"No. It doesn't matter. I need your horse."

"What?"

"Your horse. I need to borrow it. There's trouble."

"Are you hurt?" Sarah asked dreamily, inspecting the blood on Mrs. Fletcher's skirts. "I have some bandages if you—"

"For Christ's sake, the damned *horse*, woman!"

"All right, calm down!" Sarah said, looking no more awake despite the charwoman's outburst. "My horse is gone. Your friend Mr. Grady and the young lass took it. I told them not to be too long. Do you think—?"

"You need to come with me," Mrs. Fletcher said gruffly, grabbing Sarah by the sleeve. "And bring a weapon of some sort. Your husband's rifle if you have it."

Sarah pulled away, finally awake, and annoyed. "I beg your pardon? You just woke me out of bed. I'm not going anywhere."

Mrs. Fletcher clenched her teeth and stepped close enough to make Sarah's eyes widen. "Yes you bloody well *are*. We're goin' to see the man responsible for your husband's death."

Sarah paled.

***

The village slept, swaddled in a cocoon of blissful ignorance. At every door, sleep-narrowed eyes radiated hostility at having been woken up to a harsher reality.

And at every door, Mrs. Fletcher's story changed:

"A child is missin'..."

"There's a murderer on the moors..."

"They say Grady has caught the Beast of Brent Prior..."

At every door, sleep fled quickly. Overcoats were slung on, weapons were gathered and the horses saddled.

Within a half hour, thirteen men, seven youths and five women, including Mrs. Fletcher and Sarah Laws, armed with an array of weapons, from sickles to shotguns, crossed from the muddy village road onto the moors, the unified light of their blazing torches like a shield against the night, and whatever it cloaked.

31

THEY WERE CLOSE. KATE KNEW IT WITHOUT LOOKING BACK over her shoulder. She could feel them coming, as if their hunger had preceded them in tangible waves that brushed with wicked promise against the nape of her neck. They dragged at her eyes, willing her to see them and let the fear cripple her, but she refused, her legs like pistons as they desperately tried to maintain the speed her brain demanded.

Then, through the mist ahead she caught sight of something.

Fire.

More of them? she thought with dread clutching at her heart. Had those men she'd seen only represented a portion of a greater number? The idea that they might be spread across the path ahead was almost enough to drain the fight from her. As it was, she allowed herself to slow, but not by much. She was wheezing now, her lungs singing with the pain of every breath.

Another few feet and the fire separated; became a number of smaller flames, and beneath them round warm faces were crumpled up in concentration, peering into the dark.

A few feet more and something inside her pleaded with her to stop, to change direction and hide until she could be sure these people were not the enemy, but her legs weren't listening and carried her forth until at last she slowed, then stopped and stared, irritated that the clouds her breath made were occluding her view of the gathering.

She knew them.

The elation was late in coming, held up at the door by caution, but after a moment spent catching her breath, she allowed relief to numb her.

She was close enough now to see that the lights were indeed torches, held high by concerned looking folk on horseback, all of whom she recognized. And there, amongst them, though Kate scarcely dared believe it, stood the reassuring bulk of Mrs. Fletcher, talking animatedly and gesturing at the darkness around them.

Kate closed her eyes, her thundering heart setting off fireworks behind her eyelids, then opened them again and cried out with as much force as she could muster, "I'm over here, Mrs. Fletcher!" Despite her exhaustion and, not content to wait, Kate began to jog toward the crowd.

I'm going home. They didn't catch me. I'm going ho—

The tattoo beat of galloping feet behind her, getting louder, and louder still and she turned with a gasp of horror as a creature carved from the night sky itself, a nightmare with full moons for eyes leapt for her, its jaws open wide. She was dimly aware of more moons floating out of the dark and then she lunged forward, away from the creature and toward the crowd.

"Mrs. Fletcher!" she cried, and then her feet were gone from under her. She went down hard, the loamy earth thudding against her jaw, sending a fiery ache up through her teeth. Specks of light pulsed in her eyes and she moaned, then quickly rolled over on her back.

They were there, two of them, standing before her, limbs spread wide, bellies low to the ground, and following behind them, like a man out for a late evening stroll, was Stephen Callow, his hands joined behind his back, eyes on the crowd still crying out to the dark.

"You almost made it," he said, and the cheerfulness was gone from his tone. He almost looked worried, which made no sense at all to Kate, though she would not have been surprised to learn her ability to judge expressions, or anything else for that matter, had faltered over the last few hours. But still, there was something different about the man's eyes now, something almost gentle about them, an evaluation she found absurd.

"Where's Grady?" The question wouldn't leave her until she asked it, even though she didn't want to hear the answer.

"Dead," Stephen said. "By his own hand."

She remembered the single gunshot and almost smiled despite the swell of grief and sorrow that rose within her. Though she had known deep down that he was lost to her, she had also known he would fight to the end, and he had, refusing to let them take him. Memories tried to overwhelm her, a cold river flecked with icy regret, and she stopped it, let the anger burn it away.

"So, what are you waiting for? Let them kill me, you coward." Her tears were hot and silent. "Do it!"

As if they'd been waiting for this very command, no matter who issued it, the creatures began to advance, their drooling mouths spread wide. Kate closed her eyes, blinding herself to the pale fire as it threw her shadow over her shoulder. She began to pray, not for salvation, but for Grady, and Neil, and her father, and her beloved Mrs. Fletcher.

Behind her, the muttering of the crowd seemed closer, but it didn't matter now. They would kill her with one swipe of their claws and be gone, woven into the fabric of the night, before her would-be rescuers discovered her bloodied remains.

"Stop."

Kate opened her eyes.

Callow was scowling. "Leave her be."

The creatures exchanged glances but after a moment in which she was sure they'd defy their master, they retreated, and moved to flank Callow. His eyes moved back to the orange glow growing ever closer as the search party scanned the dark. "Your friend told me something," he said. "Which I suspect was a lie specifically designed to try and save you." He sighed. "But I can't take the chance that he was telling the truth. So tonight, you go home." He stepped close to her, his dark fissured flesh twisting to accommodate his bitter smile. "But we'll be watching you closely, monitoring your progress, and if the groundskeeper lied, then we'll come for you. Do you understand?"

There were a million things she wanted to say, every one of them an insult or a challenge, every one of them a rock she wished to throw in his face for what he had done. But he was letting her live, and while it didn't seem much of a mercy considering all he had taken away from her, she bowed her head and nodded once.

As Callow turned and began to walk away, the animals at his heels, another question occurred to her and she called it after him. "What did Grady tell you? What was your mistake?"

For a moment it looked like he wasn't going to respond, wasn't going to satisfy a curiosity that would combine with grief to haunt whatever time she had left to live, but then he stopped, and looked over his shoulder at her.

"He said Sylvia didn't give birth to a boy."

And then he was gone, perhaps fearing the return of the flames that had disfigured him, and moments later Kate found herself weeping amid the attention of many voices and many hands. Mrs. Fletcher sobbed and hugged the breath from her and asked more questions than she could answer.

"I thought I'd lost you, but thank the good Lord, you're safe now!"

Yes. She was safe, for a while, but ahead, in the dark where no one else was looking, she saw her brother's eyes burning in the dark like lanterns as he glanced over his shoulder at her. And in those lights, she saw the promise of his return.

***

As they led her away swaddled in blankets and sipping at brews she could not taste, she numbed herself against the agony that waited behind her eyes for its chance to become her, and in those moments, as she walked within the villagers' comforting lights, leading them to where Grady lay dead, she felt something cold in the pit of her stomach, something that sent dark tendrils into her brain and forced her to acknowledge its presence.

Mrs. Fletcher dropped to her knees and wept over Grady's body.

Kate caught sight of Tabitha Newman, hurrying to join the crowd, rushing to find the charwoman, and declining a kind offer to be assisted when someone pointed out the dried blood on her blouse.

The villagers encircled the corpse, weapons at the ready, but there was no need. The creatures, and the master of the moors, had no business here tonight.

Kate knew this to be true, just as she knew Grady had told Callow the truth.

The ache in her stomach proved it, for it was nothing so simple as grief, or regret, nothing so paltry as worry, rather the first stirrings of a great and terrible power.

ABOUT THE AUTHOR

Born and raised in a small harbor town in the south of Ireland, Kealan Patrick Burke knew from a very early age that he was going to be a horror writer. The combination of an ancient locale, a horror-loving mother, and a family full of storytellers, made it inevitable that he would end up telling stories for a living. Since those formative years, he has written five novels, over a hundred short stories, six collections, and edited four acclaimed anthologies. In 2004, he was honored with the Bram Stoker Award for his novella *The Turtle Boy*.

Kealan has worked as a waiter, a drama teacher, a mapmaker, a security guard, an assembly-line worker at Apple Computers, a salesman (for a day), a bartender, landscape gardener, vocalist in a grunge band, curriculum content editor, fiction editor at Gothic.net, and, most recently, a fraud investigator.

When not writing, Kealan designs book covers through his company Elderlemon Design.

A number of his books have been optioned for film.

Visit him on the web at www.kealanpatrickburke.com

Printed in France by Amazon
Brétigny-sur-Orge, FR